Five reasons w
love this book:

Romance, mystery, and the
supernatural in one thrilling story.

Joss Stirling is the winner of the
Romantic Novel of the
Year 2015.

Angel, Misty, and Summer are
at the hottest festival of the
year. Join them!

Two souls collide, and nothing
will be the same again.

Find out how one song can
change everything.

Angel gets more than she bargained for when she meets Marcus Cohen. Here's a sneak peek at their first encounter:

'Welcome to the yurt. Can I see your pass please?' The attractive girl on the reception desk glanced down at the envelope in my hand. Her brunette hair was swept up in a French plait and she was wearing vibrant red lipstick—no sign that she was roughing it in a sheep field.

'Oh, yes, sorry.' I put down my violins and cracked open the seal. 'And the winner is: Angel Campbell!' I tugged out the blue lanyard and hooped it over my head.

She didn't get the joke—or if she did, thought it too lame to be noticed. 'Please wear your pass at all times and make sure you do not leave it lying about. We take security very seriously.'

'Absolutely.'

'I'm here to help you with any of your needs—booking taxis, questions about how things run, changes to the performance schedule: you name it, I'm the person to come to.' Her smile was automatic.

'Thanks.'

'The refreshments in this tent are available for you free of charge.'

'Great.'

'But we would appreciate it if you respect the privacy of other performers. This is the space where our guests are supposed to be able to relax and not worry about the press snooping on their activities.'

How had she sniffed out my fangirl propensities? 'I understand.' I was itching to ask her about Gifted but somehow I just knew that would go down like garlic bread at a vampire's dinner party. She turned away and began leafing through pages clipped to a board. I hovered.

She lifted her gaze back to me and raised a brow—Lord, how I wish I could do that. 'Is there anything you need now?'

'I was just wondering who else has arrived already.' There: that was nice and vague.

She glanced down at her list. 'You are the first from your group. We've had a few early arrivals, mainly those supporting the show tonight.' She ran through a few names, many of whom I had seen on YouTube or heard live. 'The big names for this evening aren't expected until after three.'

'And . . . um . . . Gifted—anyone from that group here yet?'

Her expression hardened. 'No. They don't perform until Friday as I'm sure you know.'

'I just thought they might send someone in advance, you know: to check things out?'

'Well, they haven't registered yet. They won't be here until tomorrow at the earliest.'

Someone cleared his throat behind me.

'If that's everything Miss Campbell, I have to get on. I've other guests to see to.' Her eyes rose to the person at my shoulder and her smile warmed thirty degrees.

'Right. Thanks.' I bent to pick up my violin but a hand was already on Freddie before I could reach for him. I straightened and found myself looking up into a pair of ice-blue eyes in a tanned face, topped by a spiky fringe of gold-shot hair. My lips moved before my brain caught up. 'Oh my God!'

The guy's lips quirked into a smile, revealing cute bracket lines either side of his mouth. 'Not God: Marcus Cohen.'

Walked into that one, hadn't I? 'I meant . . . ' What had I meant: you are so gorgeous that I couldn't help myself?

For Lucy

OXFORD
UNIVERSITY PRESS

Great Clarendon Street, Oxford OX2 6DP

Oxford University Press is a department of the University of Oxford.
It furthers the University's objective of excellence in research, scholarship,
and education by publishing worldwide. Oxford is a registered trade mark of
Oxford University Press in the UK and in certain other countries

Copyright © Joss Stirling 2015

The moral rights of the author have been asserted
Database right Oxford University Press (maker)

First published 2015

British Library Cataloguing in Publication Data

Data available

ISBN: 978-0-19-274348-0

1 3 5 7 9 10 8 6 4 2

Printed in Great Britain

Paper used in the production of this book is a natural,
recyclable product made from wood grown in sustainable forests.
The manufacturing process conforms to the environmental
regulations of the country of origin.

Angel Dares

Joss Stirling

OXFORD
UNIVERSITY PRESS

Chapter 1

Flicking through the jewellery case, my fingers picked a silver Celtic knot to go on my left index. With four different rings on each hand, a jingling ankle chain, and my crystal droplet necklace, I was fully armed for the performance.

'*With rings on her fingers,*' I sang, checking my reflection in the bulb-lit mirror backstage. '*And bells on her toes.*'

Laughing at myself, I twisted to ensure the short silver-grey skirt did not ride up too high.

'Looking good, Angel: looking good.' I blew my double a kiss, Marilyn Monroe style. At least, I looked as good as I could. Frustrated by a genetic inheritance from parents who were more like hobbits than full-sized people, I have learned to boost my confidence by telling myself such truth-bending compliments just before going out on stage to sing in front of a packed house.

Eeek: don't think about that!

My phone clucked. *We're standing front left. Break a leg. S, M and A.*

I hugged the phone. My badgering had worked. I had warned Summer, Misty, and Alex that if they didn't come to the gig early and get right down the front to support me in my hour of need, I would do something awful to them—too awful to say (and I hadn't yet thought up my revenge when I made the threat). They were my closest friends, sharing the secret of having a savant gift. Summer's power gave her the ability to shadow minds—the mental version of what a spy did when trailing a suspect. Familiar with my thought patterns, she probably knew my likely retaliation before I did. I typed a quick reply. *Great. See you after. xxx*

Once I had slipped the phone back in my sequined handbag, I realized I had nothing left to do but worry. Not good. I usually ignored nerves by keeping on the move and chatting but no one else was sharing the cupboard-like women's changing room as the rest of the band was in the men's. The Hammersmith nightclub didn't run to many luxuries backstage—my guess that this dingy room served as storage space was confirmed by the mop and bucket of dirty water leaning against the clothes rail—but the club did still segregate the sexes, more's the pity. Checking the time, I saw I still had ten whole minutes to go: ten minutes to wind myself up into a state where I could no longer sing the backing vocals. I was tempted to go and join the boys but then I'd have to breathe the same air as Jay, which was equally bad for my pre-show preparation.

I picked up my black violin and tested the tuning. It wasn't my favourite instrument—that was my battered old folk fiddle—but this one worked best for rock as it could be plugged into an amplifier. I ran quickly through a scale, warming up my fingers, then moved into the opening refrain. Jay, the lead singer of Seventh Edition, had big aspirations for his band and wrote music that really needed a whole orchestra to support the drums and guitar lineup. He was right that the music we made together had huge potential but the group was still touring the semi-professional circuit, yet to get that big break. Jay had had to make do with a female violinist and a male saxophonist rather than the National Symphony Orchestra. To be honest, he was a difficult guy to like as he had fallen into the bad habit of vastly over-estimating his own talent. He was good but much of the best came from other members of the band, contributions he rarely acknowledged. As I was never slow to tell it how it was, I knew I would have been given the push months ago if he hadn't needed me so badly. Singer/violinists were hard to find.

A quick knock sounded on the door. Speak of the devil: Jay Fielding himself had come to call on his lowly backing singer.

'Everything OK, Angel?' He rubbed his long fingers together, a sign of unusual nervousness. Normally he liked to pretend he was king of the world and our lord and master.

I put the violin back in its case. 'Yes, fine.' I didn't like him coming alone to see me. Not only did he give me the creeps, I had a little routine I kept to before going on stage; any disruption to that made me feel superstitious about the performance.

Jay prowled the room, his eyes scrutinizing my appearance in an uncomfortably intimate fashion. Possessing an ordinary face with mean grey eyes, topped by extravagantly swept-back blond hair, Jay did not set my heart going pitter-pat as he hoped. I thought I had made that plain the last time he had cornered me.

'It's a big night tonight.' He stopped beside me and bared his teeth in the mirror to check all was pearly white. Too perfect to be natural, that set must have made some cosmetic dentist a lot richer lately. Fortunately for him, Jay had wealthy parents to sponsor his attempt to make it in the music industry. They were as brash as he was about his ambition.

'Um, yes, very big.' I twisted the Celtic knot wishing I could teleport away from him. *Beam me up, Scottie.*

He smoothed an eyebrow, loving himself in the glass. 'I didn't tell you before but the promoters for the Rockport festival are out front looking for acts for the summer lineup. If we impress, we might end up on the bill.'

Now that news was worth the invasion of my space! 'Really? Awesome!' I bobbed on my toes, clutching my hands to my chest—the room didn't allow for a more expressive dance of happiness. 'I can't believe we might get our break at last!'

He stopped my movement with a hand on my waist, clammy fingers caressing the narrow band of bare skin. 'So, Angel sweetheart, you'll be a good girl for me tonight?'

His patronizing tone made me want to sink my teeth into the straying hand. Although only twenty, three years older than me, Jay acted like I was his to command. But I couldn't spoil the concert by drawing blood now. 'I'll do my best, Jay.' Pushing gently against his chest with my palms, I tried to take a step back but he prevented that by putting his other hand on my waist so we stood face-to-face.

'How about a kiss for good luck, babe?'

Various replies ran quickly through my mind, ranging from 'not in this lifetime' to 'yuck'.

He tipped his head to the side, eyes looking at me through his fringe. Did he think he looked more persuasive in that pose? 'Come on, Angel: I know you're sweet on me.'

'You do?' How on earth had he drawn that conclusion? 'But—'

He nodded, his quiff bobbing 'yes' double-time like it had a mind of its own. 'Yeah, I've seen the way you look at me across the rehearsal room.'

What? He'd mistaken mild amusement for adoration, had he?

'Babe.' He leaned in for a kiss.

I jerked back. 'Jay, take your hands off me,' I said sharply. What was it with guys? This was not the first man to try groping me in a dressing room. I had a good repertoire of self-defence moves, but I always tried reasoning first.

'You don't want me to.' Jay nibbled his way to my neck, teeth threatening to leave a love bite.

'Yes, I absolutely do.' Every time I pushed him away from one part, he opened up a new attack elsewhere like some kind of writhing sea monster with too many tentacles to fight.

'No, you don't.'

'Just get your hands off!'

'Hey, don't be like that, babe. It's just us—no need to pretend you don't want this.'

OK, enough already. He had been warned. Not having the muscle to move him, it was time to bring out the heavy guns of my power. Eyes fixed on the mop bucket, I called the water to me, an amazing feeling of connectedness where the H_2O molecules in my body reached out and pulled the water to them. The dirty water rose up like a dull brown snake from a charmer's basket and wound its way across to Jay. Concentrating hard, I directed the coil of water to the back of Jay's neck.

Down.

Obediently, the water slid down his spine, soaking through his shirt and jeans, gushing out to the floor.

'What the . . . !' Jay leapt back from me, ardour cooled. 'I'm wet.'

Yes, you so are. 'Oh, Jay, you've got water running out of your trousers!' I shrieked with false sympathy. I put a finger to my chin. 'At least, I hope it's water.'

'Fecking hell.' Shaking the excess from his shoes, he glared at me. 'What else would it be?'

I waved my hands in the air. 'Oh you know: nerves get to us all.' His face was so outraged the giggle I had been repressing bubbled to the surface. 'Hadn't . . . hadn't you better go change?'

His expression darkened as he heard my laughter. 'You

bitch, you did something!' He stabbed the air with his forefinger.

'*Moi?*' I asked innocently. 'What could I do: you wouldn't let me go, remember? If there's a leak, blame the roof in this dump, not me.'

Jay scanned the ceiling but it showed no sign of water damage, but neither could he explain how I had been responsible for the sudden deluge from behind. 'You . . . you . . . don't laugh!'

I nodded to the clock. 'Sorry, Jay, but you really should go change. I hope you have another outfit?'

Squelching to the exit, Jay turned. 'This isn't finished!' He slammed the door behind him.

I leaned back against the dressing table, hugging my waist in glee. 'That was fun.'

The gig went surprisingly well considering the backstage antics minutes before we were due to start. Jay had found a set of dry clothes, though the T-shirt looked wrinkled—probably dug out from the bottom of one of the band member's bags. I could forgive Jay quite a lot when he got in front of the microphone. Though no Brit award contender, he did have a gift for songwriting and knew how to charm an audience. My part went well, with my violin solo in the track 'Star-Crossed' getting its own round of whistles and applause, led no doubt by my lovely friends. I could see them clearly from my position stage right: Misty notable for her bobbing mop of pale blonde curls; Summer dancing with a chic untouchable Audrey Hepburn air; gorgeous dark-haired Alex, Misty's soulfinder, showing that a South African student could break out a few impressive moves when called upon. The air positively crackled when Misty and Alex danced together— even I noticed it up on stage. One of the challenging aspects of being a savant is that you have a partner born around the same time as you who is connected through his or her gift. If the match is a good one, like my friends, then the experience is amazing: your own gifts flourish and you find new things you can do together in a blending of powers. That's not to mention the chemistry of attraction woven into the link: that is off the charts if Misty and Alex are anything to judge by. We savants can wait all our lives to find that special person who completes our gifts; Misty and Alex had stumbled over each other at the ridiculously young age of sixteen.

Some guys have all the luck.

I took a swig of my water bottle as we readied ourselves for the last set. That wasn't fair of me: Misty had not been so lucky as she had practically had to die to get Alex. I was excited about the idea of meeting my partner one day but I didn't think I had it in me to risk so much, not even for a soulfinder.

The final number came and Jay took the applause; I bet he had practised that bow as it was the classic pose of the rock star clutching his guitar like a girlfriend. He then swept an arm to the rest of the boys in the band, but turned his back to me so I was edged out. He was such a loser. It was still worth it to have that priceless memory of him soaked to the skin. I had to be very careful how I used my gift as savants were supposed to keep their powers secret from ordinary people and mine was a more obvious gift than many, but I gave myself a pass on this occasion. Only a saint would have resisted the temptation of putting Jay in his place.

'You've been a great audience.' Jay replaced his guitar on its stand. 'Thank you and good night!' He ran off stage, pushing me aside as he headed for the wings.

I was prevented from tipping over the edge of the

platform by a quick grab from Matt, our drummer. Lacking the pretensions of the guitarists and saxophone player, Matt had managed to cling on to his place in the band despite the multitude of fallings-out that Jay had instigated. That's why we were called *Seventh* Edition: once upon a time there had been a *First* Edition. 'Hey, Angel, what's up between you and Jay?'

'Hound dog Jay wanted a snog before the show,' I said blithely. 'I turned him down.'

Matt patted my shoulder in sympathy as we walked into the wings. 'So how did he get wet a minute before we went on?'

'Poetic justice I'd say.'

Matt grinned. 'He can be so retro in his attitude to girls. You shouldn't have to put up with stupid stuff like that.'

'Oh, don't get me wrong: I don't put up with it; I stomp on retro males and dance on their graves.'

Matt tapped his nose. 'I consider myself warned. You are a warrior: Joan of Arc of the dressing room.'

He was a sweetie, always finding the right thing to say to boost my confidence. Most people assume I have bags of the stuff; only astute guys like Matt know most of it is me sassing to pretend I'm not afraid. 'Thanks, petal.' I went up on tiptoes and gave him a kiss. 'We did good tonight, yes?'

'Yep. We did good.'

We grinned at each other and parted to talk to our guests backstage.

'Angel, you were wonderful!' exclaimed Misty, giving me a hug. As my friend was burdened with the gift of being unable to lie, I knew the compliment was sincere. 'You stand out like a burning beacon of pure talent!'

I chuckled. 'Thanks, sweet pea.' Only a little taller than me, she was a comfortable person to embrace.

Next in line was Summer. 'That violin solo in "Star-

Crossed" is very special—it makes my toes tingle every time. Who composed it: you or Jay?'

So she had realized, had she? Summer was alarmingly penetrating even when she did not exert her gift for mind reading. 'Jay would have it that he wrote every note but actually most of it came out of a jamming session when I improvised. He won't acknowledge that though.'

Misty frowned, her freckled nose creasing in an adorable fashion. 'Do you want me to go stand next to him and ask him?' If she did that, letting go of the control over her gift, she would have him confessing all his most embarrassing truths.

'So tempting, but no need. I'm happy working with the guys he's managed to bring together—I think we've really got something good going. So I guess putting up with his ego is just the price I have to pay.'

It was Summer's turn to frown. 'That's not the only price he asked, is it?'

I bit my lip. If Summer had dipped into my thoughts she would have picked up on my relishing of the dressing-room dousing. 'It's OK. I cooled him off.'

Alex put an arm round my shoulder. Because I'm short, I think he comes over especially protective of me in a big brother way. 'Did that jackass do something? Do you want me to put him straight?' Alex has an awesome power to persuade with just the power of his voice.

'It's OK, Alex: I did that myself and enjoyed every moment.' I told them about the encounter, producing the hoped-for gales of laughter. The others backstage began to cast envious looks in our direction as we were clearly having the best time. Jay threw one dark scowl my way but carried on with his earnest conversation with a couple I had never seen before. His gaze told me we still had to settle our accounts.

That could wait. I checked Summer's watch: eleven. 'I'd best go and get changed. Meet you back here in ten minutes?'

Dipping into my changing room, I quickly stripped off my stage clothes and dressed in more comfortable low heels, leggings and tunic dress for the cold ride home on the Underground. Packing up my jewellery, I stuffed everything into my bag and headed for the boys' room. I found the band all gathered around Jay, who was in the middle of his usual post-match analysis of the gig.

'Just saying goodnight!' I said, poking my head round the door.

'Wait a minute, Angel: you should be here for this,' said Matt. 'Jay said he's got an announcement.'

Jay folded his arms and kicked back on his metal-framed chair. 'She can go. It doesn't concern her.'

If he wanted me to go, then of course I had to stay. 'No, it's fine: I'd like to hear the news. I've got time before the last train.'

'All right then.' Jay swung tauntingly on two chair-legs, eyes fixed on me. He was up to something and it wouldn't be great for me. 'I've some spectacular news: the Rockport promoters have invited us to be part of the lineup this year. They're coming back to me tomorrow with the terms and conditions but they've hinted that they're generous.'

'Oh wow!' My exclamation was lost among the hoots and shouts of glee from the band.

'It's our big break, guys. The lineup this year at the festival is sweet. They've got confirmation that Gifted are going to play.'

'Really!' Gifted were only one of my favourite bands—indie but with an appeal to the mainstream. They were said to be awesome live but I'd never had a chance to see them. Now I was not only going to be able to watch but also I was part of the same lineup, rubbing shoulders backstage. I was going to have so many fangirl moments I was going to embarrass even myself.

'So we've got to work hard over the next few months—polish our presentation, write some new songs.' Jay sounded like a commanding officer ordering his troops into battle. 'I don't want us to waste this chance. Can I count on you?'

Of course, we all offered our support. Jay may be a jerk but he'd got us this far.

'There's just one change to announce now. I told the promoters we were coming as an all-male lineup—it plays better in the publicity. A girl detracts from building a female fan base.'

'What!' I exploded.

'Hey, you can't do that!' exclaimed Matt.

Jay shrugged. 'It's done. Move on.'

I saw red. 'You're . . . you're just doing this because I wouldn't let you kiss me!' The water in the bottle on the dressing table behind him started to bubble but I was too irate to rein in my temper. Thankfully, no one noticed, as they were focused on my outburst. 'That's sexual discrimination—harassment—both! I'll . . . I'll sue you!'

Jay smirked. 'Good luck with that. You don't have a contract. You've been singing with us because I asked you. You were never really one of Seventh Edition.'

First I had heard of it. Was he forgetting all those other times when he'd asked me to do stuff 'for the sake of the band'?

'That's not fair!' protested Matt. The other band members looked embarrassed but no one else was brave enough to speak up in my defence.

Jay rounded on the drummer. 'Oh I see: she's been giving it up for you, has she, Matt? That's why you're defending her?'

Matt snarled. 'That's disgusting and not fair to either of us.

Some of us can have a relationship with a girl more evolved than that. She's a mate.'

Jay crossed his arms. 'Fine: feel free to follow her out of the door. Drummers aren't so hard to find.'

No, no, my lovely evening was all going wrong! I couldn't ruin this chance for Matt. I'd known Jay would probably kick me out one day; my friend deserved to be with the band when it made its break, even if he had to share the limelight with a wart on a rat's bum like Fielding. I squeezed Matt's shoulder and pressed him back in his chair as he was about to storm out with me. 'No, stay,' I said in a low voice. I then turned to direct a scornful look at Jay. 'You'd be stupid to get rid of Matt: he's the only one who's stood by you all these years. Shame you have no loyalty to match. Good luck finding yourself another violinist. You'll have to change the vocals too but you know that: no price feels too high at the moment, does it, to get even with me?'

Jay's eyes twinkled maliciously. 'I'll find someone to take your place, no problem.'

'I wouldn't be so sure.' Nothing left here for me now, I grabbed my handbag from the floor. 'Enjoy Rockport, *Eighth* Edition.'

Chapter 2

Several months later, I awoke to a Saturday morning in May with a blank weekend ahead of me. Oh how I missed performing! Going to sixth form at my school, doing a bit of waitressing to make some money, hanging out with my friends: all seemed very tame after the excitement of almost making it. Now I knew how it felt to be one of the guys on those talent shows kicked off before they became a familiar face—or Pete Best, the drummer booted out of the Beatles before they became famous.

OK, maybe I'm exaggerating but you know what I mean.

The only people who were happy at my falling out with Jay were my parents. Mum and Dad made coming over average their mission in life, compensation for having to hide the secret of being powerful savants. You wouldn't expect it if you met them but Mum can manipulate air and Dad has an awesome telekinetic gift. They are also each other's soulfinder. With that combo, you'd think they'd both be out fighting crime or something flashy but they have the character profile of tortoises. Sure, they love each other but frankly it is such a comfortable affection that they have settled into being plain old Mr and Mrs Campbell of Putney and are gloriously happy in that rut.

They must wonder what trickster god was in command of fate when they had me for their only child.

'So, love, what are your plans for the weekend?' Mum asked me as we ate breakfast together. 'Revision I hope?'

I was in the middle of my exams so of course it was revision. 'I'll study my music. That's on Monday.'

Her pretty pale blue eyes smiled contentedly at me from under the fringe of her blonde bob: her chick was in the nest so she was happy. I think if I announced that I never wanted to leave home she would be exultant. She was fearful of anything that lay outside her front door, which was funny considering how she could blow any bad guy to kingdom come with her power.

Dad came in wearing his blue towelling robe and slippers that had begun to go at the toe, but heaven forbid that you suggest he replace them. His light brown hair stuck up in tufts. In a habit of long standing, my mum sent a little breeze to smooth it down. 'Morning, Angel! How's my little girl today?' His robe gaped open as he kissed me, revealing the UK dates from an old AC/DC tour on his T-shirt.

I got up and stacked my bowl in the dishwasher. 'Fine, thanks.' Except that I wanted to howl with boredom. Don't get me wrong: I love my parents to pieces but they are just so calm, sitting side by side like two cows chewing the cud; in bovine terms, their daughter was more bull in a china shop.

Dad took my place and called muesli into his bowl with a flick of a finger, grains arching through the air in a cool cereal-bow.

The phone rang. I grabbed it from the stand. 'Campbell home for retired rockers, how may I help you?'

'Angel.' It was Misty. 'Why aren't you answering my texts?'

I lowered my voice to a dramatic whisper. 'Because I am on a secret mission behind enemy lines and can't risk exposing my cover.'

Misty gurgled with laughter. 'Yeah, right. Or maybe you forgot to put your phone on charge?'

'That might be a possibility.' I am notorious for forgetting stuff like that. I mean to do it then get distracted by a thought or a musical phrase and off I go.

'Look, I know you must be revising, but can you come out this evening?'

I did my happy dance. 'All work and no play makes Jill a dull girl,' I said in my best pious tone.

'You—dull? Never.'

'Where're we going?'

'I meant: can you come over to mine?'

'Oh.' I love the Devon family but it wasn't quite what I had in mind. I was thinking more club and loud music.

'It's just that Will Benedict's in the UK and wants to talk to you.'

'Oh!' That was more like it. Two of Misty's aunts had become linked by soulfinder bonds to the Benedict family from Colorado, seven amazing savant brothers. I loved all of them with hopeless devotion and rued the day that their parents, Karla and Saul, had stopped having sons before they had one my age that I could nab as my soulfinder. Will was the middle one of the tribe: a square-shouldered guy in his mid-twenties, who in the UK would have been up for a rugby squad selection thanks to his rugged frame and defensive instincts. He was from the wrong country for sport. His hunkiness would be wasted on American football as all that muscle would have to be hidden by padding and helmet. 'He wants to see me?'

'Yes.'

'Me especially?'

'Yes.'

I gave a squeak of pleasure.

'He's got something to ask you—a favour.'

'Intriguing.'

'That's what I said but he was too far away for me to make

him tell me the truth. I've found Skype defeats my power. He was being very mysterious.'

'Then I can't wait to find out. What time do you want me?'

'Around seven. Come for supper. I'll ask Summer too.'

'Lovely-bubbly. See you then.'

I put the phone down. 'Is it OK if I go over to Misty's tonight?'

'That's fine, dear,' said Mum placidly.

'I'll give you a lift,' offered Dad.

'You two are the best.' I kissed Dad's cheek and wafted out to get dressed, telling myself off for my ungenerous thoughts about my parents earlier. I was so lucky to have them. Three fireballs like me in the house and the place truly would explode.

One of the best things about being a savant is the way our families interlink. Will Benedict was no blood relative to Misty and the rest of the Devons but because two of his brothers were soulfinders to Mrs Devon's sisters, he was naturally considered one of the clan and expected to stay with them whenever he was in the UK. And because Summer and I were friends with Misty, we were then added on to the chain so I could claim a kind of sisterly relationship with the Benedicts. Look round the savant world and you'll see similar chains stretching from family to family, so in a way we are all one big extended tribe. Add the fact that we can all talk to each other telepathically, then you can see how close bonds might grow.

When Misty showed me in, Will was sitting on the back terrace with Alex, enjoying a beer in the late sunshine. Hand on heart, as much as I love my country, I have to admit that England is pretty dud when it comes to climate; but this was one of the few days in the year when we managed perfection: garden ablaze with flowers, light mellow and tinged with pink, spot-on temperature for sitting out.

Will put down his beer and got up when he saw me. 'Long time no see. How's my favourite hellraiser?'

I looked round, pretending to seek another person behind me. 'She isn't here so I'm sorry, William, but you'll have to make do with me.'

He chuckled at the William. No one else called him that, not even his mother when she was cross. 'Come here.' He gave me a hug, lifting me off my toes. 'How've you been, Angel Clare Dora Campbell?'

I wrinkled my nose against his T-shirt. I hate my full name. When Victor Benedict, Will's older brother, pointed out that my initials were AC/DC, none of his brothers let me forget. I can't imagine what my mum had been thinking, agreeing to that. 'I've been fine, thanks.'

He set me down so I could exchange a hug with Alex.

'*Howzit, bru?*' I asked him in my best South African accent.

He nodded with approval and bumped knuckles with me. 'You're learning.'

Misty came out carrying a rattling tray of drinks. She tripped over the doormat but Alex saved the glasses with a well-timed dive. He had quickly learned to anticipate her chaos-creating moments.

'Thanks, Alex.' She juggled the tray to the table and sat down next to him with a sigh. 'Mission accomplished. Help yourself.'

I picked up a can of lemonade, not bothering to use a tumbler. 'Is Summer coming?'

'She couldn't get away this evening. Her mum's having one of her episodes.' Gloomily, Misty rubbed the condensation off the side of her glass. Summer was very tight-lipped about her home situation: she didn't even invite us—her best friends— to visit her there; but we had guessed enough to know that her mother was not well, suffering from some kind of mental

17

illness that placed heavy demands on Summer as the only daughter. When we asked if we could help, Summer always refused so we were left with offering silent, loving support.

A thought came to me. 'Will, I know you have something to ask me but I was wondering: could you first just check that Summer's OK? You know, no threats against her?' Will's power is to sense danger. He is also skilled at protective tactics. Naturally that had led him into starting a career when he left college offering personal protection to people and places associated with us savants. He was already making quite a name for himself.

Will arched a brow in question, brown eyes reflecting his concern. 'You're worried about her? What's the story there?'

'Not sure—Summer keeps her secrets—but would you mind?'

'No problem.' He uncrossed his legs and closed his eyes, fingers pressed against both temples. He leaned forward, a little like someone in the attitude of prayer, giving me a rare glimpse of the top of his head, which was a swirl of wavy thick brown hair. After a moment, he opened his eyes. 'She's OK, Angel. I get the sense of a long-term problem—not exactly a threat or a danger but something volatile—yet nothing is setting off alarms tonight.'

Feeling a lot more relaxed, I grabbed a handful of crisps. 'Thank you. Sorry for abusing your professional skills.'

He winked. 'That's only fair as I want to make use of yours.'

'But I don't have a profession—unless you count waitressing.' I tapped my foot against Misty's. 'I make a better one than our hostess-with-the-mostest.'

Misty nodded solemnly. 'That's true.'

'Misty makes a gorgeous waitress, trust me,' added Alex, kissing her forehead. From the intent look between them I could tell they were exchanging little messages about the night they had discovered they were soulfinders. Misty had been ineptly serving drinks then too, but who could blame her as she had more important things on her mind?

Will cleared his throat. Stroking Misty's knee, Alex sat back with a twinkling smile. Misty was looking a little flushed.

'I meant your music, Angel,' Will said, returning us to his request.

'Oh.' I exchanged a glance with Misty, dipping quickly into telepathy. *Did you tell him I was booted out of the band?*

No. I had no clue what he was thinking.

'You see, Angel, you are the only person I know who's involved in that scene over here. Zed has links back in New York but I can't wait that long for the group to go there.'

I rubbed my cheek against the can, wondering if I'd missed something. 'What group?'

Will opened his mouth then closed it again.

'You're not making a lot of sense, *bru*,' said Alex. 'Why not back up and start again?'

Will grinned and took a swig of his beer. 'OK, sorry. It's just that I'm nervous.'

'You!' I laughed. Will was the most unflappable person I knew. 'How can that be?'

'My soulfinder.'

'Oooh!' I jumped up and did another of my happy dances, scattering crisps in my wake. 'What's she like? Where's she from?' I plonked myself on his knee and kissed his cheek in pure delight for him. 'Can I meet her? Does she have a gorgeous younger brother?' I waggled my brows at him and then bounced up to return to my seat.

Will counted off his replies on his fingers. 'I don't know yet. Possibly Amsterdam. I hope so. No idea.'

Deflated by the lack of detail, I sank back on the cushions. 'Oh. You don't know very much about her, do you?'

Misty kicked me. 'Angel, you're jumping the gun again.'

'OK, I'll behave. Will, back up and tell me all about her.'

Will and Alex exchanged an amused look.

'Scout's honour.' I held up three fingers in a pledge sign.

Will grinned. 'I can't believe they ever let you in the scouts—those poor guys wouldn't know what hit them. OK, I'll start with Crystal.'

'Great.' I hugged my knees to my chest, settling down for the story. 'Misty's soulseeking aunt has identified your soulfinder for you.' Crystal was blessed with the gift of sensing where our other halves could be found.

'Not quite. She's known for a while that mine is based in Amsterdam but my soulfinder spends most of her time travelling. No sooner do I make plans to go hunt for her than the direction changes. It's been driving us crazy until Yves—'

'The gorgeous geek,' I supplied. The second youngest Benedict brother was a knockout combination of brains, kindness and good looks. Sadly he was also too old for me and had already been snapped up by my mate, Phoenix.

'Suggested,' continued Will with a wry smile, 'that he write a little programme cross-referencing her movements with international events. We had a theory she might be an aid worker or a government representative but that was wrong. The closest match proved to be . . . ' He paused to take a swig.

'Yes?' I asked breathlessly.

'Proved. To. Be.'

'Yes!'

Alex made a drum roll. They were winding me up on purpose, the pesky rats.

'Proved to be the tour dates of Gifted.'

I shot from my seat like a rocket. 'Your girl's in the band!' I landed with a thump. 'But—wait a moment—they're all guys.

Not that there's anything wrong with that if you swing that way but . . . '

Will's smile broadened. 'We think she's on the support staff: tour manager, technician or promoter, not a performer.'

'Oh. That's good too. Have you got a name or a face?'

'The Savant Net doesn't have any candidates on our books that fit the profile but, as you know, not everyone is connected to the Net. There are quite a few women of the right age that might be her as the entourage to the band is large: make-up, hair, wardrobe as well as the managerial staff.' He leaned forward. 'What I need is a member of a band with backstage access at Rockport who can meet all the people and narrow down the field of possibilities. I imagine there'll only be one, maybe two savants among them so it shouldn't be too hard once inside the gates. Problem for me is that the band is so famous they keep ordinary members of the public far, far away.'

'I see.' I felt awful that I was going to let him down.

'And Zed said he foresaw you performing at the festival the other day—just a snatch but he said you sounded great. That gave me an idea of asking you to be my spy.'

'He did?' That was weird: Zed's predictions were rarely wrong.

'So what do you say? Will you help me find her?'

I rubbed my knees with the flat of my palms. 'Of course, but the thing is . . . '

'She got kicked out of the band because she wouldn't snog the lead singer,' Misty said bluntly.

Will put his beer down with a thunk. 'What? Who is this asshole?'

'And where does he live?' Alex finished for him.

As much as I would love to send my two heroes off to wipe the smile from Jay's face, I didn't think that would help Will. I held up a hand. 'Let me think a moment.' I'd kept in touch with Matt and he had told me that Jay hadn't yet found anyone to replace me. The ones he had tried out had left after quickly discovering they had serious artistic differences with Jay: namely, they were decent musicians who didn't like bullies. Jay would be getting desperate so might be ready to let me back into the lineup. The only problem was he would expect me to eat humble pie as I begged for my place and I'm not a natural at swallowing my pride.

But Will was such a great guy. If I sat back while his lady flitted off to the next tour destination, delaying their meeting by months, then I'd feel like an amoeba. And I really did want to perform at Rockport if I was as good as Zed said I sounded.

Sometimes future predictions make themselves come true just by being spoken aloud.

'OK, Will, I'll do it. I think I can talk my way back into the band.'

Will was scowling. 'I don't want you to have to pay too high a price to help me.'

'Don't worry: I won't let Jay stick his tongue down my throat. I have my defences.'

'You do?' He looked a little doubtful, taking in my diminutive stature and pea-sized knuckles compared to his biceps and boxer fists. I know I don't look very threatening.

'Tell him, Misty.'

My friend grinned. 'She extinguished his passion with a dunking in dirty water last time. Just imagine what she'd be able to do by the seaside.'

I wriggled my fingers, making Will's beer do a little loop in his bottle. 'I'll release the wrath of Neptune if Jay so much as looks at me the wrong way.'

Will admired the storm I had whipped up in his bottle— the froth was erupting from the top like a volcano. 'I believe you, AC/DC. You're one scary savant.'

Point made, I let his beer subside. 'So just give me a day or two and I should have secured a backstage pass. You, William, will not be leaving the UK without the love of your life if this guardian Angel has anything to do with it.'

Chapter 3

On reflection, it was much easier to promise to suck up to Jay
Fielding than to carry it out. First part of the operation was to
phone Matt and see how things were with the band. I caught
him on Sunday just before practice.

'Hi, it's Angel. How's my top drummer?'

Matt grunted.

'That good, hey? How goeth the hunt for my replacement?'

'Complete washout. We're not the same without you,
though Jay would rather walk over broken glass than admit
it. The last violinist broke a bow over Jay's head, he was that
pissed off with our great leader for saying he wasn't as good
as you.'

So Jay did rate me, at least behind my back. 'So there's still
a vacancy?' I let that hang out there for a second, knowing
Matt would put two and two together.

'You still interested? I'd've thought you were happy to
keep clear. If you come back, you know what Jay'll think.'

I suppressed a shudder. 'But I have you to protect me,
don't I?'

Matt sighed. 'I can't be watching your back all the time,
Angel.'

'That's OK, he's mostly attacked from the front.'

'You shouldn't joke about it—someone should teach him a
lesson. He can't get away with treating girls like that.'

'But when you hit fame and fortune, there'll be so many groupies knocking on his dressing-room door, too star struck to know better, the rest of us will be safe. Jay simply won't have time.'

'Or he'll think he's even more God's gift to girls.'

Sadly, that was true. 'Look, I don't want Jay to spoil this chance for me. I backed off for a bit but now I'd like to return. I earned my place on the band just like you guys—you know I did.'

'You'll hear no argument from me. We're just not that good without you. But I think Jay's aware you upstage him—as far as guys watching are concerned, at least. You'll have to make some pretty convincing arguments for him to give in.'

I pondered for a moment calling Alex in to assist with his savant powers. Problem was, now he knew Jay had pushed me out of the band for rejecting his smarmy advances, Alex might just make things worse by settling the score. I'd have to rely on my own charm. 'I'll drop by the rehearsal tonight and see what happens.'

'Your funeral,' said Matt glumly.

'Don't you want me back on side?'

'Of course I do. But I worry about you, sweetheart.'

'You're a good friend, Matt. Thanks. But I can look after myself. Jay's the one who should be worrying.'

The band rehearsed in a room in Imperial College where Jay was supposedly studying electronic engineering. At least he knew how to wire a mixing desk so his university place wasn't entirely wasted. I lingered outside to listen to how they sounded without me. I could hear a lot of expletives from Jay and dark grumblings from his band mates. I could not resist celebrating the discovery that my enemy was suffering. Let's face it: I never was in the frame for a sainthood.

They tried 'Star-Crossed' but without the violin solo it

came across as lame: all clever music tricks and no heart. Time for me to make my entrance.

'Hi, guys!' I said breezily, taking off my coat and opening my violin case. 'Do you want to try that again?'

Jay stood speechless. Matt grinned and started playing. The drum intro kicked everyone into action before Jay could stop them. I swooped my way through the solo, adding a few embellishments I'd thought of during the months I'd been away. When we came to the end, I let my bow drop by my side.

'So?' I asked. I pasted a huge Angel-sure-of-herself smile across my face.

'Angel, that was great!' said Kyle, our bass player, toasting me with his bottle of water.

'Cool. I've missed you,' admitted Richie, our saxophonist.

'Not bad,' said taciturn Owen, the second guitarist. High praise from him.

We all looked to Jay. I could see he was weighing up bawling at me for invading his rehearsal without an invitation versus making use of me.

'Guys, give Angel and me a moment,' he said. 'We've done enough for one night so I'll see you down in the bar.'

Obediently the band packed up and filed out. Matt gave me a warning look as he left. I checked the room for water sources but sadly the fire extinguishers were the CO_2 sort. An awkward silence fell.

Jay stood his guitar against the wall. 'You've got a cheek coming here.'

I ran my finger over the clasp of my violin case. 'Cheek? That sounds like me.'

'I suppose you want me to take you back?' Jay leaned against the door, blocking a quick exit. He was doing a good impression of being intimidating.

'Matt says you haven't filled my place yet so I thought we could do each other a favour.' It was much harder than I expected to meet his eyes.

'So you expect me just to forget what happened?'

Predictably, he wanted me to crawl. 'What did happen, Jay? You had an accident.'

'And yeah, you laughed at me.'

In his mind, that had been my real sin. He had no idea I was responsible for the accident in the first place.

Humble pie time. Will Benedict, I hope you are grateful. 'I'm sorry I laughed at you. I was nervous. Before the show I always get giggly—you know what I'm like.'

He gazed at me, probably wondering what else he could extract from me in the way of humiliation. 'You're still not one of us.'

My heart sank: I'd failed. 'OK.' I put on my coat, picked up my violin and headed for the door, hoping he'd let me pass without contact.

His hand gripped my elbow. 'But if you're nice to me, I'll bring you back for a trial period—on a session musician basis.'

I wanted to spit at him but forced myself to remember why I was doing this. 'You'll let me play at Rockport?'

'Yeah, but you won't be mentioned in the lineup. I'm serious about you cramping our appeal to female fans.'

'That's not fair.'

'It's the only deal I'm offering.' His fingers were digging in painfully.

I don't think I'd ever despised anyone so much as I did him at that moment. 'Then I'll take it.' I tugged to get my arm free.

'Part of the deal is being nice to me.' He pulled me closer.

Crap. 'I am being nice to you, Jay.' I hadn't scratched his eyes out yet.

'Nicer than that, honey.'

The door shoved behind him, toppling us both forward. Matt appeared with a trolley.

'Oh sorry,' he said, not in the least apologetic, 'just loading up my kit before my car gets a parking ticket.'

Saved by the drum kit. I freed myself from Octopus Jay. 'Let me help you. Jay says I can appear with you at Rockport: isn't that great?'

'Yeah. Thanks, mate.' Matt gave Jay an over-friendly punch on the shoulder. Jay winced. 'She's like our secret weapon, isn't she? A great find you made when you selected her.'

That's right, Matt: appeal to Jay's vanity. Make me into his discovery.

'I suppose I did. Yeah, I was the one that found her.' I could see Jay was already planning to use the line in interviews. 'See you in the bar after you've packed up?' Jay's eyes swept my entirely ordinary jeans and jumper combo, managing to make me feel tainted.

'Tragically, I've got to dash.' Hold back on the sarcasm, Angel. 'I've got a music exam tomorrow.'

Matt ruffled my hair. 'Good luck. You know I forget you're still in sixth form—way younger than the rest of us.' I picked up his subtext: Jay, you are a creep picking on schoolgirls.

'Not that much younger,' grumbled Jay, who liked no one to remind him that he had said goodbye to his teens.

'Well, thanks anyway for having me back,' I said brightly. 'I'll see you at the next rehearsal. Let me grab that for you, Matt.' Picking up the snare drum, I made a run for it with Matt's kit before Jay changed his mind.

Surveying the belongings scattered on my powder-blue carpet between bed and window, I ticked off the list of things I had to bring: wellies, tent, clothes for mud, clothes to perform in, clothes to party in, towel, toiletries. What else? Problem was I was so excited I couldn't sit still long enough to remember.

Mum came in carrying a pile of folded laundry. 'I expect these to end up in your chest of drawers, not on the floor, young lady.'

'Yes, Mum.' I gazed vacantly into the half-empty wardrobe. There was definitely something missing.

Mum stood among the flotsam and jetsam on my carpet sea, hands on hips. 'And is all that supposed to fit in your rucksack?'

'That's the plan.'

Mum hummed and started filling the bag with her usual methodical ease. 'I'm a little worried about you going off to that festival. I've heard about these things—don't take any pills people offer you.'

Wise advice but I really already knew that. 'I won't.'

'And try to get some sleep. Scientists have proved that our best sleep is the two hours before midnight.'

'Uh-huh.' Sleep could wait.

'And don't talk to any strangers.'

'I'll be with Will Benedict when I'm not with the band, camping along with Misty, Summer, and Alex. You like them, don't you?' I added a little travel case of jewellery to the pile.

Mum rifled through my heap of things. 'Are you not planning to change your underwear?'

I snapped my fingers. 'That's what I forgot.' I pressed a smacking kiss on the top of her head. 'Thanks, Mum. You must think I can't cross the road safely without you.'

She bit her lip, repressing her urge to agree. 'I was going to see if I could do something about the local weather for you—divert a few winds to a few miles down the coast.'

That would exhaust her—and was unethical. Savants aren't really supposed to use their powers to arrange the world for their own convenience—large-scale use was for emergencies only. If Mum adapted the weather at the Rockport festival to stop her daughter getting damp then some poor farmer in Africa might not get the rains she needed: everything is interlinked like the theory about the butterfly wings causing the hurricane. 'Please, don't. If it rains, then so be it. Wading through mud is part of the experience. I'll be fine.'

'We're only a phone call away.'

I chuckled. 'I know, but this is Brighouse-by-Sea we're talking about. You know: sandy beaches, bucket-and-spade kids, pensioners with flasks. It's not as if anything will happen to me, is it?'

Jay had made it clear that, as 'not one of the band', I was responsible for getting myself to the festival. No place in his minivan for me, he announced at our last rehearsal. Had he heard about the photo of him I had stuck to the dartboard on the back of the shed door? I found that great therapy. Seventh Edition's loss was my gain as Will had hired a car so he could drive us to the south coast and I'd far rather travel with my friends. The plan was to arrive in good time for Wednesday, the first day of the festival. Gifted weren't expected to pitch up much before their performance on Friday. I had a gig on Thursday and Will wanted to give me time to prepare the ground and get to know my way around backstage.

Poised by the window next to the front door, I was out of the house even before Will tooted the horn outside. The others were already in the car: Summer in the front, Alex and Misty in the back.

'Hi, guys!' I jumped down the steps and shoved my tent in the boot, ignoring the fact that it was full to the brim already. It would fit somehow. Dad followed with my rucksack. He and Will had to unpack to fit everything in.

'I can't imagine how you're going to carry all this stuff,' Will marvelled. It was true that my rucksack was as big as me and possibly heavier.

'Excuse me: *performer*.' I tapped my chest. 'I have to be prepared for my public.'

'She just wants to impress Gifted,' said Misty shrewdly. 'Once they are in the room, you'll not get another word of sense out of her.'

'It's not my fault they are all so . . . oooh . . . talented and hot.'

'But most of them are way too old for you,' said Summer.

'But that's not the point: I admire them as musicians.'

'Yeah right,' muttered Alex.

I plonked myself next to Misty. With my two violins on my knee, it was a squeeze, but we managed it.

'Two?' asked Alex.

I patted the black rock violin. 'One for stage—and the other because . . . well, just because.' I had had a strong hunch that I should bring my folk one too. Savants learn to listen to instincts.

'Angel doesn't like to be parted from Freddie,' explained Misty.

'Freddie?' Alex looked doubtfully at the battered case that held my second instrument.

'No, she hasn't got some creepy ventriloquist doll in there!' laughed Misty, obviously having read Alex's mind through their telepathic link. 'Freddie the Fiddle.'

'I should explain I named it when I was nine, in honour of rock legend Freddie Mercury.' The problem about having such old friends is that they never let you forget an unfortunate nickname or silly thing you did when at primary school. At one stage, it had even been painted in Tipp-Ex across the lid. 'I've not called it that for years.' At least, not when other people were present.

The boot crunched closed. I hugged my violins closer to my chest, relieved I'd had the foresight to keep them with me.

'Give me Freddie,' said Summer. 'I've room by my feet.'

'You can have Black Adder.' I passed her the rock violin. 'Freddie stays with me.'

Dad tapped on the window and I pushed the button to bring it down to say goodbye.

'Have a lovely time, all of you. Bring her back in one piece,' Dad said to Will.

'Yes, sir. Thanks for the loan of your daughter.'

Dad smiled doubtfully and then stood back to let us go. My parents may be reluctant to let me out of their sight but they don't get in the way when they know I really want something.

'I'll text when we get there,' I shouted out of the window.

Summer, as the most responsible English person present, was on navigation. She tapped the destination into the satnav. Will pulled out of my road and headed for the South Circular.

'So, how long's the drive?' he asked, rolling his neck.

'It's quite a journey. We should be there in about three hours,' Summer told him.

His shoulders started shaking with laughter.

'What?' I asked.

'We're setting off at the crack of dawn to drive for just three hours? I drive three hours in Colorado to pick up groceries.'

'Brighouse is a long way from London,' Misty said.

'Alex, help me out here, bro.'

'Small-island mentality, Will. You'll get used to it. Misty's trained me into thinking that anything over half an hour is an expedition requiring months of planning, scheduled stops and emergency supplies.'

Misty elbowed him. 'Not true.'

He squeezed her arm. 'OK—a day's planning.'

'Don't knock your host country, William,' I said in my best reproving manner.

Will tapped the brim of an imaginary chauffeur cap. 'Yes, ma'am.'

'Left, William, we drive on the left!'

'Oh, yeah.' Our car selected the correct side of the quiet suburban road. 'Just checking you were paying attention.'

We arrived at the campsite at lunchtime, joining the long queue of festival-goers filing into the field for parking. Cars had to be left some distance from where the tents were to be pitched so that meant we had to carry all our stuff for what felt like a mile. Will took pity on me and shouldered my rucksack as well as his, but that still left me toting two violins.

'I hope you've got somewhere safe to leave them,' warned Summer.

'I imagine there will be an instrument store backstage.' I edged round a puddle—wellies were packed, weren't they? Summer, of course, had on sensible rubber ankle boots with Monet lilies on them, whereas I was optimistically wearing sandals.

Misty laughed and nudged Alex.

'What?' I asked. They were telepathically whispering again.

Misty blushed slightly. 'I was just telling Alex: imagine, Freddie and Black Adder can nestle up to Kurt's guitar.'

'You think?' Many of my daydreams featured me and Kurt Voss, lead singer of Gifted, jamming together and, well, other stuff.

'No, I'm joking, Angel. You'd be lucky they let you anywhere near their gear—must be a security nightmare with so many crazy fangirls out there.' She grinned at me. 'I wonder what they'll say when they find one has slipped through the net?'

I stuck my tongue out at her. 'I'm not going to do anything

crass. I'll be professional—you know, politely interested? But first, I'm going for the mysteriously aloof girl haunting the green room, looking soulful with some dark delicious secret. Kurt will become fascinated by me and want to find out more.'

Misty snorted with barely suppressed laughter as Alex and Will chuckled out loud.

'What?'

Summer fell in step beside me, neat black backpack settled comfortably on her shoulders so she still looked fresh. 'I think you'd be better off being yourself, Angel. The strain of trying to be aloof will probably kill you.'

That was likely true. My shoulders slumped. 'I expect they won't let me within a mile of any of Gifted. But anyway,' I lifted my chin, 'I'm doing this for Will. *It's all about you, it's all about you, baby.*'

As I struck up the classic track, a favourite from my childhood, Alex joined in, adding the harmony. Will laughed and beat time on my backpack. Misty and Summer added their voices to mine on the main tune. Singing, we entered the campsite.

Chapter 4

I approached the performers' entrance a little fearfully. I would not put it past Jay to have failed to request a pass for me. That would be so like him: offer something then whip it away at the last moment to make me suffer and have to beg my way into his presence.

In the Portakabin, the security guard, a great black bear of a man, frowned down at the newcomer carrying two violins. I suppose I was possibly the only performer to arrive on foot and alone.

I put down Black Adder and showed him my letter of engagement. I had to go on tiptoes to reach the window, which made me feel like Frodo the hobbit arriving at the Inn at Bree where the big people live. 'Hello, I'm Angel Campbell. You should have a pass for me, I hope?'

He took the letter from my fingers, scowled at it as if it had just bopped him on the nose, then he looked through a box of envelopes. He tugged out one with my name typed on the outside. Phew. Checking the address against the letter, his face broke into the first smile it had probably seen since England won the World Cup.

'Miss A. C. D. Campbell?'

'Yes?'

'Initials AC/DC?'

'Er, yes.'

He flourished the envelope. 'Best group ever.'

I'd discovered another old rocker—that figured, seeing the job for which he had volunteered. 'So my dad says.'

He handed down my letter and envelope with much more warmth than he had first shown me. 'Welcome to Rockport, Miss Campbell. If you need anything, just let me know. I'm Al.'

'Nice to meet you, Al. Can you point me to the instrument store?'

'No problem. Head straight through the green room—that's that circular tent. On the far side you'll find several locked storage units. Your envelope contains the code for the one your band has been allocated.'

'Great.'

He leaned forward over the edge of the window to take a better look at my luggage. 'Who you playing with, pet?'

'Seventh Edition.'

His face registered his disappointment. 'Haven't heard of you.'

'Haven't heard of us *yet*,' I corrected.

He chuckled. 'I'll try to catch you on stage then.'

Pleased with that encounter, even if it was all thanks to my absurd initials, I walked swiftly to the green room. The festival site stretched over several fields and ended abruptly at the low cliffs of Brighouse-by-Sea. The short springy grass saw flocks of sheep more often than musicians in residence. There was still plenty of evidence underfoot of their habitation in little traps of dried droppings. Lovely. The performers' area was established to the left of the main stage. That was famous for being built jutting out over the cliff with the stunning backdrop of the sea. Shelter was provided by the pine woods that curved around the site so from above, in the helicopter shots, the site looked like a half moon of green bitten out of the dark forest. Once filled with people, music, and lights, it was going to be stunning. I couldn't wait.

I pushed open the flap of the tent to be greeted by the faint tang of incense. Turkish carpets covered the ground, muffling sound.

'Welcome to the yurt. Can I see your pass please?' The attractive girl on the reception desk glanced down at the envelope in my hand. Her brunette hair was swept up in a French plait and she was wearing vibrant red lipstick—no sign that she was roughing it in a sheep field.

'Oh, yes, sorry.' I put down my violins and cracked open the seal. 'And the winner is: Angel Campbell!' I tugged out the blue lanyard and hooped it over my head.

She didn't get the joke—or if she did, thought it too lame to be noticed. 'Please wear your pass at all times and make sure you do not leave it lying about. We take security very seriously.'

'Absolutely.'

'I'm here to help you with any of your needs—booking taxis, questions about how things run, changes to the performance schedule: you name it, I'm the person to come to.' Her smile was automatic.

'Thanks.'

'The refreshments in this tent are available for you free of charge.'

'Great.'

'But we would appreciate it if you respect the privacy of other performers. This is the space where our guests are supposed to be able to relax and not worry about the press snooping on their activities.'

How had she sniffed out my fangirl propensities? 'I understand.' I was itching to ask her about Gifted but somehow I just knew that would go down like garlic bread at a vampire's dinner party. She turned away and began leafing through pages clipped to a board. I hovered.

She lifted her gaze back to me and raised a brow—Lord, how I wish I could do that. 'Is there anything you need now?'

'I was just wondering who else has arrived already.' There: that was nice and vague.

She glanced down at her list. 'You are the first from your group. We've had a few early arrivals, mainly those supporting the show tonight.' She ran through a few names, many of whom I had seen on YouTube or heard live. 'The big names for this evening aren't expected until after three.'

'And . . . um . . . Gifted—anyone from that group here yet?'

Her expression hardened. 'No. They don't perform until Friday as I'm sure you know.'

'I just thought they might send someone in advance, you know: to check things out?'

'Well, they haven't registered yet. They won't be here until tomorrow at the earliest.'

Someone cleared his throat behind me.

'If that's everything Miss Campbell, I have to get on. I've other guests to see to.' Her eyes rose to the person at my shoulder and her smile warmed thirty degrees.

'Right. Thanks.' I bent to pick up my violin but a hand was already on Freddie before I could reach for him. I straightened and found myself looking up into a pair of ice-blue eyes in a tanned face, topped by a spiky fringe of gold-shot hair. My lips moved before my brain caught up. 'Oh my God!'

The guy's lips quirked into a smile, revealing cute bracket lines either side of his mouth. 'Not God: Marcus Cohen.'

Walked into that one, hadn't I? 'I meant . . . ' What had I meant: you are so gorgeous that I couldn't help myself?

He didn't wait for me to embarrass myself further. 'Here: this is yours, I think?' He thrust Freddie at me. 'Sorry, but I'm in a hurry. Henry, do you have a message for me?'

Henry—she who manned the reception—fluttered and

batted her eyelashes at him. Even her cool efficiency melted in the heat of the dark-blond god's wry smile. 'Oh, yes, Marcus. Margot Derkx called by and left this for you.' She handed over a folded piece of paper.

Marcus 'OMG' Cohen flicked it open. 'Sweet. See you later.' He strode off. Never had SuperDry beanie, long-sleeved grey T-shirt, and faded jeans looked so good.

'Was that really him?' I asked, patting my heart.

Still feeling the warming after-effects of his visit, Henry smiled conspiratorially at me. 'Yes, Miss Campbell, that was Marcus Cohen.'

'Call me Angel.'

Henry pursed her lips. 'Angel: really?'

'It's my name.'

Henry shrugged. 'Well, Angel, keep an eye on that one. He's headed for big things.'

'You don't have to tell me that.' I'd seen his face in the music press often enough and even cut out a photo to add to the guys who made the Wall of Buffness in my bedroom. 'He plays with that new group, doesn't he?'

'That's right. Black Belt. They're touring with Gifted. The three of them released their first album at Christmas. Very hot property at the moment: we were lucky to sign them along with Gifted.'

'Very hot,' I agreed.

Despite herself, Henry let out a humanizing giggle. 'Uh-huh. You'd better call me Henry—short for Henrietta.'

'See you later, Henry.' I headed for the storeroom. This mission for Will looked like it might have some excellent side benefits.

Having seen Freddie and Black Adder safely stowed, I texted my friends that I was going to hang around for a while to acclimatize. Helping myself to a juice, crisps and a couple of sandwiches, I found a table outside the yurt and tried to look as though I belonged. The places rapidly filled up with new arrivals grabbing a late lunch before the sessions began on the second and third stages. Main stage didn't kick off until seven thirty. No sign of Marcus Cohen. A man in a leather jacket took a spare seat next to me without asking, too busy checking his emails and smoking to bother with courtesy. I was amused to hear that, when he took a call, he managed to use the f-word in every sentence with mind-boggling variations.

'Angel!' Two meaty hands landed on my shoulder, making me jump.

'Matt! You just got here?'

'Yeah. Jay got lost near Exeter.'

'You're supposed to turn off way before Exeter.'

Matt grinned. 'That's what I told him.' He put his beer and packet of crisps next to me. 'Who's your friend?'

'No idea.'

The man frowned at us as if it was our fault for talking at the table I had been occupying before his arrival.

'Have you met Joey Reef and Fresh Chance?' Matt waved to a couple of guys cutting a swathe through the milling crowds with their loose-hipped stride. They diverted from their path to join our table. 'They're both from London too.'

'Hey, Matt: how's it going?' The taller of the two brushed hands with the drummer. An impressive six-foot plus, he had shaved black hair, dark brows and stubble sculpted into sharp lines. Not that I'm shallow or anything but, on the strength of his appearance, I made a note to catch him later in performance.

His friend wore his hair in little dreads, had thick-rimmed black glasses and a Che Guevara cap. 'And what's a girl like this doing sitting with you, man? Your luck changed?'

'Fresh, this is Angel. She's in Seventh Edition with me,' Matt explained.

'Angel.' Fresh perched on the table between the leather jacket man and me. 'Fallen among us to make my dreams come true?'

I shook hands. 'You might be a teeny bit disappointed if you're expecting me to work miracles.'

'How's that Jay guy treating you?' asked Joey, leaning on the back of my chair, making me feel like a piece of cheese in a man sandwich. 'Matt says he's a pain in the ass.'

'He treats her like rubbish,' said Matt.

'No fair, man.' Fresh stole a crisp. 'If I had a girl like Angel on my side, I'd treat her right.'

'He doesn't have your good sense and impeccable taste,' I told him.

'Do you mind?' interrupted the leather jacket. 'I'm trying to work here.'

Not bothering to look round, Joey laughed derisively. 'Yeah, we do mind.'

The man stood up and flicked ash in our direction, before stomping away to another table.

'I see he's been to the rock school of charm. Is that like Jay's dad?' asked Fresh.

'No, that's Barry Hungerford, record producer,' said Jay, arriving just in time to see the exchange. He was smirking: someone else's mistake always cheered him up.

Both rappers swore—something they did with great invention and fluency. 'Oh, man. He's only got five of the top fifty hip-hop artists on his label,' moaned Fresh. 'I didn't know he would look so . . . '

'Miserable?' I suggested.

Jay took one look at our little cluster, and then the space next to Barry Hungerford on the far table, before heading over to join the bigger fish.

'Don't worry, guys,' I said, patting Fresh on the knee. 'If he wants to sign up rappers then he'll want you with, you know, an edge? Politeness isn't a selling point in that market.'

'You've got a smart girl there, Matt. Let me get another round before that dumbass Jay drinks all the good stuff,' offered Joey, moving swiftly to cover his embarrassment.

I held out my empty. 'Why, thank you. So generous with the free bar.'

Grinning, he took my glass. 'Watch it, Angel. I'm an edgy rapper, remember.'

'I'm quivering in my boots—or I would if I were wearing them.'

'Yeah, right.' He sauntered off, slapping hands with several acquaintances.

By the time the lights came on to illuminate the outside tables, we had gathered quite a crew. Henry had joined us as she came off duty, having been drawn in by Joey's jokes as he passed to and from the bar. Fresh, Joey, and Matt had many friends from the music scene—sound and lighting technicians as well as other artists, so we numbered about twenty, the largest group by far among those joining the early-evening lull in festival events. It was amazing having so many talented people together in one place, sparking off each other. I felt a little drunk on the excitement. Somehow I found myself singing with Fresh, doing a cover of a favourite track, that led to a couple of others getting out their acoustic guitars and then I was dancing on the table with Henry. Don't ask me how that happened, but we made a surprisingly successful duo. She confessed that she had volunteered for the festival because she had ambitions as a performer herself. It wasn't until I jumped down that I realized Marcus Cohen had taken a seat at Barry Hungerford's hostile encampment over the other side of the decking area and had been watching us. I suddenly wasn't so sure I had been impressive: to a guy headed for big things, perhaps I just looked as though I was trying too hard to catch the record producer's attention? I swear Hungerford's presence hadn't been any part of my motivation: it's just I can't sit still when there is so much music to enjoy.

But Marcus still looked so gorgeous and a little bit lonely stuck on the boring table.

I nudged Henry. 'Go ask Marcus to join us.'

Tucking a stray strand of brunette hair behind her ear, she glanced over at him. 'No, I couldn't.'

'Why not?'

'I'm too shy.'

'Geez, Henry: you've just been strutting your stuff in front of an audience of strangers. No way are you shy.'

'With him, I am. You do it.'

'Me? He doesn't know me.'

'He only knows me as staff. I'm not supposed to approach the guests.'

That was the moment when I wished I could raise a brow like she did. 'Really?'

'You lot don't count. You're . . . ' She blushed. 'Normal.'

Not quite, but I understood what she meant. We were the festival qualifiers; over at Hungerford's exclusive table were the top seeded players—and Jay.

I rubbed my palms together. 'Right: I'll do it.'

'Angel!' I don't think she believed I had the guts for it and now she looked quite worried for me.

I jiggled my clothes straight. 'It's OK. I won't be creepy stalker. I'll be friendly.' I was already regretting this but something was eating at me. The guy deserved a break. He was sitting with smarmy Jay and charmless Barry as well as three other serious-looking business people. Our side of the patio was having way more fun.

As Fresh and Joey broke into a rap battle with Matt drumming on a chair, I made my way over to the far table. I had already decided an indirect approach was best.

'Hey, Jay, how was the journey?'

Jay rubbed his jaw, puzzled at my sudden desire to talk to him after my ice cube manner of the last few weeks. 'OK,' he said finally.

'Do you want to join us?' I waved to my little party.

'I might later.' His eyes went to Barry, who was still busy with his emails and phone calls. Jay had been keeping the producer furnished with drinks and snacks, playing errand boy in the hopes of getting a chance to make his pitch.

'And what about you, um, Marcus?' I asked, aware my cheeks were torpedoing my attempt to seem cool and collected.

He shook his head. 'Thanks, but no thanks.' Marcus' expression was broadcasting irritation, scowl lines furrowing his brow under the beanie. He made me feel like an autograph hunter on Hollywood Boulevard pestering an A-lister.

Arms across my chest, I squeezed my elbows. 'We wouldn't make you sing—or dance. Only hopeless extroverts like me get to do that.'

'So I saw.'

Ouch. 'Right, so that's a "no" then?'

'Yes, it's a "no".'

It took a lot for me to walk back to our party with my head held high. I had mistakenly thought Marcus was OK when he had made the crack about OMG when we first met; but it turned out he considered himself above us. He went down in my book as more like Jay than Matt.

'No luck?' whispered Henry, who had been watching my diplomatic mission.

I shrugged, boosting my smile by extra sass. 'His loss.' I

jumped up on the table again and slapped Joey on the head. 'Sing something we can dance to, why don't you?'

Joey broke off his battle and jumped up next to me. 'Hey, girl, let's show them all how Londoners do party time.'

The guitarists struck up a fast club number, Matt cranked up the beat, Fresh did the vocals and the rest of us danced along.

See, Marcus Cohen, we didn't need you or your approval to have a good time.

The party broke up as the evening programme began. Most of my new friends were needed to man the soundboard or lights so had to leave for the technical checks. I was just saying my goodbyes to Fresh and Joey when my phone clucked and Misty's text came through.

Do you want pizza?

They'd be wanting an update and I'd let time run away with me. I'd rather drifted off mission, hadn't I? Texting a quick reply, I hurried back to the campsite. In my absence my friends had pitched the tents and got everything organized so they were now more than ready to dive into the festival.

'Everything OK?' asked Misty as I arrived a little out of breath. She and Summer were waiting for me by our tents; Alex and Will had already left to join the snaking queue at the pizza van.

I was going to say 'yes' but out came a big fat 'no'. 'Misty, you're not keeping control!' I squeaked in protest.

She frowned, checking her power. 'Sorry. I forgot because I was worried about you. You've been gone for hours. What happened to you?'

'I told you where I was. Outside the green room.' I grabbed a pink sweater for the cooler evening from my rucksack in the girls' tent.

Summer tugged the hem of my skirt straight as I backed out of the zip-up door flap. I always seem to manage to get myself in a mess. Probably not unconnected to the fact that I had been dancing on tables until ten minutes before. 'Take a moment and explain,' she suggested.

I stood up and took a breath. 'OK, OK. Most of the performers are great—we had an awesome time—but there are a couple who really get on my nerves.' I ran my fingers through my shoulder-length bob, giving it a quick comb. 'Jay as you know is a pain in the butt, but I also bumped into this other guy. He kind of made me feel . . . ' I pulled a face, ' . . . too pushy.'

Misty gave me a one-armed hug. 'The jerk.'

'What did you do?' asked Summer.

'I just asked him to join our party.'

'Party?'

Something about Summer's calm questioning made me wonder how I might have struck an outsider. I was beginning to regret my irrepressible urge towards exuberance. 'Well, I was having a good time.'

'Yes?' Summer exchanged a smile with Misty.

'We were singing and, er, dancing.'

'Dancing?' asked Misty.

'On the picnic tables.'

Summer laughed. 'For some guys that might be just a little too much, you know?'

'I guess. But I meant it as a friendly gesture.'

Summer hugged me. 'You, Angel, are the friendliest girl on the planet and we love you for it. If this guy can't appreciate you, then that's his problem.'

I nodded fiercely. 'Exactly what I said.'

'Who was he?' asked Misty. 'I just need to know so I can hiss his act.'

'Marcus "OMG" Cohen—he's in the band supporting Gifted.'

'He really calls himself that?' asked Misty dubiously.

Rooting through my tote, I pulled out a sparkly turquoise scarf with a flourish and flung it around my neck. 'No, but I did, sort of, and by mistake. When you see him, you'll understand.'

Misty's phone buzzed. She glanced down at the message. 'Forget him; much more important is whether you want pineapple with your ham?'

'Too right: who needs rock gods when there is pizza? Tell Will that I want as many toppings as possible.' I ordered extravagantly partly in defiance of guys with the Marcus Cohen approach to life. As far as I was concerned, life was for living, not for sitting on the sidelines, and if that meant overloading the pizza, then I was in.

Chapter 5

Alex and Will had bagged us a spot on some hay bales by the pizza van.

'Hi, guys! Sorry to abandon you all afternoon!' I called cheerfully, jumping up on the nearest bale to give each a hug.

Will offered a hand to help me down. 'How can I complain when you're here for me? Any progress?'

I cracked open the nearest pizza box. 'What flavour?'

'Every flavour—as you requested.' Will snagged a slice and took a bite. He chewed thoughtfully. 'It tastes kinda . . . confused, but good.'

Tasting a piece, I agreed with his assessment. 'My sort of pizza then. I did find out, Will, that Gifted are expected later. They don't perform until Friday but will rock up tomorrow. I met one of their support band so I guess some of the team will be coming ahead and then the big stars. If they're doing a big show there must be technical rehearsals the morning before when all us happy campers are sleeping off our late nights.'

Summer wiped her fingers on a serviette. 'I've been thinking: that name—Gifted. They've been around a while so I never questioned it before, but do you think that, if they're like us, that the name is deliberate?'

'You mean so in-ya-face no one notices their gifts?' asked Misty.

Alex frowned, his dark blue eyes pensive. 'I've never heard a whisper about them on the Net before; have you, Will?'

'No, and, trust me, I checked thoroughly before I left.'

'But it would explain part of their phenomenal success, if it's true,' added Misty. 'There's no other band like them.'

'If it is a clue, isn't the real question who else might be in on the secret?' I asked. 'We've already ruled out the band members on grounds of gender, so if Gifted are like us, maybe there's also another in their circle?'

Will sat forward, excited by the new lead. 'And gifts often run in families—just look at us. I'll need to go back and examine the links between the band and their entourage. And we may just have discovered a bunch of savants who work independently of the rest of us: that's a good outcome whatever else happens. The Net could help them stay undetected.'

'Oh, we can do much better than that.' I picked up the last piece of pizza, thought twice about my tight skirt, and handed it to Will. 'As much as I like tidying up the loose ends of the savant world, we're really here for love, and don't you forget it.'

'No danger of that.' Will held out the pizza. 'Go on: take a bite. You know you want to.'

'I'll be the size of a house.'

'Eat all you like and you'd never make more than a decent-sized dog kennel, Angel. Go on.'

Grinning, I nibbled a corner then pushed it back at him. 'Really, I'm stuffed.'

While the guys finished up the pizza, I looked round, enjoying the sights of the festival. Brightly coloured flags fluttered overhead against the flush-pink sky. Strings of lights decorated the stalls and food concessions, adding a magical element. The folk-tent flaps were thrown back and a woman with long dark hair strummed a guitar, singing to the small gathering of fans. She was good, giving a modern twist to a traditional song. Might be worth listening to from inside.

Before I could make the suggestion, Misty gasped and grabbed Alex's arm.

'Don't use telepathy!' she hissed.

'What? Why?' I asked.

'It's him—over there! No, don't all look round. Alex, you check. You remember him?'

Alex soothed her by putting his arm around her shoulders and rubbing her sleeve. 'Who, *bokke*?'

'That creep Eli Davis: the man in that anti-savant group who cornered us at my school. He had that device that registered telepathy, remember?'

'He's not someone I'd forget in a hurry.'

'I know Uriel took it off him but I wouldn't put it past him to have others made.'

Alex's face took on a hardened expression, quite unlike his normal easygoing demeanour. His resolve was clear: no one was going to mess with us on his watch. His eyes swept the crowd but there were so many people milling around finding a single man was almost impossible. 'I can't see him, *bokke*. Can you mind-shadow him, Summer?'

My friend shook her head. 'I have to see or sense him first.'

'Will?'

Our friend closed his eyes, reaching out with his gift. 'You're right, Misty: he's here. The threat level has crept up when I wasn't paying attention, but not for us. I sense a . . . malevolent presence but I don't think he has any idea we're around. He's after another target.'

'The same one as us, maybe?' asked Summer in a low voice.

'I guess.' Will tapped my knee to get my attention. 'Angel, I'm sorry to have to rush this, but you'll need to move quickly tomorrow and see if you can make contact with someone in the Gifted entourage as soon as the advance guard arrives. If he's after them, they'll need to be warned.'

I swallowed. I had hoped to have a chance to do this more subtly. 'But don't they have bodyguards for that kind of thing?'

Will shook his head. 'Davis and his gang aren't here to attack; their agenda is to expose savants. A group cut off from the rest of us won't have been warned through the usual channels to keep him at arm's length.'

'He poses as a journalist,' added Misty. 'He can get backstage on his credentials.'

'Not just poses: he *is* a journalist,' corrected Alex. 'That's his angle: he's looking to break one of the biggest stories of the century, revealing our existence to the general public.'

'And he's unlikely to be here alone,' concluded Will. He took out his phone. 'I'll text my brothers to let them know Davis is active again—see if we can get some backup.'

'That's good,' I said, shivering, as goosebumps stippled my skin.

'But until then, Angel, I'm afraid you're our best hope. Use your link to the support band and see if you can get an introduction to the rest of the Gifted crew.'

I exchanged a quick look with Misty and Summer. 'Um, I don't think that's a very good idea.'

Will's forehead creased in a frown. 'Why not?'

'That guy from the support band, he doesn't like me.'

'Impossible. Everyone likes you even when they find you . . . ' Will rubbed his chin, searching for the right word.

'Too vibrant for their sad little lives,' finished Misty.

'Aw.' I jumped up and twirled Misty in a circle. 'I love you, guys. OK, I'll remind the killjoy rock god that I'm sensational and he really wants to bring me into the inner circle of one of the most famous groups on earth.'

Summer stood up and joined our little girl huddle. 'That's right—you tell him: resistance is futile.'

'And if that doesn't work, I'll talk my way past security and have a word,' offered Alex.

'Let's see what Angel can do first.' Will turned his phone so I could see the screen. 'Here's the mugshot of Eli Davis my brother circulated last year. I'll send it to you.'

Misty wrinkled her nose. 'Yeah, that's him. Dark hair, big nose, dresses like you would expect from a journalist—smart casual. Carries a notebook. The thing that gives him away though is his hostility—I'm sure you'll sense that. He really hates us savants.'

'Do you think he knows about me?' I asked. If he were backstage, I'd have to plan what to do if I ran into him.

'He was at the Cambridge debate when you were there, but I doubt he would have paid you any attention. He was focused on Misty and me,' said Alex.

'I don't think he ever saw us together, did he?' Misty bit her lip. 'He did spy on me so I can't be sure, but I think you'll be safe from his attention as long as you don't use telepathy.'

'That sucks. You mean I can't talk to you about developments backstage?'

'Of course you can.' Will waggled his phone. 'Remember these devices?'

'Smart arse,' I muttered. 'OK. I'll move as quickly as I can tomorrow. I've also got an ally on the reception desk: she might help if I put my request right.'

Will tucked away his phone. 'I'm going to scout around and see if I can track Davis. Alex, keep an eye on the girls for me?'

'Sure.'

'And we'll keep an eye on him,' I added, not having much patience with this macho stuff the Benedicts were into.

'I think we should get under cover,' said Summer. 'Cut down the chances he'll run across Misty and Alex.'

She had thrown me an easy ball to get my wish of hearing the guitarist. 'Then we should go to a small venue. Folk tent, anyone?'

'Folk?' Alex didn't look too keen.

'Bob Dylan, Mumford and Sons, Taylor Swift—they all started on this circuit. You never know who you'll see before they hit the big time.'

Taking a longing look at the bands striking up on the main stage, my friends loyally followed me into the tent. It was just a shame we arrived as the guitarist finished and the accordion player took over. I would have to apologize later.

The next morning over breakfast of croissants and coffee, Will reported that he had not run across Davis in his search of the campsite.

'The threat level went down overnight so I'm guessing he's staying offsite.' Will blew the steam from his purple Thermos mug. 'But to be safe, no one is to use telepathy until we know for certain if he still has one of Dr Surecross's detectors. They register surges in psychic energy so your other gifts are also out unless you know how to mask the energy pattern.'

Misty went pale. 'He's bound to find me then. You know me: I'm hopeless at control.'

Alex brushed a tender kiss over her cheek. 'Don't worry: I'll help you with that. I'll *persuade* you to keep a lid on your truth power. I can do that keeping everything very low energy.'

She smiled with relief. 'Thanks, Alex. I would hate to be sent home because I was a liability.'

'You OK with the rules, Summer?' asked Will.

She nodded. 'Of course. You wouldn't notice me using my power.'

In teasing mode, I nudged Summer with my toe. 'Yeah, she is the crocodile of savants: skimming undetected under the water then, snap, her mind has you in her jaws.' I mimed the action, spilling a little coffee on the grass.

'Gee, thanks, Angel, for the flattering comparison,' laughed Summer.

As I joined in the laughter, my plastic cup tilted and a stream of coffee threatened to pour out on my bare legs. I summoned it back with a click of my fingers. The droplets of water separated into little globes and bobbed into the cup.

'Angel,' said Will.

I looked up, surprised at his severe tone. 'What?'

'No displays of power.'

'Oh come on: that takes next to no energy!'

'But it's hardly normal, is it? If you do that without thinking and someone else sees, then you've blown it.'

Playing with any liquid containing water was second nature to me so I went immediately on the defensive. 'I don't do it in front of strangers.' Misty flinched: my lie making her teeth hurt. 'Well, only when they really really deserve it.' She winced. 'Or I think I can get away with it,' I ended. Misty's tense shoulders relaxed as I finally gave the complete truth.

Will shook his head in disbelief. 'I can't believe no one's caught you. My parents taught us all not to let anyone see what we can do. Our safety was too important.'

Now I felt protective of my parents. 'So did mine! It's just that . . . I don't listen very well.'

My friends smiled, too ready to forgive me my faults when I knew I should act more responsibly.

'I'm sorry, Will. I'll be more careful. You're right: I've been caught before but I've always been able to pretend it was some cool conjuring trick like those magicians you see on TV.'

'If Davis or one of his people sees you, they'll know at once that it's no illusion.'

'I get it—I really do.' Feeling a little crushed, I did my usual thing of bouncing up with an even wider smile. 'Now, I've had my knuckles well and truly rapped, I've got to go blag my way into the Gifted inner circle if anyone's arrived yet. Wish me luck.'

Will stood up and hugged me. 'Sorry to be a grouch.'

I savoured his big brotherly embrace. There were just some things you couldn't have as an only child: an older brother grumbling at you was one of them. 'You're no grouch. Well, maybe you are, but I deserved it.'

'Be careful, Angel. You're the only one of us on your own—I don't like that.'

'I'll be fine. I'll text and let you know how I get on.'

Head held high, I hurried off to the performers' area. Al was on the desk again, attention on a little TV screen. I thought it might be CCTV then noticed it was playing a rugby match. I yanked my pass from my shoulder bag and slipped it over my head.

'Hey, Al, all quiet on the western front?'

He looked up and grinned. 'If it isn't Little Miss Alternating Current. How's things, AC?'

'Great. Anything exciting happened yet today?'

'If you think the arrival of the Gifted tour bus is exciting, then yeah.' He scratched his generous belly and yawned. 'Their majesties have decided to pitch up early to catch some of the other acts.'

'Don't you like Gifted?'

'They're not bad.' He leaned over the edge of his counter. 'Believe me: that's a compliment from me.'

'See you later.'

'Take care.'

Walking across to the yurt, I hugged my arms to my sides, feeling a little chill in the early-morning air. So Gifted were here: all I had to do was worm my way into their presence. Hah—piece of cake. They were probably over in the celebrity camping area as that was where the other tour buses and motorhomes were parked. Some groups had hired big trailers called Winnebagos, a mobile home from home. No sleeping on sheep droppings for the headliners. My spirits lifted when I realized I knew someone who would know exactly where they were set up.

'Morning, Henry!'

Henry looked up from her mug of tea, shadows under her eyes. She looked rough; even her lips were without their usual sheen of perfectly applied lipstick. 'Hi, Angel. Had a good night?'

'Yes, it was fun. I checked out the folk tent with my friends.'

'Hear anything good?'

I grimaced.

'You should've come to the main stage. Total Zone were playing.'

'I know—I could hear them.'

'They were great.'

'Looks like you made a late night of it.'

'Those other friends of yours—Matt, Joey, and Fresh— don't seem to need sleep. Matt insisted I stay.'

I chuckled. 'I bet they're sleeping it off now—not like you, with a job to do. Shall I go throw a wet flannel at Matt in revenge?'

She pursed her lips, remembering she was supposed to be the prim watchdog on the yurt entrance, but then her mischievous side won out. 'Would you?'

'Can you show me where his pitch is?'

She pulled out a map of the camping ground. Boy, aren't I

the super spy! I didn't even have to ask. Her red polished nail tapped a spot. 'Matt's here. Joey and Fresh are bunking down next door.'

I took out my phone. 'Mind if I take a photo of that? I'm rubbish at remembering where things are.'

Her hands splayed over the map. 'I'm not supposed to show anyone.'

'Just imagine: lovely cold dripping flannel, sweetly sleeping drummer thinking he's safe till noon . . . ' I let the picture hover temptingly.

She removed her hand. 'Oh, go on then. Just don't let anyone else see you've got that.'

'Promise.' I quickly snapped the plan. 'Wait five minutes and expect to hear the girly screams.'

Enlarging the map with a swipe of finger and thumb, I saw that each plot was neatly labelled with the occupant or band name. I had to go ahead with the wet flannel thing just so Henry didn't suspect my ulterior motives. Best to get that done first. I grabbed a bottle of water from the yurt fridge and made my way through the network of duckboards laid between camping spots. I passed the tour vans and motorhomes on my way to the more distant area handed out to the less famous names. As Al had said, Gifted had rocked up that morning. Their silver tour bus was parked alongside four Winnebagos. No slumming it under canvas for Kurt Voss and his band mates. There was no activity around the doors so perhaps they too were sleeping in. Checking the map, I saw that the fourth Winnebago was given over to Black Belt. Gifted clearly looked after their support act—that was nice of them. Most new bands weren't treated so well.

I reached Matt's tent. It would have been easier to use my gift and snake the water in without being seen, but I had promised Will that I would lay off using my powers. I'd have to go for the conventional approach. Not having a flannel to hand, this would involve direct application. Taking the lid off the bottle, I crawled in. Matt was lying on his back, snoring. Leaning over him, I tipped a little stream of water onto his face.

Yelling, he sat up like he'd been electrocuted, his flailing arm knocking me flying. The bottle catapulted from my hand and hit the side of the tent. 'What the—!'

I put my finger tentatively to the side of my face. 'Ouch.' That hadn't gone very well. I'd only gone and hit my head on a metal tent peg.

Matt scowled at me from his sleeping bag. 'Angel, what the hell are you doing here? Why am I wet?'

I threw him a towel. 'Sorry. It was supposed to be joke—payback for keeping Henry up all night.'

He rubbed the water off his face then noticed I was still clutching the side of my head. 'You hurt?'

'Just a little.'

Swearing, he scrambled out of his sleeping bag. 'You twit: you need more practice at playing practical jokes. They're not supposed to backfire and injure you.' He turned my head to the light coming through the doorway. 'Not too bad: just a bump.'

I'd imagined it being really funny; instead it had turned out just pathetic. I didn't learn, did I? Always failing to look before leaping. 'Sorry.'

Matt huffed, his early-morning wits only just catching up with him. 'Henry's pissed off with us?'

I nodded, picking up that my friend was more than slightly interested in Henry.

'I'll have to make it up to her then.'

'Chocolate or flowers.'

'What?'

'If you want to impress her. And pretend the joke was really funny—show her you've a sense of humour.'

He grinned. 'I must have a good one if I'm still friends with you.' He ruffled my hair gently. 'Get lost, sweet pea. Some of us are trying to sleep.'

Reversing out of the tent, I dusted myself off. OK, so maybe I wasn't as funny as I liked to think. But I'd got my map—it hadn't all been a waste of time. Next stop: Marcus Cohen. Summer had said I was irresistible. Even though my confidence had taken a knock at my totally lame execution of the joke, I had no choice but to act like I believed it.

Chapter 6

I stood at the bottom of the short flight of metal steps leading up to the Winnebago door. Oh Lord. I bit my knuckles, running various lines through my head.

Hello, remember me?

Hi there. Do you want to have coffee?

Marcus, can you give me some tips at making it in the music industry?

Nothing sounded right. He was going to hate me—and probably call security. I might even get my pass taken from me for stalking one of the stars.

Think of Will. I walked up the steps and raised my hand to knock. Dang: I couldn't do it. I turned and hurried back down the stairs.

Stop it, Angel! You're no coward. Get it over with.

I put my hand on the rail, towing my reluctant body back up the steps.

'Hey, honey: got a problem?'

I swung around and found myself face to face with Kurt Voss, lead singer of Gifted. Lanky limbed, shock of black hair, piercing green eyes, in his early thirties, he was Zeus in the rock god Pantheon. I opened my mouth but nothing came out except a squeak.

Smiling, his eyes dipped to my pass. 'Angel—real name or nickname?'

'Real,' I whispered. Inside, fangirl Angel was screaming and begging for him to sign her festival programme, T-shirt, skin—anything.

'You want to see my man, Marcus?'

Come on, Angel: get your act together. I could bypass Marcus entirely if I could make friends with Kurt.

'I was trying to pluck up the courage,' I admitted, giving him what I hoped was my best gamine grin. Summer swore my dimples were my true 'access all areas' card. I leaned forward and lowered my voice. 'I don't think he's that impressed by me.'

'You sure about that?'

I nodded. 'I think he thinks I'm . . . ' I frowned, trying to put myself in Marcus' shoes, 'lightweight.'

Kurt chuckled. 'You may be right. Marcus is far too intense for a guy who's only seventeen. I wasn't half as serious at his age. I tell him to lighten up all the time but he's got this mission, you know?' He grabbed my hand—Stop press! Kurt Voss was holding my hand!!!!—and towed me up the steps. 'Let's go see him together.'

I pulled back, thinking how I'd probably never wash that hand again. 'Oh, but I don't want to interrupt.'

'I wouldn't miss this for the world, darlin'.' He rapped on the door. 'Hey, Marcus, get your ass in gear. You've visitors.'

The door flew open and Marcus appeared in the doorway clad only in jeans. If my jaw hadn't already been on the floor since Kurt took my hand, it would have fallen there. Oh boy. My day was getting better and better.

'Kurt! You just got in?'

'Yeah. Made good time from Hamburg.'

Marcus then realized I was standing next to Kurt. 'What's she doing here?'

'That's no way to talk about a guest.' Kurt muscled his way into the Winnebago, tugging me along with him. The place was dim, curtains still pulled. It smelt of a guy's deodorant and toast. A guitar leaned against the bench sofa, a scattering of paper with musical notations on the table. 'I found her trying to screw up the courage to approach the lion in his den and, being a noble kind of guy, thought I'd give her a helping hand.'

In the middle of pulling a T-shirt over his head, Marcus's blue eyes snapped to me. 'You were coming to see me?'

I shrugged, feeling about a centimetre tall. 'I guess I was.'

'I could do with coffee. Got any on the go?' asked Kurt, rifling his way through the sheets of music.

Marcus' gaze now shot to his work-in-progress. Kurt scanned the title and lyrics and grinned. 'Had a new inspiration, Marcus?'

'It's not finished yet.' Marcus tugged the paper out of Kurt's fingers and shoved it in his guitar case. Lid closed and locked, he seemed to breathe more easily. 'I'll get you that coffee.' He paused, shoulders rigid, then turned to me with his movements screaming reluctance. 'You want something?'

As grudging as the offer was, I couldn't refuse as it was the excuse I needed to hang out with them. 'Coffee would be great.'

'How do you take it?'

'White, no sugar.'

Kurt opened the curtains and cracked open one of the windows to let some fresh air into the place. The sounds of the festival rumbled like thunder in the distance. I perched on the sofa, smoothing the fabric of my skirt flat on my thighs.

'So, Angel, what band are you with?'

'Seventh Edition. You won't have heard of us.'

'What do you do?' He sat across from me, foot resting on the opposing knee. I had to keep pinching myself: Kurt Voss was actually acting as though he was interested in what I had to say.

'Vocals and violin.'

'Cool. You any good?' He laced his fingers behind his head.

'Er . . . ' How to answer that without sounding a complete egomaniac?

Marcus banged three mugs of coffee on the table between us. 'Her boyfriend says she's very talented, but the guy's such a dick I'm not sure I'd take his word.'

'What boyfriend?' I scowled at Marcus. 'Matt and I are just friends.'

'Matt? I've no idea who that is. Just how many guys are you stringing along?'

I spluttered in outrage: that was completely uncalled for! 'None, thank you very much!'

'I'm talking about your boyfriend, Jay Fielding—remember him? He bored me rigid about you yesterday; he said you were his great discovery, owed everything to him.'

Kurt chuckled and sipped his coffee.

My temper soared. 'Jay Fielding? Are you out of your tiny little mind? The guy is a gold-plated egotistical gobbet of slime!'

Marcus's eyes glinted dangerously. 'So what does that make you? You're the one shacked up with him.'

'Shacked up? Who said that? I live with my parents, you idiot!'

Kurt cleared his throat, breaking into our quarrel. 'I take it, Marcus, you met Angel just yesterday?'

He nodded, face dark with rage.

'Then why are you so angry with her?'

'Because . . . I'm not angry.' Marcus took an angry sip of too-hot coffee and winced.

'No?' Kurt flicked his eyes to the guitar case.

I stood up. 'Look, let's get something straight here before I'm the one putting a fist through something.' Preferably Marcus' face—or Jay's, as he had started this whole stupid rumour. I settled for stabbing a finger at Marcus. 'I am not—nor am I ever—going out with Jay Fielding and I'm definitely not living with him. I'm still at school for Pete's sake and I live at home. Not that it is any business of either of you.' I glared at Kurt, who was chuckling quietly on the sofa.

Oh my word: I'd just sassed my rock hero. I had to be mad.

'I hear you, Angel.' Kurt pushed my coffee closer. 'Sit down. Marcus will stop being a complete moron when he realizes he's made a mistake about you.'

'Unlikely. I would have thought that moron setting was Marcus's default mode.'

Kurt roared with laughter at my quip, while Marcus fumed and moved to a spot as far from me as the living space would allow.

'Did you want something, Kurt, or did you just drop by to stir things up as usual?' asked Marcus.

Kurt stretched his arms above his head lazily. 'Just came to tell you the tech is at eleven. You OK with that? I must be getting old because all I can think is how nice it is to have a day or two in the same place for once.'

There was a quick rap on the door and two more people appeared—an Asian boy with black hair longer at the front and an auburn hunk with impressive biceps. Putting two and two together, I recognized them as the other members of Black Belt. From my deep research of the subject—I had read the Wiki entry last night—the smaller one was called Michael and he played drums. The big guy was Pete and he multitasked on keyboard and bass. I deduced from the muscles that he also did a fair bit of heaving kit in and out of vans. The band members were all from Liverpool and had met as kids when they had all been enrolled in the same judo class, hence the cute name. After they hit their teens, they started making music together. The rest, as they say, is history: Black Belt had been talent-spotted a year ago. I could only sit back and gaze with envy at their meteoric rise.

'Hey, Kurt, how was the trip?' asked Michael. His gaze slipped to me. I was beginning to feel very out of place. These guys already knew each other so well and now I was sitting among them blending in as well as a penguin among pelicans.

'Great, thanks. Have you met Angel yet?' Kurt gestured to me. 'She's my new best friend as she really gives as good as she gets.' He winked at me while my heart did a little tap dance. I knew he was teasing but still, it's not every day a girl gets called Kurt's new BFF.

'We've not met yet, no. Hi, Angel.' Michael lifted his hand in greeting. Pete nodded in my direction. I was getting the message he was not the talkative type.

Now I was in the inner circle, I racked my brains to decide what I should do with it. From the thunderous expression on Marcus's face, he wasn't going to rush to invite me back. I had to make some progress so I would still be welcome. Making myself useful seemed a good way to go.

'I'm so excited to meet you guys. I've heard good things about your band. Have you had a chance to look around the festival yet?' I asked.

Michael took the spare place next to me, too polite to ask what the heck I was doing here. 'Not yet. We rolled in late last night. Marcus, you gone exploring yet?'

'No,' growled Marcus.

Michael's eyebrows raised in surprise. 'What's wrong with you, man?'

Marcus dropped his shoulders, trying to rid himself of his tension. 'Nothing. I was caught up writing a song.'

Michael smiled. 'I see.' He turned to me. 'Marcus gets these moods. Nothing will stop him once he has an idea—kinda like a hen laying an egg. Can't be shifted till it's all over.'

'Ignore little red hen then, if he's not got time for fun. I could show you round later if you like,' I offered, making the invitation general. 'I've already found a great place for pizza.'

Pete put two more coffees on the table, having helped himself and Michael to a cup. 'It's OK, Angel: we've got our own caterers. Easier than fighting off the autograph hunters.'

'Oh.'

'Not that we don't all like pizza. We should ask chef to make it tonight; what do you say, Kurt?'

'Fine. I like pizza and he will insist on serving that French fancy stuff to impress us.' Kurt's eyes twinkled with mischief. 'You want to join us, Angel? You can bring your band mates. I'd like to meet this Jay guy who's got on Marcus's wick.'

'Wow. I mean, yes of course.' My usual confidence was recovering. I couldn't sit still when I had just secured an invitation to dinner. I bounced up and had to stop myself doing a happy dance. I settled for hugging myself. 'Thanks so much.' I wrinkled my brow as I imagined the evening ahead. 'And I apologize profusely in advance for Jay. He is quite impossible to like—but he is talented so you'll have to forgive him. When should we show up? We're due to perform tonight at seven on the second stage; can we come along after that?'

Kurt smiled at my eagerness. 'Sure. We've not got much on tonight—just a few interviews. I'll give you my number so you can text me a reminder before you go on. I might just come see what you guys can do.' I took my phone from the front pocket of my tunic dress and he tapped his contact details into the handset.

Oh my word: I had Kurt's number and a promise he'd try to come along! I tucked the phone back and held it to my thigh. 'You'd be very welcome.' I was going to explode.

Marcus's tidy little man cave was going to have one huge girl-whirlwind rip through it if I didn't get out. 'Thanks . . . and . . . er . . . I'd better go. Right now. Quickly.'

I could hear Kurt and Michael laughing as I exited. I hadn't managed to hide my enthusiasm from them, not even spreading a shred of sophistication over my delight. I jumped down the steps and twirled on the duckboards between the motor homes, relishing my wonderful news.

'Angel, wait up!'

Oh great: I had been caught by Marcus acting like a kid in her first party dress. 'Yes?'

'You left your bag.'

I turned to find him holding out my blue sparkly shoulder bag with the silk fringe. 'Oh thanks.' Feeling so happy, I even managed a smile for him. 'Not sure how I could forget it, seeing how obvious it is.'

He handed it over. 'Cut the cute act—you don't have to pretend with me. I know you did it on purpose, like everything else. Needed an excuse to come back, didn't you?'

'What?' My skin went cold.

He put his hands on his hips, thumbs in belt loops. 'Look, I've been working with Kurt now for a few months. I see how these things work. Girls like you are all over the world, trying to attract his attention, and you've decided I'm your way in. He's not careful enough if he likes someone—he's far too generous. Just be warned: his people will brush you off like a tick if they catch you taking advantage.'

I felt like I'd been sucker punched. The fact that I did have an agenda made my situation not entirely innocent but I was not guilty of anything more than genuine admiration as far as Kurt was concerned. And the secret agenda: I was looking for a girl, not a guy. I took the bag from his clutch without a word and turned away.

Marcus gave a sigh of annoyance. 'I won't apologize for being harsh. I get that you're not a bad person, Angel. You're just star struck. But I won't be used to hurt the man who has helped me so much.'

I stopped and whirled around, anger finally swamping humiliation. 'Just listen to yourself! Can't you hear how full of it you are? You assume you know me and my motivation but so far everything you've said about me is one hundred per cent wrong.'

A deep scowl furrowed his brow. 'Now see here a moment—'

'No, you listen. I've got something to say and it will be very short and pithy so it won't strain your attention span away from yourself for too long. Here it is. Eff off, Marcus. I'm at the festival because I am an artist.' I folded my arms around myself, protection against further blows. 'I might not be uber-talented like you, but I deserve my place here and any interest that Kurt might want to show me. I have no intention of using him. Can you say the same thing about yourself? Would you be here if it wasn't for him?' I tilted my chin, daring him to justify his own career skiing the wake created by Gifted.

Marcus got right up in my grid, finger jabbing at my chest, not quite making contact. 'Are you suggesting I'm exploiting him?'

I looked down at the finger in disgust. 'If the cap fits.'

His mouth dropped open. I had rendered him speechless.

'Now, I really must be off. I have a performance to prepare for—and don't you have a tech?'

Pleased to have the last word, I stalked away, leaving Marcus to get a grip on his rage.

Chapter 7

'Bow before me, mortal!' I crowed to Misty as she answered her phone.

'You've news?'

Taking a seat in the corner of the decking area outside the yurt, I checked no one was close enough to overhear. 'Am I not the best secret agent ever?'

She snorted. 'I don't think James Bond, or even Johnny English, have anything to worry about quite yet. What's happened?'

'I've only just come from talking to all the members of Black Belt and—wait for it—Kurt Voss!'

Her squeal would probably not have needed a telephone to reach me. 'You're joking?'

'Nope. I came, I saw, and I conquered. And it gets better: Kurt invited my group to have pizza with his people after our show. I've just been handed a once-in-a-lifetime opportunity to see the whole gang that travels with Gifted.'

'Kudos, Angel. You've far exceeded our expectations.'

'Thanks, Professor McGonagall. I know: don't you just love me at the moment? I almost like myself right now. Oh and Misty, Kurt's so sweet: so funny and interested in people he really needn't spare a thought for.'

'I'm really pleased to hear it. You kinda expect all celebrities to be too self-absorbed for that.'

'He said he'd come and listen to us play.'

'Aw—that's so lovely of him. So I take it that you and that Marcus guy are best friends now too?'

'Er, not exactly. Marcus thinks I'm some desperate fangirl clambering over him to bring myself to Kurt's attention.'

Misty tutted. 'He must get that a lot touring with the band.'

'Yeah, I know, but why anyone would want to clamber *over* him when he is perfectly yummy himself.' Oops.

'What are you not telling me, Angel Campbell?'

'Oh Lord, don't use your truth force field, Misty Vader.'

'It doesn't work over the phone very well so you're safe. Tell me anyway—of your own free will.'

I kicked back on the chair and looked up at the cloudy skies. 'It's just that I have a totally inappropriate crush on the guy. He is so gorgeous but the really screwed up thing is that he hates me and assumes the absolute worst. Why can I never like the guys who like me? Snobby disdain really gets me.'

'It's the Mr Darcy complex—you know, that Pride and Prejudice hottie? The more unattainable a guy is, the more you want him. Works the other way round too: guys with their tongues hanging out for girls they can't get.'

'So young, so wise,' I said with mock solemnity.

'It's being around Alex. I get educated despite myself.' I heard funny noises at her end. 'Sorry, that was me just having a quick word with Will. He was getting impatient with our boy talk and wants to know if you've remembered not to use any power.'

'Yes, I've been a good girl.'

Will took over the call. 'Davis is here. Alex persuaded his way into front-gate security and saw him come in on the CCTV this morning; now Summer's trying to pinpoint his location with her shadow power. He's not alone. I'll forward you the photo.'

'OK, thanks. To be honest, I'd completely forgotten about Davis. I've had an exciting morning. Misty will fill you in.'

'I appreciate what you're doing for me, Angel.'

'No problem—not when I'm having the best time of my life. Love to you all. See you later.'

'Take care.'

Checking the time, I tucked my phone away. It was now eleven. My group had a slot to rehearse at one, which meant that I had plenty of time to drop by the technical rehearsal for Gifted and Black Belt. I mean, if Kurt was so polite as to show interest in me, I could only return the compliment, couldn't I? And I'd make sure I stayed out of Marcus's sight.

It was easy enough to hide by the big stage. Yesterday's crowd had already flattened the field in front of it and a few members of the cleaning crew were doing a litter pickup. That still left me several banks of sound equipment to lurk behind so the people on stage could not see me—one advantage of being on the short side. It was an amazing venue with the pier-like staging jutting out over the water, providing the illusion that the band was floating mid-air. I had arrived just at the end of Gifted's big number: 'Crash and Burn'. There were three other members of the band in addition to Kurt, each legends in their own right: Channing on bass, Sonny on the second guitar and Brian on drums. The band worked like a well-oiled machine. It wasn't the song they were practising—they had played that a zillion times live already—but the levels.

The speaker beside me squawked.

'Who the hell is on the desk?' roared Kurt, demonstrating that he wasn't so patient with everyone.

A woman's voice came through the sound system. 'Sorry, Kurt: I'm there now. The festival technician is having problems linking our equipment up to his. It's almost sorted.'

Kurt saluted the technicians' box at the far end of the field. 'Thanks, Margot. One more time, guys?'

The band went through the song for a final run through. It sounded amazing to me, even plastered up against and half deafened by the speaker. A huge wall of anthem rock: it shuddered through my body like a defibrillator getting my heart going, demanding I dance and join in the chorus. I could feel the rhythmic wash of the waves just below the stage, the whistle of the wind, the swoops of the seagulls overhead: everything seemed to be dancing in time to the beat. I restrained myself with difficulty from moving, though I had to sing along to the refrain: *Crash and burn, Now it's your turn.*

The rubbish collectors all stopped to watch Gifted going through their moves—had to be some perks to a crap job after all. One started to play the litter picker like air guitar as the others laughed at him.

Peeking over the speaker, I saw a young woman come on stage with a camera and begin snapping the band. As she wasn't waved away, I guessed she had to be well known to the members. When she finished, she went over to Brian the drummer and gave him a passionate kiss. I sat back down out of sight. Rats: I hoped she wasn't the one. Discovering that Will's soulfinder was already in a serious relationship would really hash things up for everyone. But there had to be others—that Margot in the sound box, make-up artists, costume people. I crossed my fingers, wishing Will had a lucky break rather than heartbreak ahead.

'OK, that sounds fine now. Let's give the boys their go.' Kurt took the strap of his guitar off over his head and perched the instrument on its stand.

The three members of Black Belt walked out from the wings. Michael took over from Brian, adjusting the stool to his height. Pete took his place at the keyboard that had already been set up. Marcus carried his own guitar but plugged it into the same amp Kurt had been using. I was surprised to see them sharing equipment and keeping the same backing vocalists and session musicians: most bands were possessive about their extras, instruments, and kit. It just underlined how close the relationship between the two groups had become. They behaved like a family—almost unheard of in this competitive industry. It was a little hint that suggested our speculation that they might share more than music—perhaps even a gift—was not off target.

Gifted didn't leave. They stood talking together downstage while Black Belt set up. Marcus leaned into the microphone. 'Morning, campers.' He grinned at someone at the far end of the auditorium.

'Hi to you too, Marcus,' came Margot's dry voice. 'How does it sound up there?'

'There's a little buzz from the speaker on my right. Can you magic it away?'

'Your wish is my command.' The hum that I had hardly noticed disappeared.

Marcus nodded, satisfied. 'Let's give it a test run.'

It was strange to watch Marcus being so charming to his colleagues. I'd assumed he extended his 'Grinch-that-stole-Christmas' attitude to everyone, but no: apparently I was peculiarly singled out to be blessed in that department.

'What shall we play?' asked Pete, flexing his fingers over the keys. 'Out in the Cold?'

'Good call.' Marcus moved his capo on the neck of his guitar.

Kurt leaned into the mic next to him. 'Give us a break, guys. We've heard that at every tech for the last four months. Play us your new song, Marcus.'

Marcus rolled his shoulders. 'New song?'

'Yeah, the one you wrote last night.'

I could tell Marcus was really reluctant to expose something so new and raw so soon. He cast round for excuses. 'The guys don't know it.'

'We'll pick it up,' said Pete. 'Kurt's right: it'll be more fun than going over the old stuff.'

Marcus's gaze swept the field as if looking for someone. I ducked even further behind my speaker, hugging myself in delight. It looked like I was going to be present for a world premiere of Black Belt's freshly composed track. I was so glad I had taken the risk and sneaked in.

'Go on, Marcus. What have I told you? You're an artist; you know it needs to be sung before you really know if it works,' urged Kurt.

Marcus gave Kurt a ballsy grin. 'All right then. This is for you, Kurt, and ... er ... someone else.' He shifted the capo another fret and struck up the opening.

Oh. My.

It was the first time I'd been present with Marcus making any music and the experience was unlike anything I had ever felt before. The notes seemed to reach right into me and connect to my nerve endings. It was like being *inside* the song—even this simple, haunting guitar refrain. The feeling was so exposing it was almost painful. Listening to this outpouring of melody, I knew what it was like to be that major chord moving into the minor. With him, I discovered another dimension that had hidden just out of perception, a world of pure music. Why hadn't I ever seen things this way before? It was so obvious now he had showed me.

Wake up, girl! Clever Angel slapped me around the face. This was no ordinary talent; the acute sensations he generated had to be thanks to a gift. If I closed my eyes, I could sense the psychic energy pouring from him, spreading out to the listeners. We had to get to him quickly—tell him the danger he

74

was in from Davis and his fellow journalist investigators. I only managed to hold that thought for a second before the melody sucked me under again.

So swept away by the experience, it took me a while to register the words to the song.

Girl, when I saw you, everything round you shone,
Face of an angel, but I sensed the demon
Sent to torment me, say what's going wrong.
Keep your distance, baby,
Fly back where you belong.

Was this . . . was this about me? I dug my fingers into the grass, clenching my fists.

Then he moved into the chorus:

Demon Angel, got my soul on the rack
I wanna kiss you, baby, but I'm scared you'll kiss me back.
There ain't no escaping all that we can be
Move one step closer and I'll never get free.

It had to be a coincidence. My name was a common concept in songs. If I took every song personally I wouldn't be able to sit through a Christmas carol concert. But the lyrics got worse: he then sang about a whirlwind dancing—a teasing girl who flirted with everyone—a party girl. Ouch. He really didn't like his subject very much.

The song came to an end. Marcus leant towards the mic. 'There you go, Kurt. Happy now?'

'Very. The chorus needs work but it's coming along well. What's it called?'

'*Demon Angel*—kinda like the opposite of the guardian one.'

'So you've got a new muse. Any particular reason why you came up with it last night?' Kurt was smirking—you could tell from his tone.

'No reason.' Marcus glanced up at the sound box. 'Did that sound OK to you, Margot?'

'Spot on, Marcus—and the sound levels were good too,' she replied.

He grinned at the compliment to the song. 'Thanks. I'll polish it up then and maybe we can add it to the next album. Let's run through the opening to 'Out in the Cold' just to be sure there are no glitches.' Moving on as if he hadn't just destroyed me, Marcus counted in his band mates.

I turned away from the stage and sat numbly with my back to the speaker, feeling the sound pound into my shoulder blades. That little byplay in the trailer now made sense. Kurt had noticed the lyrics on the table and assumed Marcus had written it about me. But I hadn't done anything to Marcus to provoke the demon thing, had I? I'd just had a good time and tried to involve him in the fun. I was used to people finding me a little overwhelming, but no one had actually disliked me enough to say I was bad for them.

It might not be about you, I told myself.

But it felt like it was. Kurt thought it was. How could I face any of them again?

I pressed my knuckles into my eye sockets. Suck it up, Angel. You are here for Will. What does it matter what some boy thinks about you?

But if I was right about his gift, Marcus was a savant.

He was seventeen—same age as me—and I was strangely attracted to him. All I needed was to discover he also had a March birthday.

Damn and blast with bells on: I was so screwed.

* * *

76

So I did what any sensible girl would do: I ran away and phoned BFF Summer.

'Hello?'

'Summer, please, I need to use telepathy: it's an emergency!'

She laughed. It was true, I did overuse that phrase. Now it had returned to bite me on the bum like in the fable of the boy who cried wolf. 'Calm down, it's not an emergency. You know you can't take a risk like that.'

'You don't understand! I'm not exaggerating.' I dropped my voice to a whisper and checked the instrument storeroom was empty. Black cases and boxes surrounded me with no person in sight. 'That Marcus guy—I think he's a savant.'

'We did suggest it might be a possibility that Gifted and Black Belt have some savant gifts.'

Why was she so unruffled about all this? 'But Summer, he's seventeen like us and I'm irrationally attracted to him. Wasn't that what Misty said about her and Alex? She couldn't stop herself thinking about him even when they were arguing?'

Summer sighed. 'Angel, don't you think you are, you know, getting a little worked up over nothing? I would guess that several hundreds of millions of people are seventeen at this very moment. Why does it have to be him?'

'Did you miss the bit when I said he was a savant?'

'OK that reduces the odds but still—it's a stretch. What's his gift?'

'Music.'

'Angel, being musical isn't a savant gift.'

'His kind is—he seems to draw you inside the song. I know you don't think I'm very perceptive but trust me on this: I know a savant gift when it turns my insides into a shimmer of gold.' I had an echo of the feeling even as I described it.

'All Danae to the stars,' muttered Summer.

'What?'

'A line by Tennyson. The god Zeus visited Danae in a cloud of stars.'

Summer is what Matt would call 'a classy bird'. 'That's it exactly. A visitation by a higher power. I felt the music sizzle inside me even though it was a song insulting me and everything I do.'

'Oh.' Her little bubble of romantic allusion was popped by that admission.

'Yeah. This is not a one-way street of attraction going on, though at the moment he is reading it as repulsion. That's why I need to use telepathy. I can find out if he's the one. If not, I can kick him where it hurts for being rude about me. That can be his next song: "The Girl Who Brought Me to My Knees in Much Deserved Agony".'

'And if he is your soulfinder?'

'I still kick him where it hurts but tell him he is stuck with me and has to live with it.'

Summer was silent for a few moments. 'Be careful, Angel: he might not know what he is.'

'How can he not? It can't be coincidence he is hanging out with Will's girl. I've not had a chance to work out if Gifted are also gifted but the smart money is on them having hidden talents.'

I didn't need to read minds to tell that Summer was now worrying about what I was planning. My friends all regard me as a bit of a wild card due to my impulsive side, but I can't seem to help myself. I was at the back of the queue when self-control was handed out; actually, no, I probably hadn't bothered to wait around in the queue for it.

Summer sighed. 'Look, come back to the tents, Angel. We need to talk about this. If you're going to use telepathy on him, you need to be a hundred per cent sure Eli Davis and his people aren't nearby.'

She wasn't dismissing my hunch: that was good. I glanced at the time on my phone. 'Sorry, can't. I have band rehearsal now. I'll try to get away between that and our performance. If I don't, you'll be there tonight, won't you?'

'Of course.'

'When is help arriving?'

'Uriel is bring Victor from the airport when he lands this evening. They've both taken a keen interest in Eli Davis ever since Cambridge.'

'I bet. OK, must go.'

'All right, but don't do anything, you know, Angel-ish before we've had a chance to plan this.'

I wrinkled my nose. 'I should've phoned Misty. She would have encouraged me to just go for it.'

'That's why you phoned me. Deep inside, you know you needed a counter balance to—'

'To being Angel. Yes, I do, I know. I'm stupid.'

Summer hates it when Misty and I run ourselves down. She can always be counted on to bolster low self-esteem. 'You are not stupid! You are wonderful—vibrant—talented.'

'But seriously lacking in caution?'

'Well . . . yes.'

I chuckled. She understood me so well. 'Let the others know what's going on and I'll phone later.'

Seventh Edition were practising in the performers' lounge, a tent set aside for tune-up and run-throughs. I arrived on time with Black Adder under my arm to find Jay was already scowling.

'I can't see how we're expected to perform at our best if we can't get onto the stage beforehand.'

Henry checked her clipboard. 'Sorry, Jay, but the stages are either being made ready for tonight or there are already acts performing. Only the headliners get to use them in advance—we just can't accommodate all the bands who want to do their own tech.'

Jay squeezed the neck of his guitar so his knuckles went white. 'This is a crap system.'

Henry carried on with her kind and reasonable tone. 'I'm sorry if you don't like it but there is nothing I can do. Make sure you arrive at least twenty minutes before your set and check your sound requirements with the team. They're very experienced at a quick setup.'

Matt started playing the high hat, a little brush of percussion to remind Jay that time was a-wasting.

'All right, I suppose we'll have to make do.' Henry gave him a curt nod, me an eye roll at Jay's behaviour, then hurried out.

'Angel, pleased you've finally decided to join us,' snarled Jay.

'I'm not late.' I opened my case and took out Black Adder. 'Do you have my amp?'

'As a session musician, you are responsible for transporting your own equipment.' Until this point, Seventh Edition had always included my amp on the bus. I hadn't thought Jay would sink so low as to sabotage the band's sound just to spite me.

'You're kidding?'

'It's OK, Angel, I've got it here. I made sure it went on with my kit. Jay knew I had it—he just wanted you to sweat a bit.' Matt pulled it out from behind his bass drum box.

'Thanks, Matt. Not funny, Jay.' I glared at the louse and set up as far from him as I could manage without actually leaving the tent. 'Oh, I have some good news.' I kept my tone purposely airy.

'Not now, Angel. Some of us don't have time for gossip. We've got a gig to prepare for,' said Jay stiffly.

'No, really, you'll want to hear this.'

'I really wouldn't.'

'Bet you your classic rock vinyl collection that you do.'

He snorted. 'I'm not taking that bet. OK, tell us. You won't shut up otherwise, will you?'

I plucked a string to check tuning. 'I ran into Kurt Voss this morning and he has invited us back to his trailer this evening for pizzas. Gifted and Black Belt are all going to be there.' I looked up and watched the shock roll through the boys.

Jay gaped. 'Invited who?'

'Me and my band mates—but I suppose if I'm not officially in Seventh Edition, only a session musician, I don't have a band and I'll have to go alone.' I ran a scale on Black Adder.

Kyle dumped his bass guitar and scooped me up for a celebratory spin. I held bow and instrument out like wings. 'You are not going anywhere alone, Angel. That is so awesome! Hey, guys, Angel's in the band, isn't she?'

'Sure is,' agreed Richie, then played a little flourish of notes on the sax.

Owen grunted and gave a thumbs up.

'I never said she wasn't.' Matt winked at me. 'Jay?'

'I . . . ' Jay looked as though he was chewing razorblades.

I knew exactly the carrot to hold before the jackass. 'Think of all those useful contacts, Jay. Record producers, industry movers and shakers. Oh and Kurt also said he'd try to come and listen to us play today.'

'You're joking?'

'No. Deadly serious.'

Jay swallowed. 'Of course you're in the band. I don't know where you got the impression you aren't.'

This was such barefaced cheek, even from Jay, that I was left speechless.

'Girls—chicks like you—get these strange notions in their

mind, make a big deal out of a few disagreements. Irrational hormonal reaction.' He settled his guitar across his chest. 'Now we know we've got a special audience, we'd better get down to some serious practice.'

'Do you even stop and listen to yourself?' I muttered. 'You make politicians look like straight talkers.'

He ignored my insult. 'If Kurt has taken a shine to Angel, I think we'll kick off with "Star-Crossed", OK?'

Chapter 8

In the end, far from having an opportunity to talk things through with Summer and Misty, I only had time for a hit-and-run raid on my tent to grab my clothes for the performance.

'Sorry, guys: in a rush here!' I shouted as I darted past my friends seated on the grass waiting for me. They looked very comfortably settled, knocking back a few beers and some soft drinks in the sunshine. 'Jay had made us practise until my fingers were bleeding.'

'He did what?' said Will, all ready to go and pound some sense into the idiot.

'OK, I'm exaggerating,' I called out through the canvas. 'They're a little bit sore but you get the picture. Where, oh where, are my rings?' I chucked a few T-shirts over my shoulder in a vain attempt to find my jewellery case. 'I finally forced him to call a halt by pointing out that we had only two hours to get in our costumes and set up.' I didn't add that I'd also told him I needed at least that long to prepare— it was a hormonal chick thing, I claimed. Jay allowed my rebellion against his-band-his-rules. His be-nice-to-Angel mood was still lingering like a benign fallout cloud from the shock explosion of my announcement. 'Who has stolen my belt? I can't seem to find anything!' I wailed, rooting through a jumble of clothes.

Summer crawled in next to me. 'Campbell, get your butt

outside this tent. Tell me what you want to wear and I'll find it for you.'

Looking about me, I saw that I had reduced the tent to a shambles in the few seconds of frantic search, upending my bags. 'Oh cripes. The new silver dress please—belt and jewellery to match.'

Summer started putting the belongings back in my empty rucksack.

'Do you want me to help?' I hovered at her shoulder, ashamed of the mess I'd created.

'Out.' She jabbed her finger in the required direction.

I reversed out the low doorway. 'I think she's cross with me,' I told Misty, who was peering in and laughing. 'Hey, Uri, Victor, you're here!' In my haste I had blasted past the new arrivals.

'How observant of you.' Uriel, second oldest of the fabulous Benedict brothers, smiled, knowing my ways very well.

I jumped up on tiptoes to kiss his cheek. With light brown hair, warm eyes, and a wiry athletic stature, he was a gorgeous example of a man. He had a lovely, approachable air to him, like a warm bakery on a cold day. 'How's Tarryn, Uri?'

His smile broadened even further at the mention of his lady. 'Good, thanks. She's got an interview in a school in Colorado Springs the day after tomorrow or she would've been here.'

'Oh, that's great. I really hope she gets it.' It looked like Uriel and his South African soulfinder were finally getting their lives to mesh. 'Tell her I said "good luck".' I turned to the other new arrival, Victor, the scariest of the brothers who did something very hush-hush for the FBI. It was odd to see him out of his sharp suits and wearing festival gear of T-shirt and jeans, like seeing your head teacher on holiday. 'Um, hi, Victor.'

'Hello, Angel,' he said solemnly, though I think he was teasing me. As a mind reader, he would know that I was terrified of him—not what he would do to me but what he would find out about me. It felt like a foretaste of the final judgement standing before the all-seeing, all-knowing Victor.

His lips quirked, his grey eyes crinkling a little at the edges. 'You've got that wrong, Angel. I don't know everything—far from it.' He leaned closer. 'I just make people think I do—gets results.'

I grinned and gave a theatrical shiver. 'Works on me every time.'

Summer emerged from the tent carrying my dress and belt draped over one arm and shoes in the other. 'These what you were looking for?'

'Shoes! I'd forgotten about them.' Just looking at those high heels made my arches scream but a girl has to sacrifice comfort for fashion when she is performing before Kurt Voss. I let out a little squeak of excitement. 'This is just the best day of my life and I love you all to pieces!'

Will laughed. 'Now we've got that settled, do you have time to tell us what the hell's going on with you? Leave you five minutes and you have wormed your way to a dinner invitation with the hottest band on the planet and identified a suspect for your own soulfinder.' He rolled his eyes in mock exasperation. 'I thought this was about me.'

I checked the time on Uriel's watch. I had five minutes before I had to run back to the performers' zone. There were dressing rooms available for artists that were much better than trying to wriggle into that dress in a metre-and-a-half-high tent. I plonked myself down on the grass and took a deep breath.

'OK, here's how it happened.'

When I finished my summary of the day, Victor was already on his phone.

'What are you doing?' I asked.

'Texting my colleagues. If these guys are unregistered savants then they're in danger and could be a risk to our community. I'm checking them against the grey list.'

'Grey list?' asked Alex. He was sitting with his legs and arms around Misty so she could use him like a backrest.

'The one we keep off the Savant Net. Some people ask not to have their names out there.'

'A secret annex to an already secret list,' mused Alex.

'Like being ex-directory,' suggested Summer.

'Good idea if you're mega famous like Kurt,' I said.

Misty threw a daisy at me. '"Kurt" is it now? On first-name terms, are you?'

I grinned and threw it back. 'Absolutely. You should've seen me rub Jay's face in it when I announced I was Kurt's new BFF. He's even let me back into the band on the strength of it. He couldn't resist the ace chance to schmooze.'

That set off a round of not very flattering comments about my lead singer.

I jumped up and brushed off the seat of my leggings. 'Sorry, guys, but I really have to go.'

'Just a moment!' Will grabbed my hand and tugged me to a stop. 'I know you want to test out whether this Marcus guy is your soulfinder—of course you do—but promise me you'll only do it when you are sure you're in the clear. I don't know how sensitive that psychic detection device can be.'

'It picked up your telepathic messages to me when you were commentating on Alex's debate at my school, Angel,' said Misty. 'Davis didn't know at the time it was you though, so I guess it works in a largish room and is not very focused.'

Will nodded. 'So best to be cautious, OK, sweetheart?'

There was so much going on, my head was whirling. I spelt out my agenda for them, tapping each finger. 'Right— no irresponsible telepathy, check. Give one show-stopping performance to impress rock god, check. Avoid kicking Jay in the you-know-whats at after-show pizza party, check. Ditto to said rock godling with insulting song, check. Find Will's soulfinder, check. Have one hell of an evening, check.' Giggling, I grabbed my costume and shoes from Summer and started jogging back to the security gate.

'Jewellery!' called Summer.

I turned and Alex lobbed me the travel case. I caught it against my chest. 'What would I do without all of you, hey? See you later.'

Nerves made my insides ripple like wobbly jelly. I leaned against the stairs leading up to the stage from backstage, taking deep calming breaths like Summer had tried to teach me. Normally I would play with the water in my bottle, making it spin and bubble to settle my mind, but I couldn't risk it. Banned from my usual pre-show ritual, I had to make do with yoga breathing—and I suck at the mindfulness stuff that everyone else seems to like. Stop and be quiet: that's when I panic.

Matt ambled up, chewing on a crisp from packet of salt and vinegar. He held it out. 'Want one?'

I shook my head. 'How can you be so calm?'

'I'm not calm. This is my sixth packet. If I stop eating, I'll throw up.'

'Oh Lord, oh Lord,' I moaned, pressing my hand against my tummy. 'Why did you have to mention that?'

Jay strode over, giving us his version of a military inspection. 'Everyone here?'

'Yeah, Jay,' the guys mumbled.

'Angel, you look sweet. Nice dress.' An unsnide compliment from Jay—the world was surely about to end?

'Thanks.'

Gathering his thoughts, he looked about him. We could hear the crowd massed on the field in front of the second stage. Our performance area was built near the woods at the western edge of the festival ground. It was probably good for me that we were away from the sea. One result of my gift is that I am tuned into any moving water. The sea sets my instincts buzzing. I had enough going on without having to clamp down on the urge to play with the waves. The only downside here was the mosquitos that came out at twilight; otherwise it was a real boost for our band of newbies to make it on to the evening programme on one of the proper stages rather than a session tent. We might even get televised if the cameras were looking for some new action.

Jay laced his fingers together and squeezed them hard. 'Just play your best, guys. I've every faith in you.'

I couldn't get used to this 'nice' Jay. It was like that Lego character—good cop/bad cop. I kept expecting his head to spin round so it would be back to the normal foul character.

'You too, mate,' said Matt, filling in the awkward silence.

The lights came on stage, which was our signal to set up.

'OK, let's do this!' Jay ran up the stairs. I followed with Black Adder tucked under my arm, trying not to teeter on my heels. As we walked out on to the stage, the audience gave us a welcoming round of applause even before the announcer gave our name.

'Yo, Angel!' bellowed Will.

I shaded my eyes to find my friends right down by the barrier. The three Benedict boys and Alex formed a formidable honour guard for Misty and Summer.

'Looking good!' called Uriel.

Misty and Summer waved. Alex gave a sharp whistle. Even Victor was smiling.

Feeling a little more settled, I plugged in Black Adder and checked the tuning. The other guys in the band were doing their pre-show checks but everything seemed very efficient and there were no blips. Jay waited to meet our gaze, making sure his troops were in position. 'Good to go?'

We nodded.

Jay signalled the stage manager that we were all set.

'And now!' thundered the announcer. 'Kicking off tonight's programme we have a debut band from London. I'm sure we're going to hear much more of them after this. So give it up for Seventh Edition!'

The crowd gave us a roar of approval. I glanced over the faces, wondering if Kurt had kept his promise to come. But he wouldn't be out there among the herd of music lovers on the field, would he? That would cause a stampede if he were spotted.

'Thank you for your great Rockport welcome. We're going to start with a favourite song of ours called "Star-Crossed". I really hope you enjoy it,' said Jay, wooing the audience with more charm than he usually showed to people when he met them in the singular.

I couldn't see Kurt anywhere front or backstage, which was a shame as this was my biggest number.

Head in the game, Angel. I closed my eyes, counting myself in from Matt's percussion intro. And play.

The song was going really well. Jay delivered the lyrics with an emotional charge he would be totally unable to manage in real life, as his empathy was the depth of a kiddie's paddling pool. He reached my favourite verse just before my solo.

I see you standing at your window
My life starts again
Love falls like stars
A glitter of pain.

Then something happened inside me; it was like a key

change from minor to major. As I reached my section, I took off and began to fly. My fingers were playing—my violin was singing—but it was like they no longer belonged to me but were fellow birds in a flock of music. It was scary and exhilarating at the same time; I felt out of control, connected to the ground only by the notes resting lightly to the stave, birds on a telephone wire waiting to soar. Even stranger, I could feel this mood was flowing out of me and touching the audience. They were linked to me, enraptured as I was.

I reached the end of my riff and the crowd sang out their pleasure, subsiding only to hear the final verse and chorus. I had to nudge myself to remember to provide the harmony to Jay's voice. 'Star-Crossed' came to an end and we received a prolonged barrage of applause, shouts and whistles. Jay's face was gleaming with a mist of perspiration and pleasure. Matt gave me a thumbs up. I was still shaken, convinced some strange alchemy had taken place inside turning me into a very different sort of musician.

It was then that I noticed Marcus and Kurt. They were standing in the wings, watching our performance alongside the stage manager. Both were dressed in black so they looked like members of the backstage crew but I would recognize them anywhere, the relaxed posture of the rock god and the defensive vigilance of his younger friend.

Kurt I had expected, but Marcus?

'Thank you, thank you,' said Jay. 'And now a few words to introduce the band. Over there on the drums is my main man, Matt.' The crowd cheered. 'We have Owen on guitar, Kyle on bass, Richie on sax—and . . . ' He paused. This last was a public admission he was loath to make. His swallow was almost audible. 'And Angel on vocals and violin.'

I received a huge whoop and many wolf whistles. My friends started a chant of 'An-gel, An-gel' just to annoy Jay.

Our lead singer gave a sickly smile at my reception. 'And

I'm Jay.' He was cheered too—after all he was doing a great job this evening. Spirits restored, Jay bent back to the mic. 'Now for our next song: 'Broken Queen'.

The rest of the concert passed too quickly. I was acutely aware of the listeners in the wings but somehow my mind had managed to split in half: one part was doing embarrassing fangirl jiggles of delight but the other was lost in the new understanding of how music resided inside your bones, not in the brain. When we got to the end, the audience shouted for an encore. Jay was going to sing 'Broken Queen' but the crowd chanted 'Star-Crossed, Star-Crossed!' and he was canny enough to give in. It was even better the second time. I was ready for the swooping feeling and could go with the flock of notes this time. I even forgot about our audience of two backstage. There was nothing but the music.

As much as we would have loved to stay and prolong our spell in the limelight, the next act was gathering in the wings and we had to relinquish our spot. As the applause died down, Jay thanked everyone for being 'the best crowd ever' and led us off. We were still surfing the euphoria. The boys exchanged high fives as the roadies switched over the kit on the stage for the next act. I stood a little to one side, hand pressed to my heart, knocked sideways by the after-glow of the experience. What exactly had happened? I couldn't see Kurt or Marcus. They must have slipped away.

Jay came over and hugged me—not the smarmy type but a genuine pleased-you're-in-the-band kind. 'That was great, Angel. Do you think he was here?' He didn't need to spell out whom he meant.

'I hope so,' said Richie, muscling in for his own hug. 'I don't think we've ever played better—and you were on fire, girl!' Richie pretended to touch my upper arm. 'Ouch!'

I was about to reply when the stage manager came over,

walkie-talkie in hand. 'Sorry, guys, but I'm going to have to ask you to move along. Great show by the way.'

'Thanks.' Jay wished the next band 'good luck' and headed for the stairs.

'Strange how he can present himself as a passable human sometimes,' muttered Matt, squeezing the back of my neck affectionately.

'Alien possession—only credible explanation,' I replied.

'Just think: he might be someone that success does not spoil but improves.'

I giggled at that idea. 'I doubt it.'

Jay was waiting for us at the bottom of the stairs, and I could instantly see why. Kurt and Marcus were standing to one side, chatting together. They both looked up as my high heels tapped down the steel steps, giving me an intro like the snap of a snare drum.

'Angel! That was a great performance you and your guys put in there,' announced Kurt, coming over to give me a congratulatory kiss.

Fangirl inside was screeching: *he kissed me!*

Sensible Angel was relishing the 'you and your guys' crack, treating me as if I were the lead.

'Thanks, Kurt. I don't think you've met my band mates yet.' I did a quick round of introductions.

Kurt shook hands with each one. 'Sweet. I met your Angel this morning and just had to see you all perform together. She's a little stick of dynamite, isn't she?'

'Is that a compliment?' I asked teasingly, finally beginning to get past my breathless adulation to treat him as I would other friends. 'Sounds more like an insult. Oh, and this is Marcus Cohen. I think Jay's already met him, but for those who haven't, Marcus is in Black Belt. They're supporting Gifted tomorrow night.'

Marcus shook hands. His gaze sharpened when he reached my drummer friend. 'Matt, right?'

'That's correct.' Matt crunched a salt and vinegar packet in his jeans pocket as he dug his hands in.

'Angel mentioned you.'

'She did?' Matt looked down at me in surprise and grinned. 'Don't believe anything she said. I was not responsible for any of it.'

Marcus paused. I think he was trying to gauge the nature of our relationship. 'Well, if there's trouble, I'd guess she might be at the bottom of it.'

'You know her so well already,' chuckled Matt.

'No, he just thinks he does.' I linked my arm through Matt's, hoping to irritate Marcus. I knew Matt wouldn't take it the wrong way. It was so tempting to try out telepathy but this was far too public. I had to get Marcus alone for a moment. 'So, did you like us?'

'It was . . . ' Marcus rubbed his chin, searching for the right words. His blue eyes were like pools reflecting the summer sky. 'It was really something else.'

'Something else in a good or a bad way?' I pressed.

He cleared his throat. 'I have to say that you were impressive, Angel. I was surprised.'

Kurt appeared at Marcus's shoulder. 'Yeah, she blew you away, didn't she? At least that's what you said to me.'

Marcus looked over my head and his cheeks were definitely a little red.

I dropped Matt's arm and took Kurt's instead, giving his elbow a squeeze. 'Kurt, I know you have a million girls say this to you, but I love you—no, really—for coming here and being so nice about our performance. And that's love in a totally respecting-you-as-a-professional sense, not a creepy stalker fan way.' I pretend-frowned to show I was teasing, though under it all was, of course, a sliver of truth.

Kurt laughed. 'Thanks, darlin'. Now, we stayed to make sure you all got the invitation back for pizza. So see you at our trailer in about ten minutes, OK? Job well done, guys.'

My band mates gave a round of heartfelt thanks as we watched Kurt and Marcus walk off.

'That was possibly the coolest five minutes of my life,' admitted Richie.

I looked down at my little silver dress and impractical heels—hardly suitable for pizza. 'Ten minutes to change—oh no! Don't wait for me!' I slipped off my heels and ran barefoot to the dressing room.

Chapter 9

I was halfway out of my dress when my phone clucked. I checked the text from Misty.

Major problem. Victor says psychic energy was going nuts when you were playing. We all sensed it. And if we did so did Davis if he was in the audience. What were you doing?!!!!

I quickly texted a reply.

That wasn't me. Marcus and Kurt were watching. Do you think it was them???????

With a little distance from that magical moment on stage, I realized that Victor was right: my playing had been given a boost by some kind of psychic wave. I should have understood that myself but I had been on a musical high. I wasn't sure I liked the idea of Marcus or Kurt giving me a psychic lift. It was a little like performance-enhancing drugs and athletes, wasn't it?

Victor says you've got to warn them. He's trying to pull strings to get in to see the Gifted management but that's going to take time. Warn them tonight.

!

I know. We're all rooting for you.

And I had been so looking forward to a simple evening of pizza and soulfinder hunting. I glared at my reflection in the bulb-lit mirror.

'What are you looking at, dumbass?' I asked the pale-faced creature staring back at me. My grey-blue eyes had a catlike slant to them, emphasized by the stage make-up. I didn't like that person—she looked daunted, like she'd climbed too high up a tree and was not sure how to get down without the fire brigade.

I really, really didn't want to spoil this great opportunity I had been given—this dream come true—of getting along so well with Kurt. Marcus—well, that was a whole bundle of complicated, but even there I didn't want to bowl in and sabotage it by making what to them would sound insane claims. I could just imagine the scene.

Hey, Kurt, thanks again for coming to hear me. Oh, and by the way, do you have strange psychic gifts that you are hiding from everyone?

That would so not go well.

Marcus, I know you think I'm a little weird but have you ever considered you might be a savant? Not heard of us? Oh, well, it's like having a kind of superpower but without having to wear the spandex . . .

My insides were crawling at the prospect. I looked back down at my texts.

Please can someone get me out of this?

I waited for Misty's reply.

Victor says to tell you this is bigger than embarrassment. Will says he will promise you a lifetime of free pizza-with-everything if you protect his soulfinder and yours?? from these guys.

I swore under my breath. She was right. I was being totally selfish. Will's girl was somewhere here, ignorant of the danger. Even if Marcus didn't turn out to be my soulfinder, he was a savant and still deserved protection. He was too exposed. He might hate me for it tonight but later he would understand.

Sorry for being a cowardly lion. Tell them that Mission Impossible is a go.

My text signalled my acceptance of the task and kissed

goodbye to my totally cool new relationship with my rock heroes.

The pizzas were being served in the space between the Gifted tour bus and the Winnebagos. Someone had strung up lights and set out tables so it was like having our own private restaurant terrace with live background music from the main stage rumbling away. I hung back in the shadows for a moment, gearing myself up for this. I could see my band mates, Marcus, and the rest of Black Belt, but Kurt and his group were missing. As I watched, the furthest door of the tour bus opened and Gifted filed out. A pretty brown-haired woman in a scarlet suit accompanied them and—oh Lord, no—a journalist in creased trousers and a white shirt. Davis had got there first. I texted a quick alert and hurried forward to see if I could divert any disaster. I ploughed straight past Marcus and Matt. I must have looked like a shopper on the first day of the sales heading straight for her favourite bargain—not the impression I had hoped to make.

'Hi, everyone!' I called in an over-bright voice. I could hear Marcus's snort of laughter behind me. I'd just confirmed his view that I was a fame-hunter.

'Hi, Angel. Glad you made it.' Kurt introduced me to the rest of the band. Normally this would be a high moment in my life, demanding my sole attention, but I had my mind on the journalist at his shoulder. I was relieved to see that Eli Davis took no special note of me; he was finishing up his conversation with the woman.

'I expect it to appear in Saturday's edition,' Davis was saying. 'If I can get some mood details and photos backstage before the performance tomorrow, that would be great—some candid shots to back up the article.'

The woman checked a clipboard. 'I'll add your name to the approved list.'

'I'll be with my photographer; I'll send you his name.'

'Angel?' Kurt clicked his fingers under my nose. 'You still with us?'

I rubbed my forehead. 'Oh, um, sorry: zoned out there for a moment.'

He tucked me under his arm. 'You must be exhausted. I always am after a big show. I was just telling the guys how great you were.'

Out of the corner of my eye, I watched the woman steer Davis over to the window of the catering van. Don't tell me he was staying for pizza! 'Oh, er . . . ' What had Kurt said? Something about me being great. 'Thanks. Who's that?'

Kurt followed my gaze. 'That's Margot, our tour manager. Haven't you met her yet?'

'Not yet, but I meant the guy.'

'Just some journalist from LA. No one important.' He shrugged. The band probably met thousands of journalists each tour so he could hardly be expected to remember names. 'But Margot you've got to meet. Hey, Margot, over here!' He gave a shrill whistle and the red-suited woman turned. She waved, handing over Davis to another member of staff to entertain, and headed back to us. It was dawning on me that I wasn't the only one with an agenda this evening—and Kurt was making better headway with his than I was. 'Margot, this is Angel.'

Margot offered her hand. 'Pleased to meet you.' She had the very light accent of an excellent speaker of English as a second language. 'Margot Derkx.'

'Angel Campbell. Are you from Amsterdam, by any chance?'

She nodded. 'Yes, exactly. That's where the band is based. Tax reasons.' Now I saw her close to, I could appreciate her flawless caramel complexion and huge brown eyes. Her hair was a mass of long toffee-coloured waves, bunched back in a business-like swirl at the moment. Straight nose and full lips of mixed ethnic heritage: she should be modelling rather than running a tour.

'But you, you're Dutch?'

She didn't seem to mind my probing. 'Good guess—though I suppose the name is a clue?'

No, I just had a savant soulseeker on my side who had been tracking the band's movements.

I had so many things I needed to do here: warn them about Davis, check out Margot, check out Marcus. My head was spinning. What should I do first?

Kurt got in before I could. 'Margot, did you see the recording of Angel playing?'

That knocked me on a completely new track. 'It was filmed?'

'Yes, darlin'. You were on TV as your set coincided with a change-over on the main stage.' He grinned at me, flicked a lock of hair out of my hoop earring. 'Are you pleased?'

'Oh my God, oh my God, oh my God!'

Margot raised one perfect eyebrow. 'I'd say she's pleased.'

'What do you think then?' asked Kurt.

'I see what you mean now: she's got something.'

'Even Marcus thinks so—and he's hardly her greatest fan.'

'Oh Marcus.' Margot clucked her tongue. 'He's still not forgiven me for not keeping that Sinead girl away from him.'

My Marcus radar suddenly blipped. 'Sinead?'

Kurt chuckled. 'Don't worry: she's history, Angel.'

'More like "lesson learned", I'd say,' added Margot. 'You shouldn't joke about it, Kurt. The story she sold to the gutter press really upset him.'

'But had a great effect on his songwriting. Most of the stuff on the new album is thanks to her.'

'And I hope she winces every time she hears "Dead at Heart".'

No wonder Marcus was so suspicious: I'd entered into the frame just after the last love-rat had scurried back to her sewer. 'Poor guy.'

Kurt gave a world-weary shrug and took a seat at an empty table. 'Well, darlin', that's the danger of fame. Keep your real friends close because you'll find the hangers-on soon drop off if the money is right.'

Margot signalled to one of her assistants to fetch a round of drinks and pizza for us. I could feel the envious looks coming my way from my band mates in Seventh Edition. At least the other members of Gifted had spread out to be sociable. I could see Matt talking to drumming legend Brian: someone else with his dream come true tonight. The blonde photographer popped up and perched on Brian's knee, joining in the conversation. Eli Davis circulated like a piranha, chomping on a slice of margarita.

'So you and the band are all really close, right?' I asked Kurt, deciding it was time I got down to the business of warning them.

'Yep, like brothers. Want to strangle them sometimes, but we're tight all the same.'

'And . . . and you're held together by your music or by something more?'

Kurt exchanged a look with Margot, as if to say "now where exactly is she going with this?". 'I see more of them than anyone else in my life so I guess it's not just the music. But you must understand that: you've got your own guys.'

I gave a throaty laugh. My voice is ridiculously husky for someone of my stature and I could see Kurt found the sound amusing. 'Oh no, there's no comparison, believe me. Jay only lets me in the band because I'm useful. I'm kinda like the junior member of a coalition government to be thrown over when the punters give him enough votes to go it alone.'

'He'd be an idiot to get rid of the best thing in his band. Don't get me wrong: he's OK, but you, Angel, are very special.'

Flattery was making it really hard for me to keep on track with what I had to do here. 'Oh gosh, thanks, Kurt, I'm really really pleased you think that—and proud and all messily emotional at the same time.'

'It's just the truth. Margot, do I ask her or you?'

Margot picked at her tomato and mozzarella salad. 'Oh you, Kurt. I'm nobody.'

No, Margot Derkx, you might well be someone very important indeed.

Curiosity going bananas, I made a valiant attempt to stay on track. 'Actually, I have something I've got to ask you.'

'Let me go first, hey?' Kurt put his hand over mine where it rested on the table. 'Angel, what do you say to backing us tomorrow night?'

Mission dropped from my mind like engines jettisoned on rocket lift-off. 'Me?'

'Yes, you.' Kurt grinned at Margot. 'Wait for it. Hold on to your hat.'

I shot up to my feet. 'Oh my . . . yes, yes, yes!' No way could I not do my happy dance. Of course, everyone stared at me as if I'd lost my head—which I had. 'Oh. My. God!'

'I knew she'd do that. Pay up.'

Margot smiled and slapped a tenner in his hand. 'Not fair, Kurt. I hadn't met her when we made that bet.'

'Thank you, thank you, thank you! I can't believe you asked me.' Breathing hard, I made myself sit back down, reaching for professional and calm. Unfortunately, Professional and Calm had run away altogether, leaving me in the presence of their irresponsible substitutes, Over the Moon and Gushingly

Eager. 'What do you want me to do?' It didn't matter what the answer was. If he'd said 'wear an Easter Bunny outfit' I would have agreed.

'The guys and I have been saying we'd like to add a violin to our new single. We were going to leave it until we got to the studio, but hearing you today, I thought we'd give it a trial run tomorrow. If it works, you can record it for us.'

This was not happening to me. 'Have you written the piece already?'

'I've been working on it with Marcus. Come by tomorrow morning and I'll show you. You might have some suggestions. It has a folk feel to it, not classic rock.'

Just as well I'd brought Freddie along. I knew my instincts were good but this was way beyond anything I could have dreamed.

'I'll be there. A zombie invasion wouldn't keep me away.'

Kurt grinned and leaned back in his chair and sipped his beer. 'So, darlin', what was it you wanted to ask me.'

I opened my mouth, but I couldn't do it. Oh Lord, I'd promised everyone but if I now started spouting about savant gifts he would think I was completely crazy and take back his invitation to play with them tomorrow.

What could I do? 'I . . . er . . . just wanted to say that some friends of mine would like to talk to you.'

Kurt's expression dimmed. 'I'm fine with a few autographs but I don't really have time for a face to face. Ask them to come by after the show, hey?'

'Oh, they're not fans!' No, no: had I just said that? Talk about putting my foot in it.

He looked puzzled but amused by my tactlessness. 'Oh? Then why . . . ?'

'They're . . . um . . . security experts. They have some concerns they want to share with you.' Oh flipping heck, this all sounded so lame. What was I, a seventeen-year-old wannabe, doing talking about such things? Even I didn't believe me.

'Darlin', you feeling OK?' asked Kurt.

'Yes . . . no . . . damn: I'm digging a big hole here, aren't I?'

Margot was looking worried, reassessing my 'asset' label and considering shifting me over to 'liability'. 'Try the truth, Angel.'

'You need my friend Misty for that.' Not only was I off course I was wandering in blithering circles. Bite the bullet, Angel. 'Look, I'm so crap at explaining; I've got to let someone else do this. Margot, would you give my friends five minutes of your time? You see, there are these three Americans I'm camping with: one is a kind of bodyguard, another is a forensic expert and the third works for the FBI.'

Kurt was looking at me as if I'd just turned into a leprechaun and was performing an Irish jig before him.

'Please, I'm not pulling your leg or gone mad. Neither is this some newspaper setup or anything like that.' I gazed down at my uneaten slice of pizza. 'And I've blown it. They shouldn't have asked me to do this.'

'Who asked you to do what?' Kurt covered my hand again with his. 'Angel, are you in trouble?'

'No, but we think you might be. Please,' I swallowed against the lump in my throat and scribbled on a serviette with my eyeliner, 'please, just call this number, Margot. The guy on the other end is called Will Benedict.'

'Will Benedict?' Margot looked at the serviette like it was a dish of poison.

'Yes. He's a good guy—and not the least bit like me, I promise.' I pushed the number over to her. I glanced up at Kurt through my eyelashes. 'I know I sound crazy but do you still want me to play with you?'

Kurt rubbed his chin. 'I guess so, but there's something

about you that doesn't make any sense. You're hiding something, aren't you.'

And you haven't even seen what I can do to your beer yet. 'I'll just . . . just go. If you change your mind about me playing, drop me a message at the yurt reception. I'll leave you alone to let Margot make her call.'

I left them talking, heads close together. Life was not fair: I had just strangled at birth the most promising break I was ever likely to receive. I felt like jumping off the cliff at the end of the camping ground. Of course, thanks to my gift, I could make the sea receive me like a feather bed and then surf out of here, but the thought was very tempting. I found myself humming the refrain to 'Crash and Burn'— yep: that was my signature tune all right.

'What are you doing here stuck out on your own?' Marcus had spotted me sitting in the shadows. 'Margot flick you off?'

'Go away if you're not going to be nice to me,' I said, not caring at the moment what I said to him. Twenty metres away Davis was talking earnestly to Brian and Matt—too close for me to risk telepathy on Marcus. Anyway, who was I kidding that he could be my soulfinder? I was such a fool, messing up the one thing I was here to do. Marcus was way above my pay grade.

Marcus sat down beside me on the Winnebago steps and offered me a slice of pizza from his plate. I shook my head.

'Go on: you've not eaten anything.'

He'd been watching, had he? 'I can't.'

He put the plate aside. 'You should be feeling on top of the world, Angel. That was a great show.'

It was strange to be sitting next to him without him trying to shoot me down with his let's-despise-the-groupie barrage of words. I was so close, I could scent his aftershave—a faintly spicy smell. His hands, square and capable, rested on the knees of his jeans. You could imagine those hands building stonewalls as competently as he played the guitar. Three freckles sat in a triangle on the back of his right hand. I was tempted to trace the outline but kept my fingers laced together around my folded up legs.

Marcus was studying my profile. I could feel a little warmth from his breath on my cheek. 'What made you dance around just now? I've never seen anyone go from ecstatic to depressed in such a short time.'

'Kurt invited me to play the violin on the new single.'

'I see. Yeah, we discussed that we thought that would work but I hadn't realized he was going ahead so soon. The part's only in early draft.'

I squeezed my elbows, wanting to curl up in a foetal ball. 'You write music with him a lot?'

'That's how we met up. Margot introduced us when I—a complete unknown—sent in a song for the band to consider. It turned into "Crash and Burn".'

'I love that song!' Then I did the maths. 'Hey, but you must've been about five when you wrote it.'

'Hardly.' He smiled lopsidedly. 'I was fifteen.'

'You're seventeen now, right?'

'Uh-huh.'

I forced myself to make the fishing expedition. 'So am I. My birthday's in March. When's yours?'

'Same.'

Red flashing lights lit up in my brain. Here goes. 'Have you ever heard of savants, Marcus?'

'Savants? Are they a new band?'

Oh Lord, help me.

'No, we are ... we're people with some extra gifts that set us apart. You're one too.' I flicked my gaze over to Davis. Surely he was too busy to notice me? I'd risk it. *We can use telepathy and* . . . I held my hand over Marcus's drink. I can do this. I made the Coke wiggle out of the can and flow neatly back into the hole.

Marcus had frozen on the step.

You can hear me, can't you? Unless he responded telepathically, I couldn't be sure if he was my soulfinder. No matter the suspicions beforehand, soulfinders only know each other when they speak mind to mind. *Please, tell me you can.*

Over at the tables, Davis slipped a phone-size device out of his pocket and started quartering the area with his gaze. Oh, this was not good—not good at all.

Marcus rubbed his temples. 'Are you some kind of . . . illusionist?'

I shook my head. Don't look this way, Davis.

'I've got to be imagining things. Did you slip something in my drink?'

'No, Marcus. You're a savant like me—and I think you might be my soulfinder.'

He was edging away from me now. 'Your what?'

'My . . . ' There was no subtle way of saying this. 'My other half. We may be destined to be together.'

'Oh no: you're mad, aren't you? I thought you were just a desperate fangirl but now I get it. OK, Angel, just take some deep breaths.' He knelt before me, taking my hands in his. 'Are you on medication? Have you forgotten to take it? Is there someone I could call?'

I began to laugh hysterically, probably confirming his diagnosis. He was being so sweet but so wrong.

'I think I'd better get you a doctor. Stay here.' He would have got up but I kept hold of his hands. Screw Davis: I had to get Marcus to connect with me.

You can hear me—I know you can. You have a gift, Marcus. That thing you do with music—it's not normal. You are using psychic energy. It spreads to me too when I'm playing and you're there.

'Stop it,' he hissed, snatching his hands away and falling back on his butt. 'Get away from me.'

I can't. Just answer me. Please, I'm begging you.

His answer was to spring up and run into his Winnebago, slamming the door behind him. Crash and burn. When I looked up, I found Davis standing in front of me.

'Hello, little savant.' He waggled the device so I could see the dial. 'Care to do that again?'

Chapter 10

'So, Miss . . . ' Davis read my name off my security pass as he tucked his detector in his back pocket, 'Angel Campbell, how about giving us an interview?' Snake-strike quick, his hand whipped out and grabbed my wrist.

'I don't give interviews.' I tried to twist free but his grip was painfully tight.

Pulling me to my feet, he snatched my phone from my lap. 'I'll be taking that. By all means, do shout out with your telepathy: I'd just love to see your friends running to help you. That'd be damn good proof that you communicated with them as I've got your cell phone.'

'Let go of me!' Davis dwarfed me, being broad in the shoulders and a good deal taller. The way we were angled, I doubted anyone could see me struggle. Fear dug its claws in my gut. 'I'll get you thrown out for this!'

'Yeah, right. Like you want to attract attention to yourself with these people. You don't know them very well, do you? You see we've been watching them for a while now and we don't think they know what they are. Am I right?'

'Like I'm going to tell you anything.'

Davis started walking away from the pizza party, towing me with him. 'I think you will. I've finally got me a genuine savant I can handle. What: no freaky telekinesis or mind strikes? What's it you do, honey? My equipment was going crazy at the concert when you played. Do you burrow in our brains with music? What kind of subliminal messages were you planting, hey?'

'Let go! You're hurting my wrist. Where are you taking me?' He was dragging me further away from people down the narrow passageways between the Winnebagos. I was getting confused about his motives here. 'Is this some kind of sick joke?'

'No joke, hon. I've got some friends who are very keen to meet you. They're waiting to interview you too. Between us, we'll make you talk.'

I kicked and managed to reach his calf.

'Argh!' As he hopped in pain, I ripped free and bolted. I didn't get far before he tackled me to the ground, him landing on top squashing all air from my lungs so I had no chance to scream. He plastered a moist palm over my mouth.

'That wasn't very nice of you, was it? But now you're gonna shut up and come along with me.'

Marcus! Help! Though he didn't believe in telepathy, he was the only one close enough to do something.

The door to Marcus's trailer shot open. 'What the—! Angel!' He raced down the alleyway, heaved Davis off of me and flipped him over his thigh in a neat judo move. Davis slammed into the trailer opposite. 'Just what do you think you're doing?'

I rolled over onto my back and spat out the grass that had got in my mouth. I could feel bruises blooming on my knees, hip and elbows.

Rubbing the back of his head, Davis made a wary move to get up. 'I was just . . . interviewing her.'

'Like hell you were! I'm calling security.' Marcus's eyes blazed with fury.

'She won't want you to do that. Ask her.' Trembling with

the aftermath of our tussle, Davis stood up, arms folded, baiting me to bring in the authorities. That was his agenda, not mine.

'It's OK, Marcus. I'll handle it. I've got people I can tell.' I lifted my chin, meeting Davis' gaze.

'Yeah, you do that, and tell the Benedicts I'm not on my own this time.' He jabbed his index finger at me. 'This time I'm not backing down.' With a roll of his shoulders, Davis walked off, leaving me to face one very irate rescuer.

Marcus put his hand to his forehead and turned a circle, clearly confused. 'You're letting him walk away? The guy had you wrestled to the ground. Was it . . . was he trying to . . . ?'

'No, he wasn't molesting me, Marcus.' I got to my feet, shivers running through me.

'Then what the hell was it?'

'More like trying to force information out of me.' I took a breath. 'About savants.'

Marcus turned away. 'Bloody hell. Not this again.'

I felt a lot like crying. I'd just been attacked and I wanted a hug but the nearest 'huggee' thought me delusional. 'Explain then how you knew I was in trouble.'

'I must've heard you—you called my name.'

'You saw: Davis had his hand plastered over my mouth. You heard me in your mind.'

He shook his head, deep in denial. 'No, then it was the noise of the scuffle—or a damn good instinct.' His arm shot out and lifted my left. 'Hey, are you bleeding?'

I looked down at where he was pointing. Sure enough, there was a trickle of blood running from my elbow. I must've whacked that hard against the ground when we fell. My head swam. 'Oh. Sorry, but I don't deal well with the sight of blood.' I folded to the floor and put my head between my knees.

'Figures.' He gave a put-upon sigh. 'OK, Angel, let's go

to my place and I'll fix that up for you. Then you can call someone to come and walk you back.'

Woozy starbursts were still shooting through the black of my closed eyes. 'Give me a moment here.'

An arm went under my knees and round my shoulders. 'I still think you should report that guy. What did he mean about not backing down?' He lifted me up and carried me against his chest up the stairs to his trailer.

I let my head rest on his T-shirt, not opening my eyes. I wished I didn't feel so dizzy, then I would actually have enjoyed the experience of being swept off my feet. 'You won't like my answer. Can we park the questions until I feel more myself?'

He lowered me to a sofa. 'All right, but I will want answers, understood?'

'Yes, sir.' I opened my eyes to find him half-smiling at me, though his expression was still concerned.

'Good. The sass is coming back. Let's get you sorted.' Marcus got a first-aid box out of a cupboard. 'I just need to boil some water to clean that cut.'

'I'll do the water.'

'You should stay sitting down.'

'I won't need to stand. Just give me two bowls: one with water, one empty.'

Bemused, Marcus put a bowl of water on the table in front of me and an empty plastic one a little further off. I think he thought I was anticipating being sick. I held a hand over the water and quickly separated the molecules from impurities. With a flick of a finger, I made it jump into the clean receptacle, leaving any bad stuff behind. 'It's distilled now.'

Giving me a hard look, Marcus dealt with my party trick by ignoring it. He ripped open some cotton wool and tore off a wad. 'Do you want to clean it or shall I?'

'You.' I closed my eyes again, hurt that he hadn't even acknowledged what he had seen. Besides, if I had to deal with my own cut, I would require that second bowl after all.

He took my upper arm in his hand and gently dabbed at the cut. 'Not too bad. Won't need stitches.'

'Do you mind not talking about it? Change the subject please.'

His huff of laughter was warm on my skin. 'About getting you back to your tent, who you gonna call?'

'Ghostbusters?' I joked weakly. 'Actually, I can't call anyone as that slimeball took my phone. It'll have to be telepathy.'

There was a hiss of indrawn breath. 'And you're still not going to report him to the police?'

I winced as he found a piece of grit in the cut. 'No. I've got someone better than that on my side.'

'Who?'

'That's part of the whole "let's not talk about savants, Angel" thing.'

'I think this should be covered with a dressing. Keep still.'

I could hear the rustle of wrappers and then the application of a soft plaster over the cut.

'Completely hidden. Can you risk opening your eyes?'

I squinted down at my elbow. 'That looks very professional.'

'I learned to do first aid in the judo class I took with the guys.'

'So are you all really black belts?'

Relieved to have a normal topic of conversation to run with, Marcus gave me one of his gorgeous smiles. 'What do you think, Titch?'

'Titch? I'll have you know I am only a little under average height.'

'Yeah right.'

'Humph. I think Michael and Pete probably are black belts.

You, I'm not so sure. You strike me as too airy-fairy cerebral for the physical stuff.'

'If you weren't injured, I'd show you some of my moves and see if I could persuade you otherwise.' His voice had gone all husky. I could feel my cheeks flush. 'Wow, that came out way more suggestive than I intended.' Marcus took a step back and ran his hand through his hair in frustration.

Inside, brazen Angel was shouting *You can show me your moves anytime*. Self-conscious Angel, however, was in the driving seat. 'Don't worry—I didn't take it the wrong way.' Yes I had. 'OK, so you also have the belt. That's very cool. I was just teasing you about being too much of a dreamer. I noticed you threw that jerk off me quick enough.'

'That was beginner's stuff, Angel. You could do that.' He sat down next to me. 'Let's see the rest.'

'Rest of what?' Inappropriate Angel was making all sorts of unrepeatable lewd suggestions.

'The dings and scratches. Show me the other elbow.' Marcus did a quick inventory of my injuries. 'I've got arnica for bruises.' He got out a tube from the first-aid box and rubbed it into the blackened spots he could see. 'Anywhere else?'

'My hip—but I think I'd better get that.'

Marcus moved to the other side of the trailer as I slipped a hand under the waistband of my leggings and rubbed a little of the ointment on my left hip. I tugged the tunic dress straight. 'I'm decent now.'

'Coffee or tea?' He opened the little cupboard over the sink.
Have you got something herbal?

'Yes, I've got mint or chamomile. Margot keeps it in stock for herself.' He hadn't noticed.
Chamomile please.

He took out the packet, then froze. 'You're doing it again.'
Yes.

'Well—don't.'

OK.

'I mean it. I don't like it.'

No, you don't understand it. That guy who attacked me—he knows about our kind and wants to crucify us in the press. He suspects some of you are savants—he saw you respond to my telepathy You'll have gone to the top of his list.

'That's crap, Angel. I'm just me—nothing special.' He threw the tea bag in a mug and drowned it in hot water.

I think you might be very special, Marcus.

'You said you'd stop that.'

'Yes, I did. Would you just answer me back that way—just the once? Then I really will shut up with the telepathy.'

'No, never. And why? Because I'm not telepathic.' He plonked the mug on the table, liquid sloshing over the side. I cleaned up with a little twirl of my finger. He sucked in a breath. 'I can see you can do some weird stuff, but I'm not interested, OK? I'm fine how I am—with my music, my career. I don't want you coming in here with the equivalent of "You're a wizard, Marcus". I'm way past eleven, didn't get that letter to Hogwarts, OK?'

All my conversations with other savants hadn't prepared me for someone who just blanked out the possibility that they were one of us. What was I supposed to do now? Inappropriate Angel had a daring suggestion.

I tried my dimples on him. 'Marcus, thanks for looking after me.'

Some tension left his shoulders as I returned to what he thought was more normal territory. 'That's fine, Angel. I was just pleased I could get there in time.'

I knelt up on the sofa so my face was level with his. 'I'd like to thank you properly.'

He turned towards me, the tug between us still there despite his best efforts to ignore it. 'I don't need thanks.'

'But I do.' I leaned in, closing the gap between us. A little kiss, a brush of my lips on his. 'Thank you.'

The attraction-o-meter went off the dial; I could see the needle flicking into the red with each touch.

'Well, now you mention it, a little bit of gratitude doesn't do any harm.' Marcus slipped an arm around my waist and pulled me closer. 'No harm at all.' He returned the kiss but his was firmer, taking over my mouth with his. I hadn't expected his lips to be so warm, so soft, unlike the rest of him that was all spiky defences and strength. Golden tingles ran up my spine. All the bones left my body in a shower of sparkles. From kneeling somehow I went to sitting on his lap. His fingers caressed my cheek, the outer rim of my ear, the shape of my collarbone. 'Beautiful,' he whispered. 'Perfect.' We rested there, forehead to forehead, both with eyes closed.

What had I intended to do? Oh yes, get him to talk telepathically to me while he was disarmed by the kiss. Unfortunately, I'd wandered off track myself, wits scattered by the most amazing kiss of my life.

'Perfect?' I asked. No one had ever said anything remotely like that about me.

Marcus smiled ruefully. 'Until you open your mouth to speak. Then the crazy girl comes back.'

I punched his chest—but not hard.

He settled me more comfortably on his lap. 'This is getting complicated.'

You're telling me. 'I know.'

'I think I might like you, Angel.' He sounded almost regretful.

'In equal parts to hating me? I heard that song, you know.'

He swore. 'You didn't?'

'I was at the rehearsal.'

'It was . . . just a song.'

'It was about me, wasn't it? Demon Angel. I'm not a demon, Marcus. Not bad. Stupid. Foolish often. But right now, I'm just trying to do what's right.'

'Baby, you are really, really strange, you get that?'

'And you're not?'

He gave a gruff laugh. 'I suppose I am. We all are. You asked to park the questions earlier. Why don't we park this stuff completely and just enjoy the festival together? We're not likely to see each other after, are we? I'm on tour and you're . . . ?'

After I'd just blown my big break with Gifted? 'Going back to sixth form.'

He tapped my nose. 'Sweet. That's settled then.'

Hang on! I hadn't agreed to being his festival squeeze. I scrambled off his lap. 'I'm not a groupie, Marcus. I don't just throw myself at guys in bands for a one-night stand.'

Marcus watched me with amusement as I retreated to the other end of the sofa. 'Technically we're here for two nights.'

I knew what he was doing. He felt the attraction between us and had decided he could work it out of his system by letting it run its course over the next couple of days. He had no idea what he was really dealing with here. And his attitude made me about as cherished as a tissue from a box of Kleenex, the exact opposite to how he had made me feel when we had kissed.

'I'm not like that. Savants have one true partner in life: their soulfinder. I don't go sleeping around with any hot rock star in tight jeans. But Marcus, I think you could be mine.'

Chuckling, he stood up and pulled me to my feet. 'Baby, you think I'm your soulmate? That's cute.'

'*Soulfinder*—similar but different. It's special to savants.' *If you fricking well replied to me telepathically, you'd understand.*

'I agree we've got real chemistry between us, Angel.' He ran his hand down my back, doing that sparkle thing to my spine. I shivered, trying to resist the urge to melt all over him again.

'Stop it: I'm trying to tell you something important here!'

'Let's just see how it goes, hey? We've a couple of days. Let's not waste it.'

He bent his head to find my lips with his. The love-rat was thinking we had only two days before he said 'adios' and left me languishing. After his humiliating experience with the gutter press, he still thought every girl was a Sinead. Cynical was now his starting point in relationships.

'No, Marcus. That's not the deal.' I stamped on his toe to get free of his embrace. 'If you want a girl for that, go wander the campsite. They'll form a queue for you, I've no doubt.' This was a disaster. He didn't respect me, didn't believe me, just fancied me.

Ignoring the squashed toe, he closed the distance again. 'But you're in my trailer—not some other girl.'

'And watch me: I'm walking right out of your trailer giving you the finger, Marcus. You know, you pretend you're all emotional depth and creative genius angst but you're just like other guys, aren't you? You're not thinking of me as a person; you're just thinking how to get laid.' Oh hell, I was not handling this at all well. I stopped on the top step. He was standing in the centre of his trailer, expression unbelieving that I really intended to walk away from what he assumed had been my aim in life: getting it on with a rock star. I had to remember what this was all really about. There was more at stake than just my petal-plucked ego. 'If you change your mind about finding out about savants, just tell me, OK?' I swallowed against tears. 'You don't have to talk to me about it. I've got some friends who can fill you in without the distraction of this thing between us. And really, if you do one thing for me, keep away from Davis.' I started down the steps.

'Hey, Angel, you're not really going?'
'I really am.'
'What about us?'
Until you talk to me telepathically, there is no 'us'.

Chapter · 11

For all my storming out of the Winnebago, I wasn't so stupid as to go marching off on my own back to my tent, not with Davis and unspecified cronies on the loose.

'Hey, Matt, would you mind walking me back?' I asked, interrupting my friend mid-conversation with Brian.

'Really?' he asked with a pained look on his face. 'Really now?'

'Sorry, but I'm not feeling too good.'

Brian tactfully got up and moved off to another table. Matt watched him go with the expression last seen on his face when I told him that, no, he couldn't have the last doughnut from the box. 'You should do something about your timing, Angel.' He finally turned to look at me. 'But you're not lying, are you? You seem a little . . . shaken. What's happened, sweet pea?'

'Do you mind if I postpone that conversation until I'm feeling better?'

He got up and slung an arm around my shoulder. 'I saw you do your happy dance when you were talking to Kurt. Something happened since to set you back?'

'You could say that.' I glanced over at the alley between the trailers. Marcus was just emerging from his doorway. I quickly turned my gaze away.

'I see.' Gauging my reaction, Matt assumed my problem was with Marcus. 'Angel, he's not for you, you know that, don't you? These guys might let us in to play for an evening but they move in different circles. If you're looking for a date, then Joey said he liked you.'

'Joey?'

'You know, Joey Reef, the rapper you danced on the table with?'

A little bit of admiration warmed my chilled heart. 'Aw, that's sweet of him, but I think I might give the whole romance-at-the-festival thing a miss.'

We reached the security checkpoint and I made doubly sure there was no Eli Davis lurking.

'You're really nervous tonight, Angel. I know you were good in the concert but I doubt the crazy fans are waiting to jump on you. They'll expect you to stay the other side of the fence.' Matt marched me through the rows of tents, eager to deliver me and get back to the tail-end of the pizza party.

We reached my little encampment. I could see Will sitting on a cooler outside his tent, head bent over his phone.

'I'm good now, thanks. You go back to the guys.'

Matt squeezed my arm. 'OK, Angel. I'll just swing by reception and see if I can persuade Henry to gatecrash the party with me.'

'She'll love you for ever if you get her introduced to Gifted.'

'That's the plan.' With a wave goodbye, he jogged back the way we had come.

'Hey, Will, what's up?' I called.

'Thank God!' Will leapt up and grabbed me by the arms to check me over. 'Why weren't you answering your phone?'

'Hey, ease up a little.' I pulled my injured elbow out of his grip.

'The threat level on you went off the scale about half an hour ago. We've all been trying to call you but were shunted through to voicemail. Alex has persuaded his way backstage and is looking for you. You know you can't forget to keep your phone switched on during a mission.'

'Hang on, partner, back up a little.' I put up a hand between us and pushed him in the chest. 'Give me a chance to explain, why don't you? First, where is everyone else?'

'They've spread out looking for you. I got "abduction attempt" on my radar. We had to act fast.'

'Call them back in right now; get Alex from backstage. Eli Davis was there a moment ago.'

He sent the text. 'What's happened?'

I wasn't quite sure how to put this. 'I think it's fair to say, Houston, we have a problem.' I frowned. 'Multiple problems.'

Deciding that Will would make an easier audience than the combined ears of my friends, I quickly fessed up to the gory details of my disastrous evening.

'Angel . . . ' growled Will.

I covered my face with my hand. 'Don't say it: I know I've got absolutely everything wrong. The only thing I can say in my defence is that I was trying really, really hard to do right.'

'You shouldn't have used telepathy.'

'Well, duh, I think I kinda got that when Davis rugby tackled me and tried to drag me off for a torture-the-savant session.' My voice sounded a little hysterical but, gee, I was having one crap night.

Will touched my upper arm sympathetically. 'That guy's out of control. He seems to think having a gift means we shouldn't be granted the basic human rights not to be roughed up in pursuit of the truth.' He put a finger under my chin and tipped my face up so he could see my expression. 'You really OK?'

My 'yes' turned into a 'no' as truth-leaking Misty approached with Alex and Summer, closely followed by Uriel and Victor. 'I could do with a hug,' I blurted out.

Will obliged, tucking me against his broad capable chest and taking on the burden of repeating my story to my friends. It felt safe and comfortable hiding under his jacket listening to his voice rumble away about Davis and Marcus. Was it feasible to spend the rest of my life here?

Summer's light touch patted my back. 'I'm afraid not, Angel.' She'd been reading my mind again. 'Come on, out of there.'

Red-faced I forced myself to confront my friends. 'I'm really, really sorry, guys. I am Queen of Disaster.'

No one protested my declaration.

Victor flicked a glance at Will. 'Check there's no threat near our tents.'

Will put his fingers to his temples. 'Nope, levels have dipped again after the spike when Angel was attacked.'

Victor looked fit to kill. 'So Davis has all our numbers? Did you have security on your phone?'

'Um . . . ' I had tried a passcode for a while but got bored of entering it so disabled it.

'I see. So do you have any incriminating photos or texts on it?'

'Er . . . ' Hundreds.

'Angel, you're on a mission here. Didn't you stop to think for a second that that might be one huge security breach?'

I closed my eyes briefly against the pain of his reprimand. I had wanted to impress the Benedicts but I had just proved I had fluff for brains.

'I've seen the photos on Angel's phone,' said Summer softly, 'and most of them are normal stuff like anyone our age has: shots of friends and silly poses. He won't be able to make much of them.'

'But he'll see that Will circulated his photo to her. Thank God I thought twice and didn't let you send her the file, Will.

I thought she might not be secure.' Victor paced the space between the tents, clearly wanting to kick something. Me, probably. 'Is there anything else on there?'

Would he worry about a photo of me hosing Misty and Alex with water in the back garden—without a hose? 'No, nothing.'

Misty winced but didn't give my lie away.

'Everyone will need to change numbers and delete all contents of your voicemail before he hacks it.' Victor got his phone out.

'I didn't have your number,' I said quickly. 'Just Will, Misty, Alex, Summer, and ... er ... Uriel.' And a shed-load of other savant friends but fortunately they were mixed in with my contacts, with nothing to link them together. I'd have to warn them all—but not in front of Victor.

'OK. Uriel, take my spare SIM.' He flipped his brother a card from his back pocket. 'Send out the alert that no one should contact the compromised numbers. Absolutely no one should ring Angel's old phone.'

'Can you tell my parents, please?' I asked humbly. The last thing I needed was for Davis to trick them into giving a candid interview under the mistaken impression that he was a friend of mine.

'I'm on it,' said Uriel, cracking open the back of his phone and slipping in the new card.

Summer sat on the other side of me and nudged me with her shoulder. 'You OK?'

'Getting there.'

'You told Marcus straight out what you thought he was: that was brave of you.'

'Stupid, you mean. I did telepathy, brought out a couple of my best party tricks and he blew it all off. I don't think even parting the Red Sea would've impressed him.'

Will's phone vibrated. He pulled it out and checked the screen. 'I don't recognize the number,' he said.

'Don't answer it,' warned Victor. 'It could be Davis having got your number off Angel's.'

'No, do answer it!' I yelped, totally forgetting I was in the doghouse and shouldn't be countermanding Victor's orders. Had I really neglected to mention that I'd left Margot with a plea to ring? Way to go, Angel. 'It could be your soulfinder.'

'What?' Will stared at the ringing phone. If he didn't do something it was going to go through to voicemail, then Davis would hack it and . . . oh God, oh God. I grabbed it from him and swiped to answer. Victor made a move to cut me off but I danced out of the way. I'd better be right or he would be tying me up and sending me home in the boot of the car. 'Will Benedict's phone, how may I help you?'

'Hello, this is Margot Derkx. Who's this?'

'Oh hi, Margot.' I waggled my eyebrows furiously at Will in a 'get ready' gesture. 'I'm just with Will now. I'll pass you to him.' I handed him the phone.

He swore under his breath then took it from me. 'Hey, Miss Derkx, I apologize for this request to talk out of the blue. Yeah, she is, isn't she? No, she's not crazy and I'm not her doctor. Yes, absolutely. She's right: there is something we need to discuss—a threat to the Gifted security. Credentials? I can give you some references. My brother here has a senior officer at Scotland Yard who will vouch for him. Ah-ha. Yes, I agree: best if we discuss this face to face. Nine a.m.? That's fine. Yeah, Angel knows the way.' His voice dropped a little, entering a more intimate register. 'Looking forward to meeting you. See you then.' He ended the call and held the phone to his lips for a second.

'Well?' I squeezed my hands together, pressing them against the butterflies in my stomach.

'Promising. Very very promising.' He grinned at me.

* * *

I was sent to bed while everyone else planned the next day—sort of like a punishment, I guess, and I think Victor had just had enough of me. It happens. Summer told me it was because I needed my rest after the excitement, but as Misty stayed quiet I decided my interpretation was correct. I had some serious making up to do. Getting Margot to phone was a big tick in the plus column but unfortunately the minus was running off the page.

'Do not blow it tomorrow, Campbell.' I punched my pillow of rolled up clothes.

I dropped off with the thought that, if I took Will to meet his destiny at nine, I'd still have time to make my date with Kurt about the violin part at ten.

Will was up and ready when I tumbled out of my tent with my clothes askew. He looked great: freshly shaved, hair still a little wet from his shower in the camp facilities, black T-shirt with an open blue shirt over the top, blue button-fly jeans, and well-worn boots.

I whisked my hair upside down and gave it the old shake-and-go treatment, which would have to do until I got to a mirror. I could see Misty and Summer's bright eyes watching me from their sleeping bags. We'd agreed not to overwhelm Will on his special morning by all emerging to wave him off but both had fingers crossed on top of the covers. I gave them a salute—a promise I'd do my utmost not to mess this up.

'All set?' I asked Will.

'As I'll ever be.' He rolled his shoulders.

'No Victor?'

'I'll call him in afterwards.'

Yeah, I wouldn't want an audience for meeting my soulfinder either—it was too personal.

I attempted to dial down his expectations. 'You know it might not be her. It's just that she seems the most likely candidate.'

'I realize that.'

I took his hand, swinging it between us. 'Did I mention she is absolutely gorgeous?'

He gave a quiet laugh. 'No, but that doesn't matter. It's who she is inside that counts.'

I hugged his arm. 'Oh you are just the nicest man in existence, William. I wish my guy was half as nice as you.'

'You really think that Marcus person is the one?'

'I can't shake the instinct, even though he treats me like a cross between a lunatic and a groupie.'

'Second item on today's agenda: rearrange facial features of Marcus Cohen.'

And he would too. I could just imagine Will Benedict squaring up to Marcus and teaching him a lesson about how to treat the ladies. He was old-fashioned like that—got it from his dad.

'It's OK, Will, I can handle him. I'm going to drag him kicking and screaming into acknowledging me if it kills me. You concentrate on getting your life sorted out. Mine was always going to be a multi-vehicle pile-up whatever I did.'

Margot had left Will's name on security so Al let him through.

'Heard you weren't bad yesterday, AC,' Al remarked, filling out a pass for my companion. 'Caught a little of it on TV. Your band doesn't suck.'

'Thanks, Al.'

Will nudged me as we walked past the checkpoint. 'What was that—an insult?'

'With Al, that was high praise indeed.'

'You Brits are one weird nation.'

I dropped by reception to check there was no note calling

off my violin session. Henry was delighted to see me with another hot guy in tow—as good as the first cup of coffee to get the heart racing, she confessed as she looked through her messages. 'No, nothing for you.'

Phew. 'How was last night?'

She glanced at Will.

'It's OK. He won't rat on you to the festival organizers.'

The pent-up gossip rushed from her. 'Oh my gosh, Angel: I met Gifted. I love Matt—he totally broke me in to the most happening party on the site.'

Well done, Matt. 'I'm so pleased you had a good time.'

'He said you weren't feeling well.'

'Oh, it was nothing. I'm OK today.' I was tempted to impress the hell out of her by saying where I was going with my violin later but decided that might jinx the whole thing.

Saying goodbye, we headed out for the trailer zone.

'Where did Margot say to meet you?' I asked.

'Tour bus. She has an office set up in there.' Will pulled at the neck of his T-shirt. 'How do I look?'

'Yummy. She won't be able to resist. Now, how are you going to play this? Do you want me to hang around and smooth the way?'

He choked. 'You? Smooth the way?'

OK, that did sound a bit unlikely. 'So I should make the intros and just back off quickly?'

'Yeah, that seems best.'

We had reached the silver tour bus and were stood by the back door.

'Ready?' I raised my hand to knock.

He nodded. 'Don't tell her too much, OK? Don't mention savants or gifts right out. Or soulfinders.' He looked down at my attentive expression. 'Second thoughts, just don't say anything at all.'

The door opened and Kurt stood in the entrance. This was the first time I really hadn't been pleased to see my rock hero.

'Oh, good morning, Kurt. This is my totally sane, not at all flaky friend I told you about: Will Benedict.'

Kurt raised an eyebrow. 'Is that so?'

Will nudged me aside and held out his business card. 'Pleased to meet you, sir.'

The rock god shuddered. 'Not "sir", not at nine in the morning. Call me Kurt. Come on in, you two.'

Bang went Will's plan to get rid of me. With an apologetic shrug to Will, I stepped into the bus.

'Oh wow: this is sweet! You've got everything in here!' Kurt had led us into a mini lounge with sofas, TV screen, music centre, and guitars on racks. There was even a potted plant on the coffee table. I ran my fingers over the leaves—real, not plastic.

'Yeah, home from home for the band. There are normal seats up front but this part is for us to chill.' Kurt gestured to the sofa. 'Make yourself at home, Will.' Kurt sat down opposite us, ankle on opposing knee in his favourite relaxed pose. 'So what's the deal with Angel here? Is she on day-release? Marcus is convinced she's as mad as a box of frogs.'

I went very still. He was teasing but I sensed there was a serious question mark in his mind as to my sanity.

'No, sir . . . Kurt. There's nothing wrong with Angel. My brothers and I asked her to request this meeting.' Will glanced to the door leading further into the bus. 'Is your manager joining us?'

'When I'm sure it's safe. Angel was my decision—my risk. I brought her into our inner circle and I'll be the one to throw her out if she turns out to be bad news. I don't want Margot mixed up in any ugly scenes. My instincts about people are usually gold, but I might be wrong.' Kurt's smile was not his usual one; he was showing his cynical edge, honed after years of learning to distinguish good guys from bad.

'Oh, Kurt, you don't need to protect me—I keep telling you!' Margot appeared in the doorway, bearing a tray of coffee. Will jumped up and cleared a space for it on the table. 'Thank you.' Her eyes lingered on his face for a second—she liked what she saw, I could tell.

Use telepathy, I urged him.

He shook his head slightly, telling me he had another game plan.

I bit my tongue to prevent me saying anything rash like *he's your soulfinder, Margot! Snog him!*

'How are you, Angel? Marcus told us a journalist had cut up rough with you yesterday. He thinks you should report him.' Margot offered me a coffee. 'Milk?'

'Please. I'm fine. I'm really grateful that you took time to see Will.'

She smiled and passed the mug to me, decorated with the Gifted logo. 'I can't ignore warnings even if they come from an unlikely source. And we were worried about you. Talking to one of your friends seemed the way to go.'

Great. I had earned Will an interview because they wanted to check I was getting appropriate care for my condition. I gave a philosophical sigh. Well, it worked, didn't it?

'Now, Will, hadn't you better tell us what's really going on here? I see from your card you claim to be an expert in personal security. Angel said as much. If you're not mad, is this some drama student role-play thing? She also said your brother was with the FBI—that was kinda the straw that broke the camel's back of credulity.' Kurt sipped his coffee. He drank it black and strong.

Will placed another business card on the table. 'Commander

Downing, Special Ops, Scotland Yard. Ask him about Victor Benedict.'

Margot picked up the card, her French polished nails perfect. 'It's a London number. Is this for real? If I check this out and find it a fake, you are going to be in a lot of trouble, Mr Benedict.'

'Will. Call me Will.'

Whoa—I could feel the sparks between them and I was sitting some distance from the eye-contact zone.

Perfectly composed Margot actually blushed. 'OK, Will, I'll give the guy a call.'

'He's expecting you to contact him. Victor gave him a heads-up.'

Margot took the card and disappeared into her office. That left the three of us in an awkward silence.

'So, er, how long has Margot been working for you?' asked Will.

I narrowed my eyes in warning. He wasn't being very subtle about where his interest lay.

Kurt brushed the thigh of his jeans. 'For four years since she left college. She's my half-sister.'

'I didn't know that.' Will's gaze swivelled to the door through which she had gone.

'Well, why would you? She doesn't trade on the association but it works for us. I know I can trust her.'

I sensed there was probably a 'fingers burned' story behind that comment. In showbiz it must be almost impossible to know whom you could trust, hence the prickly hedgehog thing from him and Marcus.

'We shared a father, but he left both our mothers after doing little more than getting them pregnant. I got to know her thanks to our grandparents. And why am I telling you all this?'

'Because you know in your heart of hearts that Angel and I are no threat to you,' said Will softly.

Kurt sipped his coffee.

Margot came back with a puzzled look on her face. 'They check out, Kurt. They are who Angel said they are, unlikely though that sounds.'

Kurt sat forward, hands hanging between his spread knees. 'Hey, darlin', I might have to rethink the whole crazy girl thing. I owe you an apology.'

I gave him a relieved smile. 'Accepted. But to be honest with you, my friends will tell you I probably do edge into way-over-the-top zone so you are forgiven for misjudging me.'

'But I like that about you. So we're good, yes?' He held out a hand.

I shook it. 'We're good, Kurt.'

He turned to Will. 'OK, now I know you're serious, what's this threat you're on about and why are you using a teenager to carry your messages for you? Was that journalist thing last night connected?' His fists were clenched on his thighs. Marcus must have told him. 'Because if so I'll gladly hand you your teeth for putting her in danger.'

Not another protective male! Before I could protest, Will stepped in. 'Yes, it was connected—and yes, we were wrong to put Angel in danger. The thing was, when we sent her to you with the message, the threat level was reading as low on the scale.'

'What scale?'

Will ran his hand over his brow, face set, reminding me of a guy steeling himself for an Olympic high dive. 'I have a gift for detecting these things. I can read all the dangers around me if I stretch out my senses. I knew when she was in trouble—but I was too far away to locate her and to come to the rescue.'

Margot sat opposite Will, next to Kurt. 'A gift? Can you prove it?'

'What can I say? I know that you have in the main a good

131

loyal team around the band from what I've seen so far but I'd look a little harder into the affairs of the tour bus driver. He's showing up as suspect but it could just be a health condition. Still, get him checked out. You don't want him driving into a wall because he's having a heart attack.'

Margot laced her fingers together nervously. She could sense the atmosphere alive with savant power but she was not experienced enough to recognize it for what it was. 'I can vouch for Jim but you might be right about the health issues. That's hardly proof. I could make up a story like that.'

Kurt was having none of it. 'I'm sure it makes good advertising for your security firm if clients buy into this stuff, but come on, we're all grown-ups here; we don't need fairy tales.'

'I'm not quite grown up.' I lined up the coffee mugs. 'I still believe in fairy tales.'

Are you sure about this, Angel? asked Will.

For you, dear, anything. Holding out my hand, I grinned at Kurt. 'Watch.'

His coffee rose up and started twisting in a rope. Next I summoned my own to swirl around his—brown wrapping around the black. 'You want milk with that?' The milk curled from the jug and joined the party. 'No, you don't take it, do you?' I sent the milk back. 'I think it's cool enough now.' Our two strands of coffee unwound and returned to their original cups—mine still white, his still perfectly black. That part took a lot of concentration and practice but, gee, I'm an only child: there's not much else to do on family holidays with my folks.

'What the fricking hell was that?' (Between you and me, he didn't say 'fricking'.)

'I have a gift too, just mine is easier to see. I can manipulate water. We're both savants.' *Oops, was that too soon?*

Angel . . .

Sorry, Will.

'Savants? What does that mean?' Margot picked up the milk jug and sniffed the contents suspiciously.

'Margot, have you noticed whether you have any unusual abilities?' asked Will.

'Well, no.'

'Yeah, you do. You're awesome with sound.' Kurt reached out and squeezed her hand. 'You have to admit it. And you say you can sense a lot about other people, like whether they have talent—that's how you discovered Marcus.'

'We think Marcus is a savant too,' added Will, 'but he didn't take it well when Angel tried to tell him.'

'Not from her, he wouldn't,' said Margot. 'He thinks she's—'

'I know what he thinks,' I said quickly, before we got into another round of Angel-should-be-locked-up-for-her-own-safety.

'This talent-spotting thing of yours, how does it work?' asked Will. Lord, he was so patient! I'd've been on the 'you're my soulfinder' part already. Oh yeah, I'd tried that, hadn't I? And look how well that had gone for me.

'If I listen very carefully, I can hear people's ... people's souls. Heavens, that sounds mad, doesn't it?' Margot bunched her toffee-coloured hair back at her nape.

'Not in our world, it doesn't. Listen to Angel's. What does she sound like?'

Margot smiled at me. 'I already have. She's got a kind of bell-like tone to her—I associated that with strong musical talent, like Marcus, though his is pitched lower. She rings true for all the craziness.'

'And me? What do you sense about me?'

Oh wow: that was said in such a sexy tone, I was surprised Margot didn't leap over the coffee table and fall into his arms directly.

'You?' She closed her eyes. 'You sound . . . beautiful.'

There was silence. I would bet the entire contents of my savings account that he was talking telepathically to her at last.

'Soulfinder—what's that?' Margot asked.

Kurt opened his mouth to interrupt, probably to demand what was going on, but I shushed him. 'Please, let them do this.'

Then Will got up and went round the table. Going down on his knees before her, he took her hands in his and raised them to his lips.

Oh yeah, oh yeah, oh yeah! My celebration was entirely internal. Matchmaking Angel was jiving, breaking out all her moves, high-fiving herself.

'They're going to need a moment,' I told Kurt. 'Shall we go do the violin thing you mentioned?'

'But the threat?' Kurt did not look at all pleased to see his little sister enthralled to some stranger.

'Will is going to brief her about that when they get to that part.' I tugged him to his feet. 'Believe me, she really doesn't need you here right now. She'd find it embarrassing later to know her big brother was watching.'

Glancing over his shoulder at Margot, Kurt let me lead him away. 'Angel, no jokes now: what's going on?'

'Your sister has just met her soulfinder—that's Will in case you didn't get the big flashing love-heart signals going on between them.' I flickered my fingers in the air. 'Savants like Margot—and me—well, we have a special person who holds the other half of our gift. If you're lucky, you meet up and find that you are so much more together than you can be apart— the perfect cosmic match.'

'You really do believe in fairy tales, don't you?' Kurt stood in the sunshine outside the bus, trying to regain his balance after we had just shoved him off centre with our little revelation.

'Ask her later. You probably aren't going to believe me even though I've shown you what I can do. I'm used to that.' A thought struck me. *Hey, Kurt, are you a savant too?*

What the hell are you doing in my head?

I grinned. *Just checking. Oh my gosh, you are! What's your gift? Go on: you can tell me.*

'My gift is for kicking the ass of annoying telepathic chicks who turn my world into an episode of *Paranormal*.'

I hugged myself. 'You do have a gift—you do, but you just don't know that it makes you a savant. Why else is your band called what it is?'

'Because we were big-headed and rather fancied ourselves as gifted musicians.'

Disappointing answer. 'Then it's fate—the name is perfect. What do you do, think about it, what's your superpower?'

'Geez, do you never give up?'

'Is it embarrassing—like seeing people with their clothes off? Misty's mum can do that. Or depressing? Uriel's girl can tell you when you're going to die—so not a nice thing to know about someone but she's getting a handle on it.' His expression darkened. 'Oh God, I'm saying too much again, aren't I? Sorry, sorry. I'll shut up. I'll let Victor and Uriel talk to you. They'll help you through this so much better than me.'

'Angel, do you want to play the violin part for me or not?'

'Yes.' I mimed zipping up my lips.

'Right, forget all this mad stuff and go get your instrument. I'll meet you at my Winnebago in half an hour.'

I unzipped my mouth. 'Where's that?'

'Opposite Marcus's. I think you remember where that is, don't you?' He swaggered away, needing the break from me to put his thoughts in order.

Chapter 12

The instrument storeroom was rapidly becoming my thinking place. Shutting the door behind me, I drowned out the sounds of the festival rumbling away in the distance. Even in the sleepy mornings it wasn't quiet—the hubbub of voices, strains of bands practising, piped music on some of the food stalls, the ever-present swish-hush of the sea calling to my gift. I sat down with my back to a box containing someone's drum kit and rested my chin on my knees.

Too much was happening at once, even for me—and I'm the opposite of a person who seeks the quiet life. The discovery of a little knot of savants outside the usual network was a good result, and finding Margot was just wonderful. Even if I sicced Victor onto him, it was going to be tough teaching Kurt the need to keep his gift secret as he was already as much in the spotlight as anyone could be on the planet and I sensed he wouldn't take advice easily. Far too used to calling the shots. But then, he had managed to keep his power hidden—or didn't even realize he had one—so it couldn't be that spectacular or someone would have noticed.

And there was Marcus. I cursed myself softly under my breath. I had blown what was potentially the most important encounter in my entire life and the repair job would not be an easy one—like piecing together an eggshell after someone had trodden on it.

I reviewed my behaviour of the last two days. I had been unbearably hyper even for me, a kid zipping around in circles with too many E-numbers in her bloodstream. Even if Marcus did answer me, did turn out to be my soulfinder, was he likely to be pleased by the news? I knew that boys thought of me as a fun girl to date, but for the long haul? No, I didn't think I was anyone's dream partner.

I was going to have to change. 'Grow up a little,' I whispered, testing the concept out on the darkness. Serious, calm, and professional. More like my parents. Geez Louise. I banged my forehead on my knees, screwing up my eyes. No, no, you can do it, Angel. You have depths; you just need to show that to your serious, poetically minded Marcus. He doesn't appreciate lightweight so you can become the equivalent of super heavyweight boxer, knock him out with your newfound sophistication.

I practised a few lines.

Hi, Marcus. Oh, what's that I'm reading? I've just been dipping into my collected works of James Joyce. Say, do you prefer Ulysses *or* Finnegans Wake? I'd seen Summer studying both texts and had read a little over her shoulder so knew they would be dead impressive.

Maybe he was more an ideas guy? *You know, Marcus, I just love French philosophy. Isn't Jacques Derrida's theory of deconstruction so interesting?* Alex had tried to explain this to me at one point. I think I sort of got it.

No, 'interesting' was lame—Alex would never say that. I tried it again out loud.

'Hey, Marcus, isn't Derrida's deconstructionism *so* challenging?'

'Excuse me: did you say something?'

I opened my eyes to find a woman crowned with a coronet of silk flowers staring down at me. She must have slipped into the storeroom while I had my eyes closed.

'Oh, I was just practising . . . my songs.'

She picked up a guitar case. 'You sing about Derrida? That's cool.' With a flick of her long Indian cotton skirt decorated with sequins, she left me alone again. I breathed a sigh of relief. Just as well any kind of eccentric behaviour was OK at a festival. What exactly could one sing about French philosophers? *Der-ri-da, you make me go far, to get the gold star, with my soul-find-dah.* I giggled at the silly lyric. No, don't laugh. Be serious. Philosophy is no joke.

Oh Lord. My thirty minutes were almost up. When I walked out of the storeroom I was going to be a different girl, the sort that top bands like Gifted might ask to play for them and Marcus would not dismiss. Operation Angel Makeover was a go.

I grabbed Freddie—no, strike that: I grabbed my *folk violin*. New Angel would not have childish names for the tools of her craft. I left my hideout, determined to make this work.

'Come!' Kurt's abrupt answer was in response to my gentle tap. Normally I would beat out a little syncopated number but I was channelling my inner Summer, trying to act like she would. Poised. Not too exuberant. Charming.

'I'm back. Oh hi, Marcus.' I should have anticipated seeing him here; Kurt had mentioned they'd worked on the song together. 'How are you this morning? Lovely weather we're having.' I didn't wait for an answer, determined to plough on with my sophisticated behaviour. I feared if I stopped it would be like looking down in the middle of a high-wire act. 'I brought Fred . . . my fiddle. So, are you going to show me the music?' I held Freddie loosely by the neck and looked around for the sheets. 'It would be good to crack on with this as I'm sure you're very busy. Places to go, people to see. I don't want to get in your way.'

I finally met Kurt's eyes. I wasn't going anywhere near Marcus's gaze, that was for sure.

'Are you OK, darlin'?' asked Kurt. He ran his fingers through his mane of black hair, earring glinting piratically in his lobe. 'You're acting kinda weird.'

'Of course. I'm here, on time, with my violin, just like you asked. Why shouldn't I be all right?' I got out the rosin to smooth my bow, giving me another displacement activity. I thought I was doing pretty well on the professional demeanour front. 'Time's money and all that.'

Marcus cleared his throat. Some kind of unspoken conversation was going on between him and Kurt—not telepathy but the normal sort of meaningful glances between two people who know each other very well.

Kurt took Freddie from my fingers and put him back in his case.

Oh, rat warts. 'You've . . . you've changed your mind about me playing?'

'No, darlin', it's just that we weren't expecting you to dive straight in like that. We wanted to play you the piece, get your ideas.'

'Oh, OK.' I was getting the task wrong: they weren't wanting me just to pitch up and play like a session musician; they wanted me to collaborate. Music-loving Angel did a little whoop of joy and hip wiggle but was quickly stuffed in my inner teapot by Miss Getting-this-right. 'Yes, of course. Happy to do what's most useful. Let's see what you've got to show me.'

Marcus placed a sheaf of pages on my lap. I knew it was him from the hands. I still wasn't looking at him.

Kurt took down one of his guitars, an old battered one that had fading stickers over the soundboard. 'Marcus, why don't you sing the song to her? I'll do the harmony.'

'It's called "Stay Away, Come Closer".' Marcus picked up his acoustic guitar and began plucking the melody. Oh blast, it was happening again: as soon as he got anywhere near music, all the lights on my dashboard lit up. I found it hellishly difficult not to relapse into my usual gush of enthusiasm. Hands gripping my knees, I clenched my teeth to stop myself saying anything.

Kurt joined in with the harmony, adding a fine low tenor to Marcus's lighter voice. Part of my brain registered I was living out a private dream. What girl on this planet hadn't imagined being serenaded by two such super-hot rock stars? It was hard not to think of the words as being directed especially to me— *stay away, I want you closer*—the guy in the song was conflicted about the girl he loved, sending out mixed messages. Kinda fitting, wasn't it? At least this time the lyrics had been written long before I came on the scene so I couldn't take it personally.

They finished and I was speechless, still absorbing the shockwaves of Marcus's gift as it zinged through me, like a ball rattling through a pinball machine, hitting bells and lights in its passage before setting off the jackpot siren. I set my face against the soppy grin that my lips wanted to curve into.

Marcus groaned. 'She hates it. Maybe we should think again, Kurt? I thought we were on to a winner but look at her.'

'The guys like it; Margot rates it.' Kurt put his guitar back on its stand.

'But Angel's completely unmoved. If she liked it she'd at least be tapping her foot or something. What've we got wrong, Angel?'

Calm. Professional. Ignore the fact that your heart is racing like you've just come off a roller coaster. 'No, Marcus, it's good. Excellent. Nothing wrong with it. You're right: it's a great track.' I searched for a sensible question. 'Is it going to lead the album?'

Kurt rubbed the back of his neck. 'We had thought about making it the album title—you know, like in two levels: up top "stay away", down the bottom of the sleeve "come closer".' He turned back to Marcus. 'Hell, I thought it was a good concept but you're right, she hates it. Where have we gone off track with it?'

I felt a little hysterical. They were seriously thinking of junking an excellent song just because I didn't tap my foot? 'It's great—really. Brilliant.'

'Then why don't you like it?' asked Marcus, a little angry and a lot offended.

'I do like it—I love it.'

'No, you don't. The Angel we know does not sit like she's at a funeral when she hears music she loves! Why are you acting this way if you don't hate it?'

'Because I'm trying to behave myself!' I clamped a hand over my mouth. They were staring at me in amazement.

'Behave yourself?' muttered Marcus. 'That's a lost cause if ever I heard one.'

Kurt gestured him to shut up. 'Darlin', you don't need to be anyone but yourself with us.'

Frustrated tears were blurring my sight. 'Yes, I do. I'm annoying and impulsive. I jump in with two feet when I really should look first. Well, that all changes now—today.' I thumped my knees. 'I'm going to be calm and professional.' My attempt was ruined by the fact that I had tears running down my cheek. I swiped at them. 'Maybe not so calm, but I'm gonna make professional if it kills me. That's a great song. Don't change it. And I have some ideas for a violin part if you want to hear them.'

'That's why you're here.' Kurt gave Marcus a nod, conveying some message I didn't quite get. Marcus put his guitar down and sat next to me. Shoulder to shoulder, thigh to thigh, he mirrored my position. Kurt moved away to give us some privacy.

Marcus nudged me. 'Angel, you don't need to pretend to be something you're not. I don't think we could cope with you being all buttoned up. You're our go-to happy girl, aren't you?'

'I'm more than just a happy girl,' I sniffed. 'I read James Joyce—bits anyway—and know about Derrida . . . and stuff.' I blew my nose on a tissue he plucked from a box under the coffee table. 'I've got depths.'

'I'm glad to hear it.' His voice sounded as if he were laughing at me. 'Kurt says I owe you an apology—that he's seen proof you're not crazy, and that your gift for doing that freaky water thing is real, or the best illusion he's ever witnessed.'

I took another tissue. 'It's real.'

'Well then, now we know you're not about to be carted off by men in white coats, why don't you relax and enjoy this chance to play with us?'

Because I wanted so much more. 'But you hate me like I am normally.'

He bumped my shoulder. 'No I don't. It's like the song says: it's a case of stay away, come closer. You confuse me.'

'You confuse me too.'

He put his hand on my cheek and turned my head so I had to meet his blue eyes. The expression in them rang through me, waking every cell to full bursting life, like the reveille bugle call in my inner army camp. 'I'm sorry about last night. I said some things I shouldn't have.'

I scrunched the tissues in my hand, remembering how he had made me feel. 'I'm not easy. I don't sleep around.'

'No, you're definitely not easy. You're about the most difficult puzzle of a girl I've ever met. But you're one hell of a musician, so even if you don't want to try the other stuff with me, then let's work on what we can share, OK?'

It wasn't that I didn't want to try anything and everything with him—it was the basis on which he had proposed we went ahead. But how could I tell him that? Words failing, I settled for a nod.

'Great. So before Kurt gets bored of waiting for us to sort things out, let's kiss and make up.'

Good idea.

Baaaad idea. His lips touched mine and, as before, it turned from simple kiss to full-on embrace. His hand held me steady in the centre of my back, the other cruising my neck looking for spots to make me shiver. I could feel all the textures of his mouth as he explored mine. Barriers between us shuddered and fell. For one magical moment we were sharing the same space, the same mind.

'OMG' *Cohen*. I whispered my private name for him into his mind.

I could feel his lips curve into a smile. 'AC/DC—kissing you is like sticking a finger in a live electric socket—in a good way.'

Kurt coughed. 'If you guys have quite finished with making up, can we get on with making music please?'

Flustered, I smoothed my clothes down. It was a gauge of just how powerful was the tug between Marcus and me that I could forget I was in the presence of my rock hero. 'Oh, um, I'll just get Freddie and show you my idea.'

Marcus and Kurt both looked to the door. 'Who's Freddie?' asked Marcus.

'My violin.' I picked up the fiddle. Damn, my sophisticated Angel phase hadn't long survived the kiss. 'Moving swiftly on, shall I play the theme I've thought of? I was wondering if the violin could be like the woman's voice, answering in counterpoint to the confused lover in the song.'

Kurt grinned at Marcus. 'Told you she was worth calling in on this. My instinct is never wrong. Marcus, why don't you get your Dylan while I pick up Bruce here.' With a wink at me he took up his guitar. 'All the best players name their instruments,' he confided.

After working out the violin part and running it through a couple of times, Kurt shooed Marcus and I away as he had a meeting with his record producer. Marcus was eager to depart before the guy arrived.

Marcus held the door for me. 'Can't stand him. Barry Hungerford is the industry's biggest pain in the ass.'

I remembered the guy Joey had dissed on the first afternoon. 'I don't think he likes me very much.'

Marcus chuckled. 'Yeah, dancing on the table. That really got up his nose. If I hadn't been so insanely jealous after hearing Jay go on about his hot little girlfriend, I'd've joined you just to show him. Here, do you want to leave your violin in my trailer?'

Insanely jealous—so that was why! 'And do what after?'

Marcus looked over my head in the direction of the festival field. 'I've not been round the site yet. You offered to show me.'

I grinned. 'I offered to show your band mates as you were too uptight to accept my offer.'

He tried his big-eyes-imploring look on me and I was instantly putty in his hands. 'But you'll take pity on me now, won't you?'

'Only if we don't get mobbed by your fans.'

'And what about your fans?'

It wasn't fans I had to worry about but savant-hunting journalist types. I didn't think the Benedicts would approve of me wandering around the grounds; that was asking for trouble. 'We should go in disguise.'

He opened his trailer. 'I've got just the thing for you.'

I put Freddie next to his Dylan. They looked good sitting side by side, like they were meant to be there.

Get a grip, Angel: stop mooning over musical instruments, for heaven's sake!

A baseball cap frisbeed across the room and hit me in the chest. 'Try that.' He had given me a Black Belt hat. I tugged it on and looked at myself in the mirror. Hair covered, it made my eyes look huge.

'Sunglasses.' Marcus offered me a pair of mirror lenses. I slipped them on and immediately felt like someone the paparazzi should be interested in.

'I look *bad*,' I said appreciatively.

'Yeah, my bad girl.' He laughed. 'Every rock star should have one.'

'So, Mr Wanna-be-a-rock-star, what's your disguise going to be? How's Superman going to become Clark Kent?'

'With more than a pair of black-framed glasses.' He dug through a drawer.

'Not the beanie—you're too recognizable in that to your adoring fans.'

He threw it aside regretfully.

I saw something go by in his search and hooked it out. 'What's this?'

'That? Oh, that's a hippie wig I wore when I went as late-period John Lennon to the New Year's Eve party.'

'Put it on!' I crowed.

He pulled the long dark wig over his fair hair. It even had a headband. He smiled at his reflection and started to take it off.

'No, don't.'

'You can't be serious.'

'Marcus, look at yourself: no one is going to recognize you—not even your mother. Do you have glasses?'

He took out a pair of Lennon specs with dark pink lenses.

'To see the world through rose-coloured glasses.'

'That's amazing: you've managed to make yourself look almost unattractive.'

He tackled me to the sofa to retaliate for my giggles. 'Almost?'

'Well, it's impossible to hide so much gorgeousness even under such a loser's wig.'

He tickled me until I squealed for mercy. 'Do you surrender?'

'Yes!' I pulled the wig off his head. 'Just kidding: I won't make you go out in public in that.'

'Thank you.' He kissed the tip of my nose, and then somehow got diverted to my lips. Things were getting a little bit too out of control when we tumbled off the narrow sofa. Being dumped on my butt knocked some sense into me. I'd drawn a line with him and had to keep to it or lose my self-respect. He reached for me but I got up and returned to his closet, acting as if nothing had happened.

'How about this?' I threw him a cowboy hat.

Marcus sighed and bowed to my decision. 'That's good. With shades, no one will know me.'

I wasn't so sure—I'd know him anywhere now—but it would fool most people. 'So are you ready to rumble?'

'Let's go.' He took my hand. 'Show me what I've been missing.'

First, we explored what the food vans had to offer. You could get everything from traditional English and fast food to gourmet vegetarian and international cuisine. Marcus bought us French pastries and coffee which we ate sitting on hay bales in the sunshine. There were a few rides running already as the camp woke up, mainly of the turn-you-upside-down-and-make-you-shriek sort, which I didn't fancy so soon after breakfast, but we decided the dodgems would be fun. I tried to pay but Marcus insisted, muttering something about me still being at school and him having a worldwide hit. I elbowed him in the stomach to keep him humble. I expected him to demand to drive but he surprised me by paying for two. I soon found out why. For Marcus, the point of dodgems wasn't to dodge but to chase his partner around the rink and bump her into a corner.

'Playing nasty, are we, cowboy?' I called, rising to the challenge. 'Prepare to meet your match!' I directed my car to scoot off between other customers.

'Ye-ha!' shouted Marcus, getting into the rodeo rider vibe. He set off in pursuit as I anticipated.

He was expecting me to try to get my revenge by bumping him back; little did he know that I was far more devious than that. I teased him by skimming several times around the rink then saw my opportunity. My car shot between two converging dodgems, just squeaking through. Coming up too fast to swerve, Marcus bumped into both, and was left having to explain to complete strangers—one of whom was a butch guy with a thick bull neck—quite why he was being so aggressive. The klaxon sounded and I shimmied out of my dodgem and did a little air punch. Marcus scowled at me, then saw the funny side and laughed. Saying something about crazy girlfriends, he shook hands with the bull-necked man and high-tailed it over to me.

Girlfriend? When had that happened?

He put his arm around my waist and squeezed. 'You'll pay for that.'

'That, Marcus, was called angelic revenge. Did you really just tell that guy I'm your girlfriend?'

He looked away. 'Well, yeah, it seemed too complicated to say that girl over there who thinks we're soulmates but won't—' He thought twice and bit back the rest of the sentence. It was just as well he didn't finish or he would be singing soprano for the rest of the day. No joke when he had a televised gig that evening.

'I've told you what I want to happen. If you'd just try telepathy once. One or two teeny weeny little words would do, like "howdy, pardner".' I tried to make a joke of it by tugging his cowboy hat over his eyes.

'And we were having such a nice morning.'

'OK, OK, I'll drop the subject. Sorry. Where next?'

'You tell me.'

'I've not been down to the beach yet.' I took a leaflet from a man in a blue T-shirt advertising an organization that provided clean water in poor countries. 'Look: they're doing a charity sandcastle build now.'

'You want to make a sandcastle?'

'And you don't?' I stopped and got up on one of the bales so we were more on a level. 'Marcus, don't you ever just mess around: you know, play?'

A little notch appeared between his brows. 'I play. I make music.'

'That's your profession. I mean just have fun because it's . . . well . . . fun.'

He put his hands round my waist then slid them down a little lower. 'I can think of plenty of ways of having fun with you.'

'Geez, get your head out of the gutter, Marcus.' Not that my mind didn't spend most of the time down there with him. 'I'm talking innocent fooling around.'

He looked puzzled.

'OK, that settles it. You, Marcus, are too serious so you need a serious dose of silly.'

'A serious dose of silly? Angel, you're—'

'I know: crazy, infuriating, et cetera, et cetera. But you and

Kurt told me to be myself and this is me being me. I like the idea of building a sandcastle because it's for a good cause and I haven't made one for years. Are you coming?'

'As long as no one recognizes me. If this gets on YouTube, I'm gonna kill you.' He made a pretence of foot-dragging.

'Don't be stupid—it'd do your image wonders: the human side to mysterious Marcus Cohen; the guy who's rocking the world of rock gets down among the rocks at Rockport.'

'Enough of the rocks already.' He snorted at my idiotic headline. 'I'll supervise.'

I tugged him in the direction of the gate leading onto the beach. 'Uh-uh. I'm the expert on fun so I get to supervise. You are here strictly in your capacity as my minion.'

This time I didn't take 'I'm the rich rock star' as an excuse and insisted on paying our entry to the sandcastle competition.

'OK boss, where do we start?' Marcus asked. There were already several completed sandcastles and many under construction.

I looked over my shoulder to check we weren't being watched. Everyone was busy on their own projects. 'By the water.' I led him to a smooth spot of sand that would remain above the tide for a few hours yet, shielded by two large rocks. 'You get digging. I'll collect some shells.'

'Digging with what?'

'Your hands, duh.'

Playing his part as reluctant minion, he grumbled about getting his hands dirty and jeans sandy, but sank down on his knees to begin the excavation. 'What shape do you want this?'

'Your choice, babe: improvise.' Humming happily, I went to the water's edge. The beach had already been scavenged for the best bits of seaweed and shells so I would have to do some improvisation of my own. Closing my eyes I buried my hands in the damp sand, waiting for the waves to come in and lap at my wrists. Connected to the water, I felt the unrolling of my gift like an answering wave pouring from inside. Being by the ocean is heaven for me but also a little dangerous. At times I forget where I begin and the sea ends. Fortunately this time I never quite lost consciousness of Marcus beavering away behind me, my anchor to stop me drifting off on the tide. When I opened my eyes again, the sea's gifts were neatly stacked at my side: fresh kelp, complete shells, shiny stones, one with a hole through the centre, a piece of gnarled driftwood in the shape of a masted ship. I gathered them in my tunic dress and carried them back to Marcus.

'Here.' I dropped them by his motte.

In my absence, his imagination had been caught by the engineering challenge. He was intent on making a bridge over the moat around his hillock, swearing each time it collapsed. Muttering thanks, he grabbed a scallop shell and used it to scoop out the correct amount of sand.

'I could help.'

'I've almost got it.' Marcus grinned as the bridge stayed up this time. 'There!'

Compared to other constructions ours was on the modest side. 'I could hurry things up a little.'

'You can do that bit over there,' Marcus said generously. 'I'll do the castle.'

'That bit?'

'The town around the castle.'

Leaving him to pat his building into shape, I summoned a wave higher up the beach. With a few suggestions and nudges from my gift, the sea did the work for me, swirling, burrowing, building.

'Aren't you going to do your part?' asked Marcus a little testily as I remained seated.

'I have.'

'You won't get anything done sitting on that very excellent butt of yours.'

'Oh Marcus?' I said in a singsong voice.

'Yes? Dammit: it's fallen in again.'

'I think you should take a look around you.'

He raised his eyes to my effort. Between the sea and me, we had built a very fair approximation of a town: market square, church, lighthouse and port for my driftwood ship. As Marcus sat up, his bridge collapsed.

'You cheated.'

'Did not. I played—with my gift.' I called a wave closer to repair his bridge for him, bolstering the structure with some well-placed pebbles.

'Show me again.'

He sat behind me and pulled me into the space between his legs. I summoned the next wave and made it curl into an M. As each wave came, I added another letter to his name.

He rested his chin on the top of my head, voice rumbling away against my spine. 'It's real, isn't it, not an illusion?'

'Yes, Marcus, it's real.'

We sat in silence for a while, but this time not an awkward one. I let the waves return to their tidemark as I heard footsteps crunch behind us.

'Hey, that's awesome,' I heard one guy say. 'Can we take a picture for our website?'

We turned round to see a couple of volunteers in blue T-shirts. 'Sure.' I leapt up and scuffed out the RCUS, leaving just the M and the A. I added a curly '&' sign between the two: *Marcus & Angel*. 'Thanks for the competition.'

'You stand a good chance of winning with this.'

'Oh yeah? What's the prize?'

'Backstage passes to the Gifted gig tonight.'

I burst into laughter. Marcus took my hand and squeezed it

in warning. 'If we win, why don't you have them, mate? We've got other plans, so can't use them.'

'Oh wow. Cool—that'd be epic. I'll text you to let you know how the judging goes.'

Marcus gave the guy his number and we made our way back up the beach.

'Busted,' I whispered.

'How busted?'

'You, Marcus, are really sweet.'

'Bang goes my dangerous rock-star persona.'

'Yes, it sure does.'

'Must be the influence of my guardian angel.'

Chapter 13

Leaving our sandcastle for the tide to erase, Marcus and I went back to the main festival site. The camp was only just now waking up properly and I noticed at least five people staggering about like bears just emerged from hibernation. A good night had by all, evidently.

Marcus pulled the brim of his cowboy hat low over his eyes, checking behind him for signs he had been recognized. All clear so far.

I smiled at his clandestine tactics; he made me feel a little like we were two spies deep in enemy territory.

'Do we need to change hats?' I asked him in a stage whisper, pinching the brim of his Stetson. 'You know: fool the paparazzi with our cunning swap of disguises?'

Marcus stood up tall so I couldn't yank it off him. 'I think somehow that wearing a Black Belt baseball cap wouldn't be a very clever disguise for me—more like painting a target on myself.'

I tried to snag his much cooler hat again. 'No, that's where you're wrong, *amigo*. It's so overt, it's covert. The last place people will look for a rock star hiding out from his fans and the press is under his band baseball cap.'

Marcus intercepted my attempted snatch by grabbing me around the waist and turning me so my back was to his front. 'Or maybe most people will just think "Oh look: that guy's wearing a Black Belt hat—he reminds me a lot of Marcus Cohen—it *is* Marcus Cohen!—tweet his picture now and gather the press pack." Trust me, most people aren't as devious as you.'

'You might have a point.'

He relaxed his hold. 'Am I safe to let go? No underhand plans to steal my Stetson? It was given to me by a real 'cowboy in Texas, you know.'

'I'll leave it—for now.' I squeaked as he tickled me in punishment. 'I just think it would suit me.'

'It would swallow you up. All we would see is a little pair of feet shuffling along.'

'Big-head!'

'My point exactly. I'll get a midget-sized one for you when we go on tour to the States in September.' He squeezed my hand as we linked up to carry on walking. 'OK, I think I'm ready to hear more about this gift of yours. How does it work?'

Marcus's interest surprised me—as did the hint that he thought we might still be in contact in the autumn. I thought he was going to sit tight in deep denial but somehow seeing me play with the ocean had convinced him in a way that party tricks with drinks had not.

Feeling more optimistic about his cautious steps into my world, I laced my fingers with his. 'I'm not sure exactly. Savants—that's what we call ourselves—have gifts that come out in all sorts of different ways. My mum can control air to a certain extent and Dad can do telekinesis—you know, move stuff with his mind?'

He nodded, showing he was following, but in the manner of a judge reserving verdict until the end of the trial. He might have been thinking that I was spinning a fantasy—any normal person would without proof.

'I guess my gift is a blend of the two: like Mum I have power over something in nature—water in my case—and I must be using some form of telekinesis when I move it.' I wrinkled my nose in thought. 'Though it's not really like standard telekinesis as I feel part of the water when I'm manipulating it.' Embarrassed by his silence on the subject, I laughed self-deprecatingly. 'I know, I know, it's all a bit woo-woo dippy-hippy when I describe it like that.'

He didn't join in my laughter. 'Almost everything contains water—can you use it to harm someone?'

'The thought has honestly never struck me. Why would I want to do that?'

'It's just that the idea of people having these hidden powers is unnerving—like a concealed weapon.'

Crumbs: I was in the dock, wasn't I, M'lud? 'I suppose I could use water to help me get out of danger but I'd never attack anyone with it.' I then remembered what I had done to Jay. 'Well, not to harm them.'

His gaze sharpened, latching on to my amused expression. 'But you have used it against someone?'

Smiling, sure he would see the joke, I told him how I had doused Jay's ardour in the dressing room.

Marcus took another direction to being entertained. His glower went up a couple of notches. 'You mean that jerk isn't just all mouth—he really put his hands on you?'

At least I was no longer the target of his suspicions. I placated the growling lion by stroking his paw. 'You don't need to worry: when I finished with Jay he really was the embodiment of the phrase "all mouth and no trousers" as he had to change them.' I snorted in a burst of most unglamorous hilarity. I don't laugh in a ladylike fashion, unfortunately.

He gave in to a reluctant smile. 'I guess I stand warned.'

'That's right, Romeo: too much hands-on stuff and you'll get cooled off very rapidly.'

'I suppose I should be grateful you can protect yourself.' He looked away over my head, distancing himself. I was beginning to realize that this was how he absorbed things: find out some answers then assimilate them. I had to give him time.

We were almost back at the security check for the performers' area.

'Oh my gosh, it's him! I swear it's Marcus Cohen!' The squeal went up from a cluster of young women staking out the entrance. It was like throwing bread to a flock of seagulls: suddenly, we were mobbed as festival programmes were shoved under our noses. Marcus's cowboy hat got knocked back on his head and I was pretty much trampled as irrelevant.

'Guys, guys, give us some space here,' called Marcus, trying to keep hold of my hand in the scrum.

'Are you going to release a new album soon?'

'Remember me: I saw you in Birmingham when you were first starting out? You signed my shoulder—I had it inked into a tattoo.' The limb was waved between us, clipping me on the nose.

'Oh my: that's amazing—will you sign my arm?'

The requests came thick and fast as more body parts were bared in his direction—and some of them were hardly decent.

'Please, just step back a little, ladies.' Marcus sounded quite spooked by their intensity. At a music venue, he would rarely emerge without minders these days but I'd tempted him to walk on the wild side and felt responsible for getting him out. I slipped my fingers free of Marcus's hand, ducked backwards through the crowd and whipped off my baseball cap and glasses to join the throng. If you can't beat 'em: join 'em.

'Look—look!' I squawked in my best fangirl voice. 'It's him—it's Kurt Voss. He's heading for the food stalls—quick!'

Like iron filings attracted by a stronger magnet, they turned towards me.

'Kurt Voss? Where?'

'Oh my God, I'd die if I got his autograph!'

'He's hardly ever seen in public—come on!'

'There he is!' I started running towards the French bakery stall, provoking the diversion of most of Marcus's horde to a new target. There just happened to be an innocent tall lean guy wearing a hat and sunglasses in the queue who was about to have his quiet morning disrupted. Hopefully he would enjoy fending off the attention of young groupies baring skin for his signature. Letting them overtake me, I fell back, saw Marcus sign a few paper-based items for his real fans who had stayed behind, then hooked his arm. 'C'mon, superstar, let's get your very excellent ass back in the safe zone.'

Marcus politely excused himself from his admirers and followed me past the security check. 'I'm hiring you as my bodyguard.'

'You could do with one.' Feeling chipper about my clever ruse, I sang a snatch from the *Bodyguard* musical. Oh cripes: perhaps *I will always love you* was not the right lyric just at the moment, considering the confused state of our relationship.

Marcus pulled me to one side of the entrance to the green room yurt. 'Seriously? Does this soulfinder connection mean you will?'

I studied the middle buttons on his open shirt. 'Hey, it's just a song.'

He took a step back. 'Oh, I see.'

'But I do like you Marcus—a lot. I even liked you when you were being foul to me and treating me like crud—don't ask me why.'

He moved back and put his hand on the pole next to my head so he leaned in over me. 'I like you too. I think you might even be good for me. That's Kurt's take on you. He has this instinct about people.'

'Really?'

'It's a little like a radar for frauds and fakes. It's helped him get on in a cut-throat business. Anyway, he says I'm too serious. Do you think I'm too serious?'

Oh Lord: it was like being in a little slice of paradise being herded into a corner between the open flaps of Marcus's shirt, so close I could smell his warm scent overlaid by *eau de* salt water—a personal favourite of this particular savant. What had he asked? Oh yes.

'Maybe you do take yourself a little too . . . you know . . . ?' I toyed with a button, slipping it through its hole and letting it free again.

'And I need to lighten up?'

'Only if you want to. I mean, I wouldn't want you to think I've got an agenda to change you. I like you as you are—mostly.'

He raised his eyebrows. 'Mostly?'

I shrugged. 'Well, you wanted honesty. Go to one of the many groupie girls lining up outside if you want flattery.'

He tucked a strand of hair behind my ear. 'And what can I do to make you like me fully?'

Try telepathy? No, this wasn't the moment, Angel. Learn your lesson. Don't spoil everything by rushing him.

'Give me your autograph?' I teased. 'Where did that girl want it? Her arm?'

He bent down and kissed the sensitive skin of my inner wrist and worked his way up, lips brushing out the letters of his name. I shivered.

'That is . . . so much better than a pen.' Heavens, I was going to melt into a puddle of hopeless excitement if he carried on. 'If you do that to all your fans, you will have a very devoted following.'

'Only to you, Angel.' His mouth finally made it home and settled on mine. His kiss set sparkling a chain of magnificent sensation: lips, spine, hair on back of neck, waist . . .

A clearing of a throat broke into our little moment. I disentangled myself from Marcus to find Will and Margot waiting for us to surface. And they were holding hands! I sent a little yippee-kai-yay telepathically to Will, who winked back at me. Cat. Got. Cream. And now purring with pleasure. Margot looked rather like a wind-battered seabird just flown in on a storm, but I think she was pleased in her own way. It had to have been one heck of a shock for her. She hardly woke up this morning thinking 'Hey, let's completely change the fundamentals of my life today.'

'I see you guys are getting along well,' said Margot with a twinkle in her eye.

Not as well as I would like, I told Will. *Marcus is still in denial about his own gift and won't touch telepathy with a barge pole.*

Will grimaced in sympathy. 'No telepathy, remember,' he said in a low voice.

'Bit late, isn't it? I rather thought that particular horse had bolted as far as I'm concerned.'

While Will and I batted that one between us, Marcus was trying to figure out who this stranger was and quite why he was up so close and personal with the tour manager.

'Marcus,' said Margot, 'let me introduce Will Benedict. He's a good friend of Angel and—'

'He's Margot's extra-special friend in a way we are absolutely forbidden to mention because it gives you the heebie jeebies,' I said brazenly.

Angel, behave, warned Will.

I thought you said no telepathy?

Will gave me that exasperated look that so many wear in my vicinity. He held out a hand to Marcus. 'Good to meet you.'

Marcus seemed to like him—at least he shook his hand firmly and didn't call security. 'Nice to meet you. Sorry to be blunt, Will, but what's he doing here, Margot? We've got a big show tonight.'

'I know, Marcus, but something's come up. We're just going to fetch his brothers and then we'll have a meeting. The tour bus in five minutes, OK?' Margot patted Marcus's arm, trying to allay his suspicion. I could have told her it would take much more than that.

'Is Alex coming in too?' I asked Will, wondering if a little dose of Alex's persuasive power might help my rocky-road relationship.

'No, he's guarding the girls. Do you need him?' Will's eyes flicked to Marcus.

'Who is Alex?' asked Marcus.

'No one you need worry about. Maybe, Will, but not just yet. I'm still giving this a go on my own.'

Will tapped his forehead in mock salute. 'Just say the word.'

I nodded, feeling a little better now I had the promise of backup. I watched Will and Margot walk away together, bodies bent towards each other as they learned how to get comfortable with their relationship. It was all 'After you' 'No, after you'—so cute. Then I remembered what Margot had said: they were fetching Uriel and Victor. Oh crap. Uriel was fine—a sweetie—but, geez, when Marcus met Victor he was going to go ballistic into suspicion orbit. I had to prepare him but that might seem to him like the arsonist offering to put out the fire.

No other option available, I hooked my arm through his and pulled him further away from the thoroughfare to the green room.

'Um, Marcus?'

'Yes?' His eyes were still on Margot, a puzzled little frown on his face that I really wanted to kiss away. Unfortunately, I was probably about to make it worse.

'You know you mentioned about some gifts being a little scary?'

'Yeah?' He turned his blue eyes back on me. This near to him I had a good close up of the ring of darker blue around the almost grey iris. Gorgeous. Stick to the plot, Angel.

'Well, not all savants are soft and cuddly marshmallows like me and Will.'

'That guy is no marshmallow. He moves like he's had training.'

'You got that? OK, marshmallows like me full stop. The guys they're going to meet—Uriel's super intelligent and specializes in forensics. He's a sweetheart, too.'

'One of yours?' Yep: there went the wrinkles—even deeper as I predicted.

'Heck no: he's all hopelessly devoted to a lady called Tarryn. But the other one—Victor—he's a bit more . . . well, to tell you the truth, he scares the crap out of me.'

Angel, Angel, thy name is *not* subtlety!

'That wasn't how I wanted to say it. What I mean is he's very formidable. He works for the FBI, but maybe I shouldn't have told you that?' I thumped my forehead. 'Geez, why did they put me onto this mission: I am so completely hopeless at this!'

'What mission?'

I closed my eyes, not wanting to see his face as I confessed. 'Making contact with a stray group of savants—that's you, Margot and Kurt—maybe others but I've not explored that yet. I've tried to explain to you but that whole part of the agenda has not been going well as I suck at the delicate touch. I've only succeeded in blowing my cover with Davis and pissing you off on multiple occasions.'

'Angel, come on, you need to have a reality check. Mission? Cover? We were just pretending with our disguises, remember? To cheat the press.'

I gave up. Sorry, but every time I opened my mouth I dug yet another hole and jumped right in. If my conversation were a dairy product, it would resemble Swiss cheese. 'OK, let's park that with all the other stuff we aren't going to talk about. Don't say later that I didn't try to warn you.'

We arrived at the bus to find Kurt already in occupation of the sofa.

'Hey, lovebirds, how's it going?' he asked, running a few chord changes. 'Excited about tonight?'

'Thrilled.' I sat down opposite him and hugged my knees to my chest.

'Great: we've got Angel back and not her scary evil twin who stopped by this morning.'

I threw a cushion at him.

Marcus's gaze swung between us. 'You know you treat each other like brother and sister, don't you?'

'You're not another of my dad's strays I suppose, love?' asked Kurt with a cheeky grin.

'Nope—I guess it's just that plain old recognizing-another-clown-when-I-see-one thing.'

'No one has accused me of being a clown since . . . well since for ever.'

'That's what you need me for, Kurt: keeping it real.'

Mutually pleased with each other, we were still grinning as Margot and Will returned with Victor and Uriel. The mood instantly did a diversion into more serious territory as Kurt put on his game face: the one that said he wouldn't waste time on fools and frauds.

'Thanks for coming in, guys,' he said, immediately taking control and gesturing to them to take seats. 'I hear from Margot you've got something you want to talk to us about, touching on our security?'

Uriel took the lead—a good choice as he was instantly

more disarming than Victor. 'Thank you for making time, Mr Voss.'

'Kurt—call me Kurt.'

'Kurt. The reason we've requested this meeting is that we have reason to believe that you have a gift—something our society calls a savant power—that means you use psychic energy to change the environment around you. Will here says that Margot uses sound in incredible ways. Angel has identified Marcus as having a gift for projecting emotions through music—or something of that nature . . . '

Marcus muttered a denial but didn't interrupt.

'And she also thinks you have one too, though that's not yet pinned down.'

I cast a worried glance at Marcus even as I piped up. 'I think Kurt senses good and bad in people—seeing their true motives.'

'Darlin', that's just being a sharp operator.' Kurt stretched his arms above his head lazily.

'I think it's more than that,' I said softly. 'And I think you know it too.' We held each other's gaze. Kurt looked away first.

'OK, Uriel—it is Uriel, isn't it? Hell, I'm surrounded by angels. Who else plays on your team: Gabriel? Raphael?' I could tell from his sarcastic tone, Kurt was feeling distinctly uncomfortable. Like Marcus, his induction into the savant world was not going to be an easy one.

'Maybe, but not today. It's just us. Kurt, if you'd just hear what we've got to say, then we'll be out of your hair so much sooner. As Angel has tried to tell you, there is a threat at this festival. A group of investigative journalists are trying to find a story—proof, if you like—that savants exist and have penetrated into all walks of life. To them, we are a hidden enemy, something to be feared. They don't trust us because we are different.'

Kurt reached under the coffee table and fished out a six-pack of beer. 'I think I'm gonna need a drink. Help yourself.' He pulled the tab on a can.

'You might not be familiar with your own gift but they've identified it. They have a device for reading psychic energy levels. You—or someone in your entourage—has set off their alarms and they are looking at ways of exploiting that to their advantage. The fact that you didn't know what you really are only played into their hands, making you vulnerable.'

'I know what I am.' Kurt took another swallow. 'If I have a gift or not, doesn't change that.'

Will sat forward, clasped hands hanging between spread knees. 'Of course not, but to them it does. It marks you as an enemy, therefore a legitimate target for them to destroy.'

'Maybe they've a point,' suggested Marcus. 'With respect, you guys could be bad news. How do we know?'

Margot looked ready to leap in but Will wasn't offended. He smiled lopsidedly. 'Fortunately, Kurt here can tell you exactly what our motives are, can't you, Kurt?'

Kurt looked at Margot practically sitting in Will's lap. 'Yeah, you're OK. At least, I think so. Not getting much from him.' He nodded to Victor who was still standing by the door, arms folded.

'That's because I shield,' said Victor. 'It's part of my gift. It's also very necessary in my line of work.'

'You're the FBI guy, right?'

'Correct, sir.'

'Enough with the "sir". The Queen hasn't knighted me yet.'

Victor kept silent. The balance of power in the room tipped towards him. Somehow he made the rest of us seem like infants without doing anything.

'OK then.' Kurt cleared his throat. 'These journalists are troublemakers and we should avoid them.'

'They already have a backstage pass for tonight,' said Margot. 'Should I take it away?'

'I think it best to leave it,' said Will. 'If you take it off them, they'll only make that part of the story. I'll make sure they're watched at all times they are this side of the security fence.'

'So you are appointing yourself our security detail. How much is that going to cost us?' asked Kurt cynically.

'Free of charge.' Will grinned, taking Margot's hand in his. 'I've got everything I want right here and will do anything to protect her.'

Aw—they were so cute together!

Even Kurt seemed a little impressed. 'Then I'll leave you two to sort out the specifics—shouldn't be too tough an assignment seeing how Margot claims you've become inseparable.' Kurt stood up, our signal that we were to leave. 'I've got back-to-back interviews this afternoon, so if you don't mind . . . '

Of course we didn't dare mind. We filed out of the tour bus like a class dismissed.

Once outside, we were back in the hubbub of the festival. So hard to imagine sinister plots when the place felt like one long party.

'I'm going to have to abandon you now, Angel.' Marcus sounded apologetic. 'The guys and I are rehearsing and running through our programme, then I've got some publicity meet-and-greets scheduled. Will you be OK without me?'

Inside I was shrivelling up with disappointment but that wasn't the public face. I shrugged, digging my hands in the pockets of my tunic, taking comfort from its swirling pattern of turquoise optimism. 'Sure, no problem. I'll just go hang out with my mates and see what's happening.'

He untwisted the ribbon of my festival pass so it lay flat on my neck. 'Keep away from that journalist, won't you? I'll not be around to save the day.'

'OK, Batman, I'll manage without your heroics for a while.'

'Until later then, Robin.' He kissed me.

'Later.'

Chapter · 14

I found Matt hanging out with Joey and Fresh by the free food in the green room. That figured. They must be putting a dent in the profits of the festival with their repeat visits. I was surprised they hadn't been banned, but then I remembered that Matt had an ally in Henry, hadn't he? Wise boy.

'Hey, stranger, remember us?' mocked Matt.

I put my finger to my chin. 'Er, let me think; didn't we, like, know each other once upon a time *before* I was famous? Mack, Mick, isn't it?'

He lunged for me and rubbed his knuckles on my head. 'That remind you?'

We gave each other a hug, rocking to and fro like boxers caught in each other's hold—one of our standard moves made all the more absurd by the bantam versus heavyweight difference in stature.

'So, how's things with the superstars?' he asked, steering me over to a chair at their table. From the number of plates and bottles already on the surface they had been treating the refreshments as an 'all you can eat' buffet for some time.

'It's amazing, Matt—'

He cocked an eyebrow at Fresh and Joey. 'See, she does remember me. I knew it.'

'Kurt asked me to—'

'*Kurt*—first-name terms, best buddies—how iced is that?'

'Matt, would you quit with the running commentary, please?'

'But it's so much more fun to torment you.'

I turned to Joey and Fresh. 'OK, I'll tell you guys. Ignore the parrot in the seat next to me. Kurt asked me to play for one of their songs tonight—a new one which needs a violin. I'll be on stage with Gifted!' My voice ended in something of a squeak.

'Way to go, girl!' Joey high-fived me.

'That's awesome.' Fresh got out his phone. 'I've just got to tweet the breaking news. *Gifted risk tough public image by taking on sugarplum fairy violinist.*'

I scowled, trying to look (as Matt would put it) 'well 'ard', and pushed Fresh's mobile down. 'Watch it, Freshman. Anyway, I don't think it's official yet.' I lowered my voice to a conspiratorial whisper. 'I might be stepping on their publicity people's toes if I let this out. I'm not sure how many are in the know.'

'Hey, Angel, heard you were making a guest appearance with us tonight,' someone declared loudly behind me. I swivelled in my seat to find Brian, the Gifted drummer, approaching, arm-in-arm with his girlfriend, the photographer. It seemed my secret was no secret. Fresh winked at me and pressed send on his tweet. If he really had included that fairy joke then someone's brazils really were going to be in the nutcracker.

'Matt, how's it going?' asked Brian.

Matt's face flushed with pride that he was being name-checked by a drumming legend. 'Good, thanks, Brian. Why don't you join us?'

Brian exchanged a quick glance with his girlfriend to get her agreement then sat down. 'I'm not sure we all know each other. Angel, this is Jennifer, one of our publicists on this tour.'

'Hi, Jennifer.'

She took the seat next to me. 'Angel, so lovely to meet you. Kurt told me you were on board for tonight. I'm thrilled for you.' She smiled at me but I couldn't see her eyes as she was wearing mirror sunglasses. She had the same flyaway fine hair as I did—we could commiserate about that later. Hers was Scandinavian fair, unlike my strawberry blonde.

'Lovely to meet you too. So you're a photographer?'

She tapped the Nikon hanging on its thick strap over her shoulder. 'Among other things.' Her head turned to Joey and Fresh, who were still gawping at Brian as mortals are wont to do when gods come calling. 'And who are your friends?'

Matt grinned. 'I'm having second thoughts about introducing you to these two. Brian, you better keep an eye on them. Joey Reef and Fresh Chance.'

'Are they your real names?' asked Jennifer sweetly.

'Street names—and that's as real as it gets.' Joey treated her to a megawatt smile.

'You know something: I really must photograph you two.' She jumped up and took the lens cap off her camera, checking her light meter. 'Can you try to look tough for me?'

Their attempts to look streetwise were undermined by my crows of laughter and Matt's jeering, but I think Jennifer managed to get a couple of good shots in of them glowering at her, arms folded.

'These two don't take us seriously,' griped Joey. 'Hey, Jennifer, why don't you come hear us perform? You can get some shots of us in action if you're interested.'

'Have we got time, Brian?' she asked.

'Maybe. When?' asked Brian, checking his watch.

'It's at five in the Beatbox tent.'

'Sounds a plan. Wish I could stay longer with you guys but I've got to run.' Brian got up. 'You coming, Jen? I've got that magazine thing in ten minutes, remember?'

'Yes, of course. Angel, could I borrow you for a second?'

'Shall I walk with you?' I offered.

'Please.' Jennifer linked her arm through Brian's. 'It's just I wondered what you were doing for a costume tonight. Do you have something suitable or do I need to get an outfit brought in for you? There's probably still enough time to ask our stylists to get a motorbike courier to bring something here from London.'

'Oh.' She was right: I hadn't thought about that. 'What are the guys wearing?'

Brian snorted. 'Clothes.'

Jennifer rolled her eyes. 'See what we have to deal with? They'll be wearing casual which Margot and I will have picked out for them.'

Brian groaned.

'Sponsors, Brian,' she warned, 'remember them? The companies that pay you all a fortune to wear their stuff? But that's not an issue with Angel. I thought you might like to go for something a little more classy?'

'I'm not really a classy kinda gal,' I admitted.

'Got anything black?' she persisted.

I ran an inventory of my rucksack, feeling vindicated that I had packed so much. 'I've a short black dress and matching shoes.'

'Sounds perfect. You can't go wrong with black. One job ticked off my list.' She made a tick shape in the air. 'You'll be in the VIP changing room, of course.'

There was a VIP changing room? 'Great.'

She gave my hand a quick press. 'I'm looking forward to seeing you play.'

'Will we see you at this Beatbox tent, Angel?' asked Brian.

'Of course. Wouldn't miss it for the world.'

Having reached the Gifted trailers, I watched as they walked away. Two such lovely people. I didn't think Brian had a gift—no tingle of energy around him like there was around Kurt and Marcus, and Jennifer seemed pretty straightforward too.

Feeling the urge to have a good chat with Misty and Summer about all these exciting developments, I felt in my bag for my phone. That brought rushing back the memory of the altercation last night. Had Davis posted any of my incriminating photos online yet or was he holding fire? What should I do if he had? I'd not been entirely straight with Victor when I'd confessed my mistakes.

Two hands grabbed me from behind. I shrieked. I'd only got as far as an elbow in my attacker's stomach when I was rapidly released.

'Angel, it's just me!'

Marcus.

I clasped my shaking hands to my chest. 'Trying to scare me to death?'

'Sorry.' He looked sheepish.

I now noticed he was with his band mates, Pete and Michael, en route to their rehearsal. They were staring at me as if I had grown a second head. Great: I'd managed to embarrass Marcus on top of everything else.

'Sorry about the overreaction. I was just—surprised.'

'Remind me not to surprise you then,' said Michael, the drummer with the cute smile.

Marcus folded me in a protective embrace. 'You really OK?'

'Just feeling a little jittery,' I admitted.

He looked over my head to his friends. 'Angel was roughed up by a journalist last night when he got a little too insistent about getting an interview.'

They didn't seem surprised it had happened; they'd each had to shoulder their way through hordes of paparazzi staking out their every move since fame struck. They heaped insults on the journalist and asked if I was all right. I was now that Marcus had been kind enough to explain my freaked-out behaviour. 'Thanks, guys, I'm fine. You'd better get to your rehearsal.'

Marcus chewed briefly on his lower lip, two little frown lines appearing between his brows. 'You know something, Angel? I think I'd feel better if you tagged along. You don't mind, do you guys, I know its breaking band rules, but . . . '

'Sure. No problem,' said Pete, the big bear of the bunch.

'You can hang out with us, Angel. Lot nicer to look at you than stare at these two for an hour.' Michael gave me a cheeky wink.

I sat in the corner of the band lounge—the tent set aside for practise sessions and warming up—drinking in the experience of watching three talented musicians work through their set. They had an easy camaraderie and listened to each other very well. Their criticisms of any fault were always tactfully phrased and made in the spirit of getting it right. No one was scared to speak up. How different from Jay, who would bawl at any of us if we went a little off in our playing. They weren't slow at seeking my opinion either.

'What do you think, Angel: should we sing "Homeless" before or after "Shout Now"?' asked Michael.

· I ran the water droplet charm on my necklace up and down the chain thoughtfully. 'I think you should keep it as it is—it seems to tell a better story in that order.'

Michael gave me a thumbs up. 'Told you the girl has good taste.'

Marcus, who had suggested the change, mock-frowned at me. 'In some things.'

'Yeah, her taste in men is terrible, but there you go . . . '

Marcus made a single-finger gesture at Michael.

We walked back to Marcus's trailer for their traditional post-rehearsal snacks and drink session. Marcus's place was their unofficial headquarters as Michael and Pete were sharing the other half of the Winnebago.

'Our side is not fit for human habitation,' Pete admitted cheerfully. Arms folded, his muscles showed to advantage beneath the sleeves of his T-shirt. No, he didn't look the kind of boy to don Marigolds and set to work tidying up the man cave. More like give him a couple of sabre-tooth tigers to wrestle.

'Yeah,' chipped in Michael. 'Two guys and no one to pick up the socks, whereas Marcus here is a neat freak.'

'Is he?' Then Marcus really wasn't going to appreciate my approach to tidying my bedroom: shove it all in the bottom of a wardrobe or cover with a blanket.

Marcus binned the empty packets and wiped the surface. 'I just like control. I can't think surrounded by clutter.'

'Which is why he gets the room on his own. Can't kill off our golden goose by forcing him to live with us, can we?' Michael put his cup in the little dishwasher with a nod to his friend.

The guys excused themselves after two rounds of toast. Knowing Marcus was busy, I tried to leave with them but Michael pinned me to the sofa with a look.

'See you in half an hour for that interview thing?' Michael said, giving me a blatant cue about the band's timetable.

'Yeah.' Once the door had closed, Marcus flopped down on the sofa next to me and nuzzled my neck. 'Thirty whole minutes. Now, I wonder what we can do with them?'

Last time we had got close on the sofa we ended up on the floor. So tempting. But I had to keep my promise to myself that I would take this step by step, not rush the physical stuff when the more important matters were unsettled.

I curled into his side, arm across his waist—that didn't count. 'We could talk.'

He groaned. 'She wants to talk? OK.' He picked up my right hand and began nibbling the tips of my fingers.

'T . . . tell me about your family.'

'I'm the eldest of three.' He brushed my fingers against his lips. 'Mum and Dad are from Liverpool. My sister Sadie is fourteen, little brother Kyle is ten. Have we done talking yet?'

I tugged my hand free before I completely lost focus. I poked his chest. 'No. And when did you first realize you were musical?' I avoided the word *gift*, knowing how he hated the idea that his talent was due to something he didn't understand.

'Always have been. I went to my first live concert really young—maybe about eight—Dad's into music too and took me with him. That led to my first guitar lesson and the rest followed on from that.'

'And the singing?'

'That's from the football terraces.' He laughed at my doubtful expression. 'Seriously, when else is a boy who doesn't do the school choir thing gonna sing in public? *You'll never walk alone*—that's where it all started for me.'

'I suppose I should've guessed you'd be a Liverpool fan. I'm more of a Chelsea girl myself.'

Whipping his arm out from behind my shoulders, he made a warding-off-the-devil sign of the cross. 'Right, that's it. This relationship is officially over. I can't possibly hook up with one of them.'

'Can't stand the competition, huh? Running scared?' I went up on my knees on the sofa and ran my index finger down his cheek.

'Hmm.' He caught it and kissed the tip. 'Well, if I am going to keep you, I suppose I'll just have to put extra effort into turning you into a supporter of a real football team.'

'As long as you don't mind me trying the same thing.'

'Not a chance, girl.'

The look we exchanged could have started fires in a monsoon. Knowing I had to break the moment, I scooted back to my original position.

'Enough talking yet?' he asked hopefully.

'No. So tell me something important about yourself. I know: what's your first memory?'

He huffed. 'That's easy. Unlike a water nymph like you, I'm terrified of rivers ever since I almost drowned as a kid.'

'Oh my word: what happened?'

'I was playing by the local canal. I must have slipped out of our garden and the canal wasn't very far. I think I had some idiotic idea of feeding the ducks. Fell in, of course. Fortunately there was a guy walking his dog on the towpath that saw the accident and fished me out. After that I've always thought of water as my enemy—the dirty canal sort, anyway. What about you?'

'Almost the opposite: I remember playing with the water in my paddling pool. It was like my first friend. Mum and Dad had to rig up a screen so the neighbours didn't see.'

He didn't comment.

I toyed with a leather bracelet he never appeared to take off. 'What's this?'

'Got that a couple of years back. Kurt and Margot gave it to me when we first met. Three cords plaited—it was like a pledge that we'd stick together.'

'Kurt's been an important person in your life.'

'Both of them have. They have a real gift for friendship. Kurt could've blown me off—too young, too much of a wannabe—but he didn't: he took time and has helped me and my band mates every step of the way.'

I rubbed my cheek against his ribs, listening out for his heartbeat. 'That's nice to hear. You don't often find that kind of story in this business.'

'He's got nothing to prove, has he, so I guess he can be generous.'

I tried a baby step of progress. 'And do you think I'm right about his ability?'

Marcus's body stilled, unyielding under my ear. 'If you'd asked me before, I'd've said he was just very discerning—yeah, that's the word. Why do you have to turn normal stuff into all this mystic nonsense?'

Do not get flustered. Be calm. It's reasonable for him to have doubts. 'Because I believe it's different. Like you, he would be telepathic too if he gave it a try. Wouldn't you like to be able to speak to each other like that?'

Marcus burst into laughter. 'Kurt Voss—telepathic? The day he speaks to me telepathically is the day I wear a tutu on stage.'

'Be careful what you wish for, Marcus.'

There came a discreet knock at the door. 'Yo, bro, time to go!'

Marcus grimaced. 'I wish Michael would stop saying that. Come in!'

'I can give you as much . . . er . . . time as you need to finish up in there.'

Marcus opened the door abruptly so that Michael almost fell into the room. 'Angel and I were just talking.'

'You serious? What a waste. Hey, sweetheart, when you get tired of this one, come find me. You know where I live.' He pointed next door.

'A tempting offer, Michael, but one Black Belt is more than I can handle.' I kissed Marcus on the cheek as I passed. I picked up Freddie from where the case sat next to his guitar, deciding now was not the time to wing a performance. 'See you later.'

Marcus caught my hand. 'We're playing on the programme before Gifted. You'll be there backstage, won't you?'

'You bet.' I jumped down the steps. 'Wild horses wouldn't drag me away—though quite why they would try, I never understood.' I gave them both a cheery wave and headed back to the band lounge to run through my part.

As it got closer to five, I emerged from my private practice to find Will and Victor taking a break at one of the green room tables. They looked out of place, like two ravens among the chattering starlings, expressions sober as the glitzy flock pecked at other performers' reputations and exchanged seeds of gossip.

'Hey, how's it going?' I plonked myself down on the table beside Will. 'Where's Uriel?'

Will gestured over the top of the tents. 'He's with the others patrolling the site.'

'And your lady?'

Will grimaced. 'Managing the media pack around Gifted. She'll be here soon.'

'No sign of Davis?'

'Not yet. I wouldn't have left her if he had crawled out from under his stone.'

'Course not.' I hugged my knees. 'So what's it like connecting with your soulfinder?'

'You tell me.'

'Can't. Marcus won't even try telepathy. There's definitely something between us but I live in fear that I'm just projecting the rock-star glitter onto how I feel. But I'm working on him.'

'It's not like you to be cautious, Angel,' observed Victor.

'You noticed?' I laughed self-deprecatingly. 'I'm trying to wise up, believe it or not, Victor. Anyway, enough about me. How's Margot taken it?'

Will gave me a beautiful smile. 'Very well. She is one fine lady.'

'And did I mention gorgeous?' I teased. 'Not that that matters, of course, William: it's what's inside that counts—or so I'm led to believe.'

Will was primed to gush about his new partner given half a chance. 'It's true. She has a lovely spirit—kind, thoughtful, but she's no fool. She made me lay out the savant deal very carefully. I had to explain the small print before she would open her mind fully to me.'

'Small print?'

'The one-shot-at-a-soulfinder deal.'

'Yeah, that sucks.' I glanced at Victor, whose soulfinder was rumoured to be in Afghanistan behind bars. No wonder he was so grim most of the time. Misty told me he had a less scary side, but I'd not found it. 'Can you text Summer for me and suggest we meet up at the Beatbox tent at five? I'd like to bring them up to speed as to what's going on in my life.'

'No talking about savant business in public, Angel, remember,' warned Victor. 'Here with Will we can be sure there's no threat, but the situation on the festival site is volatile. You can be fine for a moment then find yourself in deep trouble the next.'

I picked at a loose thread on the hem of my tunic. 'I was thinking of just telling them about my role in the Gifted gig tonight.'

Will patted my knee. 'I meant to say, Angel: a huge well done! We mustn't ignore the fact that you've just landed yourself one amazing break, all thanks to your own talent. I'm sorry it's been complicated by this other business.'

I smiled archly. 'But if it weren't for this other business, I wouldn't be here. I wouldn't have met Marcus or rubbed shoulders with Gifted, so I think I'm the lucky one. And talking of other business, here she is.'

Margot was approaching with two men in suits, dark

glasses and earpieces: her security team, without a doubt. I considered myself excess to requirements, as I did not add to Will and Victor's professional image.

'I'd better go.'

'Summer, Misty and Alex will meet you by the exit,' said Will, showing me Summer's reply. They all must have got new Sims already. Only Mess-up Angel hadn't been trusted with a new phone.

'Toodlepip, William. Bye, Victor.'

'Take care, Angel,' said Victor. From his worried expression, I think he meant it.

Chapter·15

It was a great idea to go the Beatbox tent. Caught up in my personal drama, I had almost forgotten we were at one of the country's best music festivals and there was so much talent crammed into these fields, it was unreal. Though not headliners, both Joey and Fresh had their own gang of fans so the tent was packed. The arrival of Brian attracted some notice but this crowd was too cool to do the embarrassing 'will you sign my' thing; all eyes were on the battle on stage and Joey and Fresh were just up.

I sat squeezed between Summer and Misty on a bench at the front, Alex and Uriel flanking us. Fresh provided the beatbox backing while Joey did the rap—and they killed it. Totally awesome. We danced along in the front row, punching the air and shaking our stuff for all we were worth. OK, I danced along—my friends did a more restrained jig-along-in-time. Joey was amused however and directed some of his lines at me, which only encouraged me.

'Woo-woo-woo!' I yelled from on top of the bench when they'd finished, cycling my arm in the air. The applause was sustained. There was a real buzz about their performance, which must have done their careers no harm at all.

'Let's go backstage and congratulate them,' I suggested, jumping to the ground.

Summer caught my hand. 'You go—we don't know them.'

'But I'll introduce you. Come on!'

Dragging my friends along, I made my way to the back of the tent. Joey and Fresh were already outside chatting to fans. Inside the venue, the next act was just up. Poor new guys: it always sucks to follow the best, so depressing as the benches thin out.

'Joey, Fresh—you were amazing!' I barrelled through the fans and gave both a whopping big hug.

'Liked your moves, Angel: some serious shaking of that little ass of yours. If this playing with Gifted doesn't work out for you, wanna be our backing dancer?' Joey's eyes twinkled.

'I'll give it serious thought,' I teased. 'Particularly as you called my ass little. Can I introduce you to my friends—Misty, Summer, Alex and Uriel?' I stood back to let my guys say their hellos.

'Great show, guys,' Brian said as he and Jennifer arrived.

'Did you get some good shots?' Fresh asked hopefully.

Jennifer nodded and patted her camera. 'Yes, all in there. Give me your email and I'll send you some.'

'And did you get Angel here displaying her best moves?'

Jennifer smiled. 'Of course. It was hard to ignore her.'

Maybe I shouldn't have insisted on being in the front row. I'd meant it as support but perhaps it had looked just like showing off.

'Are you going to do that tonight for our set?' asked Brian.

'Absolutely not,' I promised. 'I'll be on my best behaviour.'

'Shame.' He grinned at my puzzled expression then winked at Joey and Fresh. 'I don't think she gets it.'

'Angel, it's a guy thing,' said Joey.

'Stop teasing her, Brian,' said Jennifer. 'Can't you see she's embarrassed?'

'That's me: always embarrassed *after* the event,' I muttered. 'One day I'll learn to anticipate.'

'Actually, Angel, can you spare me a moment?' asked Jennifer. 'I'd like to introduce you to some press friends of mine who are interested in covering the story about you taking to the stage with Gifted tonight.'

'Oh, OK. Sure. See you guys later?'

'We'll be there. Margot has sorted backstage passes for us,' said Summer.

'Great. I'm going to be in the VIP dressing room, apparently.' I grabbed Misty and spun her in a circle. 'Drop by and admire.'

'We will do,' promised Alex.

I squeezed Misty's hand. 'And stop me wearing a hole in the carpet as I pace with nerves, won't you?'

'Of course we will.' Misty and Summer exchanged a look: they both knew what I was like. They were my personal fire blankets, used to smothering my mini-meltdowns. 'Will Marcus be there? We've not met him yet.'

Releasing Misty, I dug my hands in my pockets and shrugged. 'He's performing just before us, so maybe not.'

'Then we'll see him afterwards,' suggested Summer. Clearly my friends had decided to give me a helping hand with my non-starter of a soulfinder relationship—if that's what it was.

Jennifer gave Summer an apologetic smile. 'Unfortunately that won't be possible. Gifted and Black Belt are rolling out immediately after the gig. They've got a couple more concert dates in the south-east and then they're appearing at the O2 next weekend and we've got to set up. We've spent longer here than we normally do at any venue. Margot wanted us to catch our breath in the middle of a long tour.'

I was speechless. Marcus had made no mention of this, though now I thought about it I remembered seeing the posters for the concert on the Underground. I just hadn't connected the dates.

Summer covered for me. 'Oh, I see. Well, maybe it'll be possible to meet him in between his session and Angel's?'

'Maybe.' Jennifer gave a polite smile that meant she really didn't think it would work out that way. I got the impression she wasn't that keen on my friends. Perhaps she thought I was trying to move in the whole tribe. Gifted staff were serious about preserving the privacy of band members. 'I'll be back soon, Brian. Are you coming, Angel?'

'Sure. Yes.'

Misty grabbed my shoulders before I left and whispered in my ear: 'It'll all work out—you'll see.'

'Thanks.' My voice sounded hoarse, my body felt hollow. I hadn't been this stunned since I was thrown from a pony in my first (and last) riding lesson.

Jennifer seemed not to have noticed she had delivered devastating news. She led me away from the congratulate-Joey-and-Fresh party. 'I said we'd try to meet the press people after the Beatbox event. Not really my kind of music, but they're good, aren't they?'

'Sorry, what?' I stumbled after her, arms crossed on my chest.

'Joey and Fresh—good at what they do.'

'Yes. They're great.'

'And they do it all with their own talent, don't they?'

'Yes, of course—what other way is there to do it?'

'Down here, Angel.' She guided me to a tent that promised Wi-Fi connections and coffee. It was busy with people sitting at the camping tables, headphones on, checking their emails. Jennifer walked straight through and out the other side.

'I thought we were meeting the press in there?' I asked, catching her up.

'No, no, too many people—too much background noise.' Her manner had changed. Around Brian she was all sweetness and concern; now she was brisk and business-like. Maybe meeting the journalists did that to her? Still, my instinct was telling me that something odd was going on.

'Who did you say we were meeting?'

Suddenly, Will's voice came into my head. *Angel, threat level around you has shot up. What are you doing?*

The light meter on Jennifer's camera beeped.

'Using telepathy, are you? We can't have that.'

Will! I'd only managed to shout his name when I glimpsed Eli Davis step out of the dark alleyway between tents behind me.

How do you stop someone using telepathy? Other than a savant gift for doing so, I hadn't thought it possible. Davis and his anti-savant brigade must have given the subject much thought, probably experimented at length because their moves felt practised.

Will, help! They've got me!

While Davis tied my hands, Jennifer, the double-crossing bitch, fixed earphones blasting a high-pitched whistle right into my brain. I tried to shout my distress call against it, tried to give Will my location, but it was overwhelming, like standing next to a road drill and trying to talk on your phone. All I could broadcast was an echo of the shrill tone.

I couldn't bear it. Too much. My head felt close to explosion, tears pouring down my cheeks.

Unable to hear what was said to me, I only felt the pokes and the slaps, the pull of duct tape on bare skin. Davis put his arm around me, half-holding me up, half-forcing me along. If anyone had been close enough to see us, they would have seen a couple assisting a girl who looked the worse for drink. They propelled me along until we reached a car. Two more people joined us but my vision was too blurred to see who they were. I was lifted up and placed in the boot, despite my kicks to wriggle free. A blanket smelling of oil covered me and the top clunked down. The car began to move, bumping over ruts, and then gathering speed.

Take the headphones off, please! I didn't know if I was screaming this telepathically or out loud. I kicked and thumped the compartment, desperate to escape the noise. I thrashed my head, trying to dislodge the earphones but they had been duct taped in place. *No, it's hurting me! Too much. Too much.*

I curled up into a foetal ball, eyes screwed shut, nails digging into palms. I screamed every savant name I could think of, hoping one cry would get through. The journey seemed to go on and on. I began to think it would never end—that I'd be locked in this torture chamber for ever.

I came to my senses when the sound finally stopped I don't know how much later. My head was at an odd angle on the ground, hair plastered on my cheeks. I appeared to be lying on a cold floor made of metal. It was completely dark. I remembered being lifted out of the car and dropped here but I had been battling to keep my wits against the whistle. The silence was deafening; I could still hear the residual roar of the noise, like the aftermath of standing by the speakers in a heavy-metal concert. I wondered briefly if my hearing had been permanently damaged.

Not important. Focus, girl: escape. First thing, make sure no one can put that sound in your head again.

My hands were still bound behind me but my legs were free. I wriggled to sitting position then dropped my head between my knees and caught the headphones between them. I swore viciously as I lost some strands of hair tugging my head free. I hadn't completely dislodged the headphones but at least they were now hanging around my neck, no longer covering my ears. The residual tape pulled and twisted on the damp skin of my cheeks until it finally dropped free.

Will? Anyone? I sent out a telepathic distress message.

No answer.

If I was going to try that again, I had to play my best game. Give my telepathic powers in my bruised brain a little time to recover. And not panic.

Oh crap: I was panicking . . .

OK, Angel: breathe. One . . . two . . . three . . . That's right, you can do this. You are not a complete idiot, even if your recent track record suggests otherwise. Davis has got hold of you. Jennifer was working for him—that wasn't hard to piece together. Why hadn't Kurt sensed she was a fake—or Margot for that matter? Too late to ask that now. I was here—wherever here was—and I needed to work out how I could escape.

So next on the agenda, explore the prison for an exit.

Feeling a little better that I'd managed to come up with a basic plan, I groped around on the floor. Cold sheet metal. Shuffling backwards on my bum, I then found a wall—corrugated. Building the mental picture, I guessed I was in some kind of shipping container. As my eyes adjusted, I noticed a pinprick of red light up in one corner, too high for me to reach. I put my foot out to break the beam and a light clicked on. After the utter darkness it was so bright. I buried my head in my knees and curled up against the nearest wall.

'So you're back with us. Excellent.' Davis' voice came from a speaker somewhere in the roof and tinny in the headphones dangling from my neck.

'Let me out, you bastard!' I screamed at him, kicking at the wall in case someone could hear me outside.

'We'll let you out all in good time. Perform well in our little experiment and the doors will open, I promise.'

I tried a different tack. 'Please, you don't want to risk your career for an abduction, surely? Just let me out now and I won't tell anyone. I've got a show to do.'

'Don't worry: you'll have a chance to star in your own little performance for the cameras. Footage of you is being streamed live from our webcam. When you have given us indisputable proof of the existence of savant powers, then you'll be free to go.'

Hope that he was going to be reasonable shrivelled up. How was I going to get out of this? 'I don't have any powers. I'm just a singer. No one would believe you—they'll say the footage is a fake.'

'Please, carry on protesting—it is what we expected. Your people hide among us, manipulating us without our consent. You must be exposed for what you are: just one part of a much bigger picture. And as for proof, you'll sing a different song when you have to use your gift for saving your own life.'

There was a clunk against the side of the container and it rocked. There was nothing for me to hold onto but I tried to grip the wall with my bound fingers. 'What's happening?'

'We're moving you down onto the slipway. As the tide comes in your container will start to fill with water. For normal people that would be a problem, but water is your speciality, isn't it? Those pictures on your phone were most enlightening. You'll have about thirty minutes to decide if you prefer to live or go to your death pretending you couldn't prevent your own drowning.'

'You . . . you expect me to hold back the sea? Haven't you heard of King Canute, Mr Davis?' If this were being broadcast live, at least the authorities would now have his name for later prosecution.

'Very witty, Angel. But if Canute had had you on his side, the story would've ended quite differently, wouldn't it?'

The container started to move, rattling as it was shifted. It ended up at an angle, fitting Davis's description of placing it on a slipway.

No help was going to come from my captors. My head felt strong enough for a second attempt at telepathy. *Will!*

Again no reply. Telepathy over any significant distance was always a chancy matter; far greater prospect of success if the relationship was a close one, the other mind well known to you. The bond between the middle Benedict brother and me was not strong enough to span the distance from the festival to wherever I was being held.

I wouldn't get many attempts at this—my head was already throbbing with a migraine from the whistle, white lights flashing behind my eyelids. I'd have to try for my strongest link—and I knew who that was even if he wasn't going to like it.

Marcus! This time I felt my message brush against someone else's mind.

Angel, where the hell are you?

Oh God, Marcus. I got the blurred impression of masses of people and bright lights.

Why aren't you here? You promised. His hurt zinged down our connection.

You really think this is a good time to hash that out? Tears of relief were running down my face, mingled with a sharp joy—so counter to everything else I was experiencing. I hadn't been imagining anything: Marcus was my soulfinder. Petrified though I was, the connection between our minds blazed between us with warming, reassuring fire.

I'm in the middle of our set here. Pete and Michael are asking why I just stopped singing. I've got an audience of about ten thousand staring right at me.

Pull yourself together, Angel. Tell the guy to get you help. *Sorry to interrupt but I'm in a lot of deep water here.* I began to laugh hysterically, blotting the tears with my knees. If this was on webcam, I had to look completely mad. *Eli Davis and Jennifer abducted me maybe an hour or so ago—I don't know for sure. They've locked me in a shipping container, which is going to fill up with the tide. Tell Will to come and get me out.*

There was no response. It was like the 999 dispatcher putting down the phone in the middle of your call.

Marcus? Please, please don't let me down. I need you to believe me.

Jennifer?

I saw my mistake: I shouldn't have mentioned someone he had known and trusted for longer than he had known me. *That's not important right now. Can we just concentrate on the saving-Angel-from-drowning part?*

None of this makes sense. You're doing this on purpose, aren't you? You already told me water was your friend. Is this another of your "get Marcus's attention" ploys? Show your power over me by making me drop everything for you?

You cold bastard! No, it damn well isn't!

He was angry with me—with me! *This isn't a good time, Angel. Give me twenty minutes and I'll be finished up here. You've got your own performance in ninety minutes—you'd better be here for that.*

He didn't believe me. He thought I was playing some ridiculous game with my gift to get his notice—to make him choose between his band and me. My soulfinder didn't care enough for me to risk his career and come save my life. My knight-in-fricking-shining-armour was abandoning the princess to the dragon and riding off in the wrong bloody direction.

He was about to end the link but I could feel his hesitation. *What's that you're feeling?* Telepathic communication between soulfinders gave each one an insight into the heart of the other—he was experiencing that right now.

I'm not sure what I'd call it: devastation maybe. I felt so tired—so disappointed by him.

You know, Marcus, I thought we stood a chance once we spoke this way, but I was wrong. I was scared that my soulfinder might hate me but actually it's the other way round: I should've been scared that I'd come to hate you. Go away, Marcus. I'll get someone else to rescue me. I cut the link.

Water began to spurt through the joint where the container doors met. These shipping boxes were meant to withstand rough weather as they spent much of their working lives stacked out on a deck. Thanks to this, the tide had not found a way in until it was already a third of the way up the sides. I hadn't noticed that I was already partially submerged. The water gushed towards me, wrapping me in the only kind of embrace I could bear just at the moment.

'Oh my friend,' I whispered to the water, 'you and me are in a lot of trouble.' I wasn't scared, not of my element, but I was terrified of the decision I would have to make.

The sea tickled my aching wrists, bound so tightly with tape. I couldn't ask it to carry in a knife or anything to cut me free—the gap wasn't big enough to let in a blade—but I welcomed its soothing touch.

Hang on though: the sea could scour off the glue, couldn't it?

Calling out to my friends telepathically all the while but failing to reach any of them, I summoned as much sand and grit as had come in with the water and directed it at the tape. Cool water protected my skin as a little whirlpool worked at the sticky join binding the tape. Gradually it loosened and floated free, like a strip of rubbery brown kelp.

'Score one to Angel,' I whispered, bringing my arms up in front of me.

'How did you free yourself?' Davis' voice crackled over the speaker system.

I made use of my unbound hands and offered him a two-fingered reply. I took the earphones off my neck and dropped them into the water. Standing up, I found the water had reached my calves and was fast rising. It wouldn't stop rushing towards me unless I ordered it to do so—and that was exactly what I didn't want to do, not while on camera.

Camera? Could I disable that somehow? I began searching for a way to reach the light in the corner. Jumping up, I fell back, still a long way short. Damn being small! I'd have to wait until I could float up there—or maybe send a plume of water to do the job for me?

Turning my back so they wouldn't see what I was doing, I used my power to wind water up the wall like ivy. It reached the camera but the light refused to blink off.

'What are you doing? We know you are using your power.'

Like I was going to tell them anything. Disappointed, I let the water subside to its natural level. The camera was waterproof, of course.

Chapter 16

Angel, are you there? Marcus's voice lanced back into my head, adding to my headache.

I told you to go away. Oh dash it all—I had to talk to the bastard, didn't I? He was the only one I could reach.

Look, I just walked off stage for you.

Well done, I shot back sarcastically. *So you've decided saving a life might be worth more than your reputation? I'm honoured.*

OK, if that's your attitude, I'll go back on. I might still be able to salvage something of my credibility if I do it now.

I hate you. I leaned back against the container wall and covered my face with my hands. *I really really hate you.*

I'm not so hot for you right now either, Angel. But there was something tender in his tone that undercut the cruelty of the thought. *Tell me what I need to know.*

I sobbed, feeling my heart break into little sand fragments and scour my chest as it came out with my tears.

Angel? OK, I'm sorry. I'm just furious. I don't want to be one of you—don't want this gift thing you told me about and I'm taking it out on you. I apologize.

He wouldn't have to worry: I'd leave him alone after this. *Just tell Will, Victor or Uriel—whoever is closest—that I'm being held in a shipping container somewhere. I don't think I'm that far from you. They've put it on a slipway and it's filling with water so I have to be in some kind of dock or marina. Footage is being streamed live so the Davis people will get evidence of the existence of savant gifts—maybe if they find the feed that'll give them a hint of where I am.*

Come again? This is for real?

Marcus, wake up! This isn't about you—I'm not grandstanding to get your attention. My life is in danger. As a savant, I've promised not to reveal my gift to outsiders and I'm being put in a situation where I'm going to have to break my word. Even so, I've limits: I can't keep out something as strong as the sea for ever. They might end up drowning me because I've never tested my powers in this way.

The sound system crackled.

'Congratulations, Angel. You've interrupted the concert, which was being broadcast live by the BBC. The evidence of gifts is mounting—when it all comes out people will know why someone like Marcus Cohen walked out in the middle of a career-making performance. Keep up the good work.'

My reply was to wade over to stand directly under the camera to make it more difficult for them to film me.

Marcus, once you've told one of the Benedicts, get back on stage. The anti-savant people are compiling evidence against you.

Marcus told me succinctly what the journalists could do with their evidence. *I've found Will and Margot. Will's calling Victor.* I then got the impression that someone new—not one of the Benedicts but Kurt, had joined Marcus. I could hear an echo of the conversation through Marcus's replies.

'What the hell are you playing at? Get back on stage!' roared Kurt. 'You don't do that to your band mates—not unless you're dying and only then if there's treatment that'll save you. Otherwise I expect you to keep going until you croak on stage. That's what real musicians like us do.'

'Hey, Marcus, bro, what's going on?' asked Michael, joining the little 'let's-get-Marcus-back-on-track' brigade. 'Pete's just making an apology—saying you were suddenly taken ill. Is that what's going on?'

I could feel Marcus balanced on a knife-edge of decision: apologize and return to the stage, letting others handle this, or stay with me.

'Look, guys, someone's got to Angel—she's in danger.'

He'd chosen me—reluctantly, kicking and screaming all the way, but he'd decided I was more important. It was hard to feel grateful.

'How do you know this?' snapped Kurt. 'You were in the middle of a song and this brainwave hit you? How the hell do you know what's up with her?'

I reached out to Kurt through my link to Marcus. *He's telling the truth, Kurt. I really really need some help here.* I sent him an image of the container rapidly filling with water—up to my waist now at the shallow end, probably over my neck at the lower side.

Victor sprinted up to Marcus and grabbed him by the elbow. 'Where is she?' His normally cold demeanour was cracked, revealing the magma of fury just below the surface.

Let me speak to Victor, I told Marcus.

Marcus shook Victor off and paced, holding his fingers to his temples. *How do I do that?*

I think you have a gift to act as a bridge—that was how I was able to talk to Kurt. You may not have realized it but you two must have been communicating on some instinctive level just below full-blown telepathy. I remembered the natural collaboration between the two when playing. *Through music I guess. It all follows if one of your gifts is to be a strong telepath.*

How does that help you?

Link with Victor—or ask him to link with you. I'll be able to join in.

This all must have looked very strange to Michael and the

backstage crew: Marcus pacing with his head in his hands, Kurt looking as though someone had dropped a lighting bar on his head, Victor close to prising the answers physically from Marcus.

While we had been talking, Margot had quickly devised a plan to salvage what she could from disaster. She started rapping out orders. 'Michael, go back and apologize—say you're having technical difficulties. Marcus got hit by a blast of full-volume feedback from his earpiece and can't sing until his hearing recovers.' Closing her eyes, she must have unleashed a little of her power because the sound system started popping and crackling, howling with electronic distress. She pointed at the backstage manager. 'Get your men on the problem. It'll be something to do with the incompatibility between our equipment and yours. Tell the crowd the concert will resume at the earliest possible moment but it is unsafe to continue for both them and the performers.'

Kicked out of indecision by her sergeant-major manner, the stage manager called his crew to get on to the task.

'So sorry, Mr Cohen, if you were inconvenienced,' he said. 'This has never happened at Rockport before.' He hurried away to the sound booth, gabbling further orders on his walkie-talkie.

'Victor, she wants to talk to you via me,' Marcus said awkwardly.

Will put a hand on his shoulder. 'Welcome to the savant world, Marcus. Just hang in there: Angel is relying on you.'

Marcus gave a jerky nod.

Victor reached out to touch Marcus's forehead but my soulfinder reared back. 'Whoa, what's this: the Vulcan death grip?'

Victor almost snarled with frustration. 'It helps me find your mind. Hold still—this will feel . . . strange.'

Miles away locked in a container, I suddenly felt Victor in my head as clear as my own presence. It was nothing like the frail connection to Kurt; Victor had moved in with all his possessions and was sitting with his feet up in my living room so to speak, probably holding the damn TV remote. If I felt this at one remove, I couldn't even imagine what Marcus was experiencing. Flattened like doormat, probably. Victor didn't bother with questions; he just rooted through my recent memories and took all the relevant data. He then stepped back a little, retreating to a less intense connection.

You've no idea where you are? Can the sea tell you anything?

Good idea. I put both hands into the water and stretched out my senses. The sea didn't perceive the coast as a human—it was like looking at the photo in negative. I could sense some shapes, some textures, nothing coherent.

Concentrate, Angel. There has to be something.

No shit, Sherlock. I left the margin of the water and sought for clues out in the deeper waters. *The seabed shelves here very rapidly—I think this must be the deepest harbour in the area—figures if there's a dock. It's got to be big enough to have machines to move containers.* I felt something else—something disturbing the water. *There's some kind of outflow here too—industrial or a sewer. What about Brigport itself? There's a dock here that gives the festival its name—used by smaller container ships, I think. It's round the headland from Brighouse-by-Sea.*

Are you sure?

I bit my lip, conjuring up a map of the south coast of England. *No. I was out of it while they were moving me. I could be anywhere. There are lots of dockyards.*

Can we work this out by a process of elimination? How far does your telepathy usually stretch?

I'm not a strong telepath—a few miles at most. But my guess is Marcus is a strong one.

He is—exceptionally so. And Brigport is the nearest container port?

I think so.

Then we'll go with that. Hang on, Angel. Try not to give anything away until you have to.

Did you hear the 'No shit, Sherlock' comment earlier?

Yeah.

Well, ditto that with brass knobs on. I was shivering with cold. *Hurry up.*

He sent the impression of a salute through our connection. *Yes, ma'am. I see you've lost your fear of me.*

Nah—just too freezing to care right now.

He dropped his end of the link and released Marcus from his . . . well . . . possession I'd suppose you'd call it. 'Brigport—we think she's there. Let's go.'

Will nodded. 'Uriel's fetching Margot's car.' He kissed Margot's cheek. 'Keep the excuses coming. Stay safe.'

'You too,' she replied, letting another squawk burst from the speakers.

Marcus ran after the two Benedicts. 'I'm coming with you.'

Victor raised a brow at that demand. 'Haven't you got a concert to finish?'

'We've got technical problems, didn't you hear?'

'You don't need to do this. Angel doesn't expect you to abandon all this—you've made your priorities clear.'

'I know she doesn't—but I'm your link to her, aren't I? Her . . . her soulfinder. She's only hearing all this because I am communicating with her somehow in my head.'

'True.' Victor gave him an assessing look. 'But you messed that up, didn't you? I saw how you treated her.'

'Vick, he'll be useful—especially if we're wrong about where she is,' added Will. 'It's not the time to discuss what's going on between them.'

'OK, Marcus, saddle up. You can ride with us.' Victor opened the front passenger door. Alex was already in the back with Summer and Misty. 'Not the whole gang. Girls—out!'

Summer and Misty just glared at him.

'We're wasting time,' warned Uriel.

'There's a third row of seats,' said Alex persuasively.

If I hadn't been so numbed by the icy water I would have chuckled at Victor's furious expression in the face of my friends' rebellion.

It's my army riding to the rescue, Victor, I told him, nudging our link back open. *And I want my friends.*

I could feel Marcus flinch a little as I added that thought. He could see that I didn't regard him as a friend: I wasn't sure what he was just then, but friend wasn't one of the terms in contention.

Victor flicked a contemptuous glance at Marcus. 'Get in.' Marcus and Will climbed in the rear. They hadn't even buckled in as Uriel floored the accelerator.

It was tiring to maintain the link to Marcus so I let it drop for the moment while I mustered my strength. If they didn't get to me soon I was at serious risk of exposure of the other sort. Could I call a warmer current to me? I rejected the idea as using too much of my power. I needed to have something left in the locker for keeping myself breathing. OK, I'd swim. Movement got the blood flowing and took the chill off the water.

There's not much room in a container to do widths but I splashed from one end to another.

'What are you doing? Is this how you exercise your control over water?' asked Davis.

No, this is just how I exercise. Let him wonder what I was up to: I had no reason to answer. After a few minutes of swimming, I tried to put my feet down and discovered that the water level had gone over my head. There was about a metre left between the roof and me. I floated on my back and drifted over to the camera. It was set behind a wire cage—no way I could get to it to switch it off.

But I could stop them seeing me, couldn't I? I had to have straw for brains not to have thought of this before. Recalling what I was wearing, I debated between leggings or tunic.

Tunic.

I wriggled out of it, grateful for my foresight to wear a strappy top underneath. Swimming back to the camera, I gave Davis a final cute smile and wrapped the sodden tunic around the camera cage.

'What are you doing? Take that cover off immediately.'

'Why don't you come in here and make me?' I sang out sweetly. It felt so good to get one punch back in after having been beaten into this position by these savant-haters. I began to sing Kurt and Marcus's song, 'Stay Away, Come Closer'.

'I'm warning you!'

'Threats are a bit redundant, don't ya think? I'm already locked up to drown in a shipping container. You should've thought a little more about how to play your cards, holding some back. There's nothing more you can do to me.'

I could hear a bump and a rasp on the speaker as if someone was grappling for the microphone.

'No—that's going too far!' The protest sounded like Jennifer. 'This is just a test—no one was to get harmed.'

'It's the only way. We've gone too far to back down now.'

'Not too far. We've not done anything incriminating; there's just the word of a girl that she was abducted—most people think she's half-cracked anyway.'

Thanks, Jennifer.

'Then there's no evidence to link us to the next stage either—nothing to stand up in court anyway, even if the savants know the truth. The live-streaming is only going to our supporters—the savants will never find it.'

'No . . . '

'I'm overruling you on this. I'm sending the order.'

The silence that followed was ominous. I sensed that in this case Jennifer was my ally and I needed her to win the argument. 'Hey, Jennifer, I'm going all wrinkly here. A joke's a joke, right? Time to let me out and we'll forget this ever happened.'

Davis, not Jennifer, came back to the mic. 'I was hoping we could do this without resorting to extremes.'

I half-choked on horrified laughter. 'This isn't extreme?'

'But if you won't show live on camera the kind of behaviour I found on your phone, then I'm going to have to up the stakes for you. It won't matter if we can't see what you're doing inside—we've cameras on the outside that will record enough for our purposes. You can't escape us.'

I felt the container lurch again. 'What are you doing?'

'We're winching you up on the crane.'

That was good, wasn't it? Up was out of the water.

'Then we're going to lower you into the deep water of the harbour so the container is completely submerged. When you survive that, no one will be in any doubt that you have extraordinary powers.'

The container began to sway free, water slopping from one side to the other, bashing me against the wall. I clung on to the camera cage to keep anchored. The water level was receding but that would be only temporary.

'Stop!' I screamed. 'You've got to believe me, Mr Davis: I don't know that I can survive that. In fact, I'm pretty sure I can't.' Arms at full stretch, I had to let go and drop down into the water. 'You must be crazy to think I can stop the sea.'

'Angel, Angel, I have every confidence you will rise to the

challenge. We need a spectacular demonstration and this is going to be amazing.'

Are you getting what this madman's saying, Marcus? I asked my soulfinder, knowing he had been a shadow at the back of my mind for some time now.

I can't believe what I'm hearing. What are you going to do? He sounded much closer.

Hope my cavalry arrives. Can you see me yet?

We're just turning into the port now.

Look for a crane working this late on a Friday night.

Angel, it's a busy place, working under floodlights, twenty-four seven.

Then—I don't know—try to feel where I am. Is anything off—a single container over open water?

Oh hell, I can see you!

His alarm was not reassuring. I caught a confusing glimpse through his eyes. A rust-red container was swaying on the end of cables at the far end of the furthest pier, no ship underneath it to accept the delivery.

Can you get to me in time?

Victor's cutting through red tape with Alex. The guys are ordering people to do what they ask.

Mind powers and persuasion: yeah, those two would make quite a team.

Hurry, please.

Angel, just hold on.

With a sudden lurch, I felt the cables spin out their full length. The container smacked the surface, paused a fraction of a second, and then began to sink, the weight of metal and half a load of water pulling it down.

Marcus!

We're almost with you. Someone must have tipped off the guy controlling the crane that we were on our way.

'You bloody maniac!' I screamed at the microphone. 'I hope you rot in hell for this.'

Silence. Davis had either fled his post at the monitor or he had cut communications.

One end of the container nosed down further than the other and the water rebalanced, leaving a pyramid-shaped pocket of air up in one corner. Silently, it slipped down in the dark waters of the harbour, taking me with it.

Chapter 17

So many times I have claimed, without really thinking of the words, that I'd 'never been more scared in my life' but this time I had no doubt I'd found a whole new level of terror. Sensing my horror, the water nearest me tried to keep away, bending into a bubble shape, preserving the little air for me to breathe. Yet I knew that the molecules could only resist so much pressure from the weight of the ocean to which they were connected. I was one small savant; they formed one vast sea wrapping the world in its blue embrace.

Angel, Angel: are you OK?

No, I'm not OK, Marcus: I'm in a container going down like the Titanic.

How much air? We can see bubbles.

Yeah, that's my air escaping. I'm in a kind of bubble inside but it's rapidly deflating.

Hang on in there.

Why do people say such incredibly obvious things to you when you're dying?

You're not dying.

Tell that to the rising water level. I'm so tired. My thoughts were drifting, a sense of unreality stealing over me, cold catching up as I had stopped swimming. *Is this like some really weird dream?*

No, it's not. I wish it were.

So tired.

Angel, come on: you mustn't give up.

Give up what? Just then, hitting the bottom of miserable, I wasn't sure I wanted to get out of the container, not if it meant facing the complete mess-up that was my life. I'd compromised savant safety with my photographs, fallen in and out of love with my soulfinder in the space of twenty-four hours, and missed out on the biggest break of my career.

Angel, don't. Summer had joined Marcus in my mind. In fact, I knew he'd invited her there, feeling he wasn't enough for me. *We'll get you out. We've your fabulous Benedict boys on your side, remember?*

That provoked a flicker of a smile, hearing my nickname for them.

And Alex too, said Misty. *He's gone with Victor to get control of the crane. They'll be lifting you out any moment now—you've got to believe it.*

I closed my eyes and swallowed against the lump in my throat. *I do if you say it.*

Marcus spoke again, his voice so much closer somehow than even my best friends, like the difference between skin and clothes. *Summer says you're exhausted—that you need energy. Can I . . . can I try and give you some of mine?*

The air had become little more than a diver's helmet around my head. Only the faint light glimmering through murky water showed which way was up. I was getting disorientated, lulled by my favourite element. Soft cold fingers of sea brushed my limbs. It wouldn't be so bad to drown. One of the better ways to die, I'd heard.

Stop it! Marcus's message was like a slap in the face. *Angel, you are going to snap out of this. It's not you—you're about life.*

But I'm just not strong enough.

Together we will be.

Perhaps. Maybe. *How are you going to help me?*

Summer thinks that I connect best through music. So I'm going to sing to you. I could hear his private thoughts, the ones muttering that of all the bizarre and stupid things he'd done in his life, this one took the prize, but he ignored all those protests for my sake. *Any requests?*

I don't want . . . I don't care . . . What was I saying? I really was drifting off like a capsized sailor flat out on the upturned hull of her boat in the middle of the Pacific.

You've got no choice as I'm gonna sing anyway or Misty here will scratch my eyes out; only flexibility is the song.

I said nothing, too cold even to imagine what I would ask for.

All righty, my choice then. Demon Angel, got my soul on the rack . . .

A little energy woke me out of my daze. *No, not that one! I hate that song.*

He was pleased: he'd done it on purpose to shake me out of my lethargy. *It's a good song.*

I hate that it's about me.

Then ask for another.

OK, if I have to. Stay Away, Come Closer.

He started to hum the intro, then softly sang the words. His gift stole along our connection. My friends tactfully retired from our shared mind-space so he could nestle me to him in the melody, wrapping it around me like a blanket. The warmth flowing from him reached my skin from the inside out, then spread a little further, helping hold the air pocket against the press of the ocean.

Hold steady, baby, he said, interrupting his song, *you're about to get rescued.*

But he'd already rescued me, hadn't he? Not that that changed anything fundamental about what was wrong between us. If anything I resented him for it.

The container began to creak and groan as it was lifted, the payload of water stressing the cables. I could feel the water reluctant to let me go but I had a counterweight now: Marcus, my anchor on shore, and I helped nudge it away.

Not today, I told the sea.

Not ever, said Marcus.

The container cleared the surface and rivulets streamed off the sides. Salt water raced for the exit, helping me by escaping through the cracks as fast as it could.

That's beautiful, said Marcus. I could see what he saw: water spurting from all directions like the rose spout on a watering can, glittering white against the fiery orange glow of the setting sun. My prison swung over the jetty and lowered smoothly to the ground, landing with a clunk. It was still half full.

Careful! I warned whoever was going to open the door.

The large bolts bottom and top were released and the doors swung open. The remaining water gushed out, washing me with it. Cushioned by my element, I landed on the concrete like a fish on the deck of a trawler, gasping and shivering. I was plucked from the ground and wrapped in two strong arms.

'Don't you ever do anything like that ever again!' whispered Marcus fiercely. He hugged me to his chest, helping warm me with his body, though he too was soaking. I guessed he had been the one to reach the door first.

A silver foil blanket was pressed around both of us as Summer and Misty moved in to the group hug.

'Th . . . thanks, guys,' I managed to say through chattering teeth.

'Let's get you somewhere you can warm up,' said Will.

'W . . . what's h . . . happening here?'

'Vick, Uri, and Alex are staying to deal with the crane driver and the local police.'

'Davis an . . . and Jennifer?'

'We don't think they were on site. It was all done remotely. Don't worry: we're onto them. Your job is to recover: get warm—rest.'

'O . . . OK.' To be honest I was too cold to care.

'Come on, baby, I've got you.' Bundling me up in his arms, Marcus carried me over to the car. 'Seems as though I'm making a habit of this.'

'It . . . it w . . . won't happen again,' I said, meaning I wouldn't involve him next time.

He wilfully misinterpreted my words. 'Of course it won't. You, Angel, are not getting within a million miles of Davis and his crew again even if I have to sic a squad of bodyguards on you.'

I didn't have the energy to argue. In the middle row of seats, he pulled me onto his lap as the other passengers took their places. There was a tangible tension in the vehicle: our driver, Will, was absorbed with talking telepathically to his brothers, picking their path through the crisis; Summer and Misty were painfully aware of my misery; Marcus by contrast was clueless how to handle me. Even in my upset I had to allow that he'd been dropped in the deep end—ha ha—discovering his connection to me during a live concert before an audience of thousands and then having to ride to the rescue. Most soulfinders get a little more space to adjust to their new reality. Physically it felt so right to be curled up with him like this; emotionally I felt we were poles apart. He was sending out such contradictory signals, still so angry, thinking of his gift like being diagnosed with a rare genetic disorder, a sentence of artistic death. He couldn't see it for the wonderful bounty it was. Cheat and fraud: these were two of the terms he was applying to himself. What must he think of me, then?

'After tonight, you'll need therapy,' I muttered, in a broken-winged joke.

It flapped clumsily between us. 'Yeah, I think I do.' He leaned down and brushed a kiss on my wet hair. 'I'm just relieved you're alive.'

'So am I.' I spread my fingers against the damp cloth of his T-shirt, wanting the contact despite myself.

We passed the rest of the journey in silence. By arrangement with Margot, Will drove the car right into the performers' zone and parked at the steps to Marcus's trailer. Margot hurried up just as we arrived.

'Oh Angel: you're really all right? I can't believe what they did to you! They have to be mad.'

'I guess that about sums it up,' I replied, shuffling out of the car.

'You get warmed up in Marcus's shower. Marcus, how are you, sweetie?'

I watched enviously as Marcus went to Margot for a hug. Of course, she was like an older sister to him. That was the problem with soulfinder relationships, I was discovering: you felt as though you should be close but there was no shared history, no depth to support it.

He's not ready yet, said Misty softly, seeing my expression, *but if you let it grow, it'll come. Alex and I got off to a rocky start too.*

Yeah, but at least he wanted to be a savant.

Give Marcus time to adjust. It'll work out.

But I'm not even sure I like him, I replied truthfully—I couldn't lie to Misty about something like this: she would know. *He didn't want to come save me.*

But he came. And it's not quite true, Angel, that you don't like him. Right now, you're angry with him, explained Summer, joining in our little girl chat as she helped me up the stairs and into the Winnebago. *He's angry with us. Neither of you can see clearly what else you might feel.*

I guess he'll need to write a few more bitchy songs about me to get it out of his system, I said bitterly.

If he has to, you should let him do it. You've had a lifetime to get used to being a savant; he's had, like, five minutes?

Summer was always so reasonable; was she right this time?

I guess.

At least you found him. She tried a smile but I couldn't find one to answer her—probably a first for me. 'Go on: in the shower with you.'

I stood under the warm spray and let the salt wash from my body. It felt cleansing, like I was a snake casting off a skin. Some of the old wide-eyed Angel broke away from me and swirled down the drain. Instead of new tender skin under the old, I decided I would emerge with a thicker hide to bear with my disappointment. At least, that was the plan; the reality was somewhat different.

Wrapped in a towel, I stepped out into the living room area. Misty and Summer were waiting for me, sitting tensely on the sofa. I looked around. 'Where's Marcus?'

'He ... er ... he had to go and finish his concert,' Misty explained. 'Margot insisted and Will thought it for the best— less chance of rumours spreading about him and his gift.'

If I strained my ears I could hear that Black Belt had indeed resumed their concert after a good hour of interruption. 'Well then, good for him. Did you get me any dry clothes?'

Summer handed me a bag. 'Margot dug these out for you.'

'Great: the ever-efficient Margot. Thanks.' I went into the little bedroom area I'd not visited before and closed the door.

You will not cry, Angel. You will put on these new things, smile and carry on.

Oh damn, I was crying.

Stop it, you spineless idiot. Where is your pride?

I'd never really been that bothered by pride before but now

it was important to leave this disaster zone with some intact. I pulled on the T-shirt and jeans I had been lent and wiped my face on the Black Belt logo of the top.

Summer tapped on the door. 'Kurt's here, Angel. He wants to check you're OK and if you are up to playing tonight.'

Kurt. Funny how my heart no longer leapt over him either. Both Marcus and Kurt had managed to siphon off all my fangirl glee and left me on empty. I came out of the bedroom and found him standing by the door, guitar in hand.

'Hey, darlin', I can't believe what those criminals did to you! Glad to see you in one piece.' He held out his arms for a hug.

I wasn't in one piece—more like a dropped Easter egg held together by its gaudy wrapper. 'Hi, Kurt.' Staying back, I dug my hands in the pockets of my jeans.

He frowned as he took in my defensive stance. 'You . . . you must be shaken up, right?'

I nodded.

'So you'll give the performance a miss then?'

I dipped my head again, hiding my anger that he could even think I'd be up to playing after that experience. Self-absorbed rock god.

Kurt clenched his fist then released it. 'I'm sorry about that but it would be too much, wouldn't it?'

I could tell he was hoping for an Angel bounce back to put everything on track to how it had been before all the weirdness had started but I couldn't oblige. 'Yes.'

'Right. OK. See you later then?'

I nodded, but I had no intention of doing so. Seeing him standing there had firmed my resolve. I couldn't return to how things had been a few hours ago: me trying to win Marcus and Kurt over to the savant world like some desperate puppy whining for their attention, rolling over with enthusiasm to make them love me.

Summer stepped into the awkward silence. 'I hope the performance goes well.'

'Thanks, love.' Kurt took one last look then left.

Summer came over to me and pulled me to her for a hug. 'You want to go.'

Of course she knew. 'I *have* to go. I want to be home, not here. Will you . . . ' I took a shuddering breath. 'Will you fix it for me?'

Summer nodded. 'Misty, can you make Angel a hot drink? I'll go talk to the others.'

I don't know how she did it but Summer persuaded Margot to provide me with a chauffeur-driven car to take me home. As Gifted stepped out on stage to make their headline performance, I was tucked up on the rear seat with Summer beside me, heading back to London. Everyone else was staying to sort out the mess of my abduction: Davis was still on the loose, Jennifer had not yet returned, and the crane driver claimed he had no idea someone was in the container. With no evidence to lay against them—even the live footage had not shown up on any part of the web Victor's people had searched—it looked as though it was purely my word against theirs as to what had happened. And none of it made any sense unless I could be open about my savant power—which I couldn't. I'd almost died keeping that secret so I was hardly like to blurt it out now, was I? Doubtless this was part of the risk calculation Davis had made.

'Are you sure you're doing the right thing leaving?' asked Summer softly.

I watched the trees lining the motorway flick by. 'Yes. I'm only bringing forward a few hours what Marcus was going to do to me. It's for the best.'

'It's not over, Angel. You can't leave your soulfinder even if you feel better putting a distance between you right now.'

'I know we'll always be connected by that but, honestly, I can't bear to stay near him. You and I both know that soulfinder relationships don't always work out. I can't be with someone who doesn't even like me very much. He makes me feel bad inside.'

Summer touched the back of my wrist. 'He's plucked the wings off our butterfly and I think I could hate him for that.'

'Butterfly?'

'That's how Misty and I think of you—you are so ... so happy, it's a joy to be with you.'

'Not so happy now.'

'Of course not. But you will be again, I promise.'

'I love you guys.'

'And we love you.'

Mum and Dad didn't question me when I arrived home—just opened their arms and hugged me, then put me to bed. I think I heard Mum muttering something about Marcus never playing under fine skies ever again, but that was just temper talking. I switched off the light and lay staring at the darkness for a few seconds. Exhausted but not able to sleep: a poisonous mixture. Sighing, I sat up and gave in to temptation, opening iPlayer on my laptop. Searching through the recent broadcasts, I found footage of the night's concert from Rockport. Thumbing the timeline to the point where Marcus walked off stage, I watched the replay. He was in the zone playing 'Out in the Cold' then froze, hand poised over guitar strings. Seeing it from the outside like this, it was incredibly awkward. He was going to have that clip come up again and again in every interview. The stillness and conflict within was etched on his face. I realized then that he had also had the tug of the audience to battle— his gift linked him to those he was playing, like my attraction to the sea. Yet he had done it, hadn't he? He might not win any prizes for doing it with grace, but he had stormed off with a face like fury to deal with my crisis.

The footage then cut to coverage of other stages while the commentators speculated on the reason for Marcus's abrupt departure. Then the conversation moved to the technical problems and some pitying comments at Marcus's expense at getting the blast from the feedback.

'Of course, that's standard decibels at a Black Sabbath gig,' joked one music critic. 'These modern guys have gone soft.'

'Yeah, but at least this generation will be able to hear when they reach fifty.'

The footage returned to the stage as Marcus, Michael, and Pete walked back an hour later. Marcus wasn't smiling—not so unusual for him as he was known to be serious, but neither did he take the front man role as he normally would. Michael made the repeat apology and explained how they were going to finish their set, putting the start time of the Gifted gig back. This didn't please the live broadcasters but cheered up the crowd. The field that had emptied during the intermission rapidly filled up as spectators abandoned the other stages for the main event.

I reached out to the screen and stroked the profile of my soulfinder. He looked so vulnerable up there, having to sing when he'd just been through such a confusing episode. As the music started though, he appeared to recover, moving down to take his position at the central mic. By the end, it would have been hard to know that anything was wrong. I couldn't tell if his gift had been as strong as usual. Maybe he didn't know how to turn it off? But I did take some pleasure in the fact that he had recovered most of the reputation damage his mission for me had caused.

He would be OK without me, that was clear. But would I be OK without him? I was going to have to learn how to live without a soulfinder.

Chapter· 18

Back at the family breakfast table, it was comforting to watch the usual morning behaviour of my parents: Dad in his rumpled T-shirt and pyjama trousers playing with his cereal, Mum already dressed checking the weather forecasts on her tablet. The only odd thing was what they weren't saying; they hadn't even asked me what had happened, which must mean that someone had already told them everything.

'Who was it?' I asked, stirring my cereal. 'Summer?'

'What do you mean, sweetheart? Who was what?' asked Mum, glancing at Dad. Gotcha, parents: you do know!

'Who told you of my complete cluster bomb of a disaster at the festival?'

'You weren't a disaster—we saw your performance. Got it recorded for you,' Dad said proudly.

I sighed. 'Not that. I meant the rest.'

Mum sipped her tea. 'No, not Summer. Victor Benedict called and gave us the full story.'

'Oh Lord, in that case, you must think me a complete idiot—and a traitor to savants.'

'Don't talk nonsense, Angel. He said you made a couple of slips—the phone being the worst. How many times have we told you to put a passcode on it?'

I slumped. 'A million.'

Mum nodded. 'Exactly, but as for what happened yesterday,

214

he says it wasn't your fault—and that you were let down by him and his brothers. They should have realized that you could be targeted after the first attempt to snatch you went wrong. But they had got it into their heads that Gifted were the real target—Kurt Voss to be exact.'

I picked up a pen and drew circles on a piece of junk mail lying on the table that promised me I'd win millions if I only entered their competition. 'Well, that does make more sense: he is mega famous and I'm nobody.'

Dad cleared his throat. 'Not so, love. You are our special ray of sunshine.'

I waved that away. 'Of course, I'm special to you guys. I meant in the world's eyes.'

'Even by that measure you've become something of a name in your own right.' Mum turned her tablet so I could see the gossip pages of a tabloid. There was a picture of me sitting on the beach with my back against Marcus's chest. It must've been taken with a telescopic lens and fortunately missed out on the sea cutting his name into the sand. Instead, it had an artistic grainy effect, which made us both look really cool. I couldn't stop the little flip of delight at seeing how good we were together. I scrolled down to read the text. *Marcus Cohen captures his own angel. Hearts are breaking in teen bedrooms across the world as Marcus Cohen gets serious with newcomer Angel Campbell (17), singer with London band Seventh Edition.* The rest of the article spun a lot from that not very much, digging up the fact that I was still at school but destined, it was claimed, for big things.

As if.

'He looks a nice enough lad,' said Mum generously. 'But he has been a fool, hasn't he?'

'No more than me. I rushed things. Spoiled what little chance we had.'

Dad huffed. 'I'm very cross with the whole pack of them.'

A statement like this was so unexpected from my quiet dad that I gaped. 'With whom?'

'Those Benedicts for a start.' He pushed away his cereal and topped up his cup of tea. 'I asked Will to return you in one piece but it doesn't take a genius to see that you've been hurt by all this—not to mention put your life at risk.'

True: pieces of my heart were scattered like confetti between here and Rockport.

He added a spoonful of sugar, forgetting he had given it up a year ago. 'And as for this young rock star—he's the last person I'd let through that door right now. Not appreciating the wonderful gift that is my daughter! He should be . . . ' Dad brandished the teaspoon at me but couldn't think of a suitable threat, not that didn't sound like it came out of a nineteenth-century melodrama.

'Made to sing kiddie songs in a silly costume on CBeebies for the rest of his life?' I suggested evilly.

Dad smiled. 'Yes, exactly.'

'But he was my soulfinder—and I messed up big time.'

'We know, love,' said Mum, putting away her tablet. 'But you're both so young: maybe when you've had a chance to grow up a bit you'll be ready to try that again. At the moment, your relationship is so off balance, what with him being so famous and successful and you being . . . '

'At school,' I finished for her.

'Not that we don't think you too can be famous and successful in your own right,' said Dad stoutly.

'But we shouldn't wish that on her, should we? Not with us being savants and having to keep that quiet,' countered Mum.

'Oh flipping heck, it's all such a mess.' I buried my head in my hands. 'You can't un-famous people—Kurt and Marcus already rate the front pages.'

'And so do you now. I guess we will have to settle for you being well known and discreet about your gift.' Mum frowned, a little doubtful.

Dad chuckled. 'That will be a new one for you, eh, Angel?'

'Don't waste energy worrying about that. It's not likely I'll meet any of them again after how I left it last night. I'm not sure I even want to. I've had my five minutes of fame and that's enough for me.'

The home phone rang. I was surprised that anyone was calling as it was still early and those that knew what had gone on at the festival would be giving me a chance to sleep in. When I didn't move, Mum answered.

'Hello?' She held out the receiver. 'It's Matt for you. Do you feel like talking to him?'

'Sure—he'll be wondering where I ran off to,' I explained. I got up and walked into the living room to take the call. 'Hey, Matt.'

'Angel cake, where are you?' His words were slurred.

'You're up early.'

'Not gone to bed—been selly . . . celebrating.' He burped. 'Hey, Henry, say hi to Angel.' There was the sound of the phone being passed over.

'Angel, why aren't you here?' asked Henry, also far from sober. 'You've missed, like, the best party!'

'I had to get home, sorry. What are you celebrating?'

'Moment.' The phone was handed back, dropped, curses followed, then picked up.

'We've only gone and got ourselves a record deal, Angel: can you believe it? That dumbass Jay is not so much a dumbass— all that hanging around Barry Hungerford has paid off.'

'Oh wow—congratulations!'

'It's for you too, Angel. Barry made that very clear—quote "the little Angel girl has to be part of the lineup" unquote.'

Even though I had been as low as low could be, I felt my spirits rise a little at that. I hugged myself in glee. 'How did Jay react to that?'

Matt snorted. 'Oh, he was *very* pleased. *Wouldn't* have had it any other way. But we've got a meeting at Hungerford's office in Soho on Monday. Can you be there?'

'Of course—just email me the details.'

'Will do. See you later.'

'No, you won't, you big lummox: I'm already home, aren't I?'

'Oh yeah. I forgot.' His brain was on slow setting. 'Why did you miss your chance to play with Gifted, tweetiepie?'

'Oh that? It just didn't work out.'

He called Kurt a bad name and hiccupped. 'That's what these famous guys are like; I did warn you. Blow hot and cold.'

I just remembered that I'd left Freddie and Black Adder behind. How could I have forgotten? 'Matt, are you sober enough to do me a favour?'

'Anything, love. You're our ticket to sweet success.'

'Can you pick up my gear from the instrument store—my amp and violins?'

'No problem. It's not like you to forget Freddie.'

'I had a lot on my mind yesterday.'

'OK, Angel: consider it done.'

'Thanks.'

I was dressed and sitting in the sunshine in our back garden when I had my next set of visitors. Mum showed Summer, Misty, and Alex out of the kitchen door, handing Alex a tray of iced homemade lemonade. She knew better than to give it to Misty to carry.

'Hey, guys!' I took out my earbuds and waved them to join me on the rug under the cherry tree.

'What were you listening to?' asked Misty, sitting cross-legged beside me and checking the playlist on my iPod. 'Oh.'

'Pathetic, aren't I?' I'd been listening to Black Belt's back catalogue on a music streaming service. 'Give me points for not watching the videos too.'

'Not pathetic; completely understandable.' Misty sipped her drink and gave a little shudder. 'So cold.'

'So good,' murmured Alex, nibbling her ear.

'Cut it out.' Misty grinned at him, which was hardly very effective at persuading him she wanted him to stop.

Feeling a lot jealous of their easy display of love, I changed the subject. 'So what happened after Summer and I left? Did Jennifer show up?'

Misty rolled her eyes. 'No, but she sent Brian a text claiming she had a sudden family emergency.'

The hollow in the pit of my stomach grew worse. 'So they all got away? I nearly drowned and nobody is to blame?'

'Seems that way,' said Alex, 'but I don't think for one second that Victor is going to let it rest there. He's on their track, convinced Davis has not given up on his idiotic plan to expose us.'

'It all feels so unfair. So I climbed in that container myself, did I? Decided it would be a hoot to try a Houdini?'

'It doesn't make sense to anyone outside the savant world so that's why the Benedicts are keeping the story quiet. They've persuaded Marcus and Kurt not to mention it to anyone and the crane driver is hardly going to want to confess he dumped you in the harbour.'

I curled my fingernails into my palm. 'But I want justice.'

'Of course you do,' said Summer. 'But as Alex says, it might not come immediately. You'll have to trust the Benedicts to do right by you.'

'My trust is rather at a low ebb at the moment.'

'I know—with good reason.' She left it at that, rather than make things worse by repeating her arguments until I got annoyed.

I flopped on my back, trying to recapture my better mood. I held up my fingers, capturing the leaves and ripening cherries in their frame. 'Oh, guys, I have something good to tell you. Jay got us a deal with Barry Hungerford, the record producer. Looks like Seventh Edition is going somewhere.'

'That's great, Angel,' said Alex. 'You deserve it.'

'So last night wasn't the only chance you were going to get, was it?' said Misty brightly, referring to my missed opportunity to play with Gifted.

'How very *Sound of Music* you are, Misty: when one door closes, the good Lord opens a window,' I chuckled, paraphrasing Maria.

'Don't knock it: sometimes commonplace sayings hold the truth.'

'You mean like absence makes the heart grow fonder?' I asked, thinking of Marcus and me.

'Or time heals all wounds,' said Summer gently. 'I think you should let Marcus process the new information about the savant world. He'll have Will on hand with Margot to keep reminding him that he's got a connection to you he can't ignore. He'll come round.'

'I'm not sure I want him to come round.' Leaving it at that, I rolled over onto my stomach and put my forehead on my arms, hiding my expression. I had that wobbly feeling around my mouth that heralded a good cry. What was wrong with me—happy one moment, in despair the next? Oh yeah, I'd met my soulfinder: that was the problem. My friends tactfully moved on to other subjects and left me to my moping.

I got up to see them out and spent the early afternoon quietly playing with the garden hose, honing my control, seeing how far I could push my powers. After the scary time shut in the container, I had to reassure myself I had some energy left and I'd not blown it all by holding back the sea. I could tell Mum and Dad were worried about me. They weren't used to me staying at home and, well, being more like them in refusing to go out. Mum kept making helpful suggestions—ring a friend, make an appointment with a hairdresser, go for a walk with the neighbour's dog—but I ducked each one. Dad did drive me to the local phone shop and waited outside while I replaced my lost mobile. The assistants in there all knew me from school. They were sweet about my appearance on television and the news stories, teasing me for becoming famous.

'The press will have forgotten me tomorrow,' I told them, attempting a smile.

From the puzzled reaction my modesty received, I knew I had to be acting very out of character. Old Angel would have been lapping up the attention. How to explain that looking at the photos of the festival was like ripping a plaster off a wound?

'They won't forget,' Sophie assured me as she packaged my phone back in its box. She had left my school last year and knew me a little from the sixth form common room. 'You were really great: we were all amazed. You were good at the gigs round here but that was something else.'

I pondered her words as I got back in the car. I'd been 'something else' because I had been plugged into the extra power of my soulfinder. Even my triumph was a fraud, now I thought about it. I was beginning to think I should bow out of the meeting with Barry Hungerford: he wasn't signing up whom he was expecting after that performance, just her shadow.

Will you just listen to yourself? snarled Angry Angel, giving my moping self a kick up the butt. Enough with the self-pity!

Forget Marcus. You were a musician before he came along. What better way to test your real talent than seeing how far this deal will take you? You don't totally suck as a performer without him so just get on with it. The guys are depending on you.

Pitiful Angel whined and licked wounds but Angry Angel took her shoulders and gave her a shake.

Pack it in! I called for order in my warring sub-conscience. Angry Angel had made some good points. I couldn't bear the thought of spending my life waiting for a guy to get his act together: that was so lame. I would climb on board the adventure that was offered, not worry about the one that had stalled on the starting grid.

I wasn't sure what I'd been expecting of a record producer's office but Barry Hungerford's was not it. His company was on the third floor of an old eighteenth-century townhouse overlooking Soho Gardens, a little park in the centre of the Bohemian district of London. We were in the middle of the theatre and restaurant district but the area still held the edge of being part of the red-light zone so I suppose the record producer thought that gave him some street cred. The stairs were narrow and the carpet on the tatty side. The only reassuring notes were the framed photos on the wall: it looked like a rock hall of fame—nearly all the most important bands and artists of the last twenty years had their mugshot here. Matt poked me in the back as on the turn to the third-floor landing we came face to face with several shots of Gifted when they were starting out. Kurt Voss looked like an alley cat back then, not the sleek and dangerous puma he had become, long black hair hanging over his eyes, a studded collar round his neck. The final photo just by the buzzer for reception was a recent one of Black Belt, Marcus looking moody as he sang, his band mates lost in the music: it was a great picture. I sincerely hoped Jennifer hadn't taken it or I would have to hate it on principle.

How had Brian reacted to the news that Jennifer had been a spy in the camp? Had Kurt even told him?

Jay rubbed his hands nervously then pressed the buzzer. A handsome young man with shaved black hair and lanky frame opened the door. He had sharp cheekbones and an expression to match.

'Hi, everyone. I'm Ali, Mr Hungerford's PA. He is expecting you—just wrapping up a call to the US. What can I get you to drink?' He ushered us into a little boardroom that looked out onto the garden square. The room was a contrast to the stairs: stripped oak floor, big table with metal legs and clear Perspex top, chairs made out of moulded plastic, probably by some up-and-coming designer. Prints of classic album covers decorated the walls. It felt a little cold. I had the odd image I was sitting in a shark's mouth, not helped by the pigeon-deterring spikes on the windowsill that looked like rows of teeth.

We made our orders. Jay had the balls to order something complicated—an espresso I think he said. I asked for water and slid into a chair at the end of the table, far from the one at the top with arms—a carver they were called in dining-room sets. I imagined Hungerford sitting there to slice and dice his deals.

Five minutes of awkward conversation passed, then Ali was back with the drinks, Barry Hungerford coming in behind. He was dressed in a navy blue Paul Smith suit so new that it surely had a few flakes of tailor's chalk still on it. A bright cerise tie throttled his neck under the crisp white collar of his light blue shirt. His short brown hair with fair highlights was swept back from his forehead, eyes steely grey and hungry for the next deal.

'Hello, everyone. Thanks for coming in. Angel, you're looking pretty today.' He came round and kissed my cheek as if we were the best of friends.

I had made an effort for the meeting, putting on a favourite pale green silk top, but the last time I had seen him he had been treating me like athletes' foot. Now I was flavour of the month. Sensible Angel whispered to me to take this as a lesson in the fickleness of fame. One day I was Hungerford's trump; next I'd be his discard.

'Thanks, Mr Hungerford,' I said, acknowledging his compliment while Jay struggled to smile at the fact he had gone over to me first.

'Barry, please.' Hungerford went to the top seat and took his place. 'Where's the fricking champagne, Ali?' (He didn't say fricking but I can't bring myself to transcribe his every swear word). 'Go fetch a fricking bottle—we're going to need it to toast our deal.'

Another suit came in—a middle-aged man who looked like a lawyer: collar and tie, intelligent face and salt-and-pepper hair.

'This is Neil: he's got the contract. Did you bring your own legal representation?' Barry directed the question to Jay.

'Er, no, Barry.' Jay looked like he was kicking himself.

'Then you'll want to have another pair of eyes look at this before you sign, but for today I hope we'll make a gentlemen's agreement—a handshake—if you like what you hear.'

Jay tried to look as if he made such deals every day. 'Yes, sure, that'll be fine.'

Hungerford passed copies of the agreement to each of us. I was the last to receive mine so was aware already that Jay wasn't pleased by what he was reading. I looked down at the first page.

'Angel Dares?' asked Jay, trying to keep a hold of his temper.

Hungerford leant back in his chair, fingers steepled. 'Yeah, the marketing guys say that name tests out well. It has an edge, gesturing to the exploratory nature of your songwriting, taking risks.'

Jay looked blank.

'And of course it highlights your main attraction and her personality.' Hungerford winked at me.

I didn't know where to look.

Matt leant closer and whispered in my ear. 'Ready to steal the limelight, Angel?'

'And I'm sure you'll recognize that Angel here is your selling point. Guys like her—girls want to be her surrounded by all these gorgeous boys.' He looked over to Ali standing at the door. 'I do like that—ticks so many boxes its fricking unreal.' He beamed at us all.

'You're moving Angel up to front man—front girl?' asked Matt.

'Frick me, yes! She'll be sharing the spot with Jay. That's fricking new and fresh—there's no other leading band at the moment with that lineup so you'll get more attention.' He took our stunned silence as assent. 'Now "Star-Crossed" has to be your first single—the Romeo and Juliet reference very classy. I'm thinking Angel on the cover in a kind of modern version of the balcony scene. Angel's already in the news as Marcus Cohen's girlfriend so a song about doomed love will play really well with the music press—human interest angle, you know?'

He was planning to turn my heartbreak into my career break.

'I don't suppose you can engineer a little falling out with Marcus on single release day, Angel?' Hungerford asked in a jovial tone, only half-joking. 'It would be worth at least a hundred thousand fricking downloads.'

Where to start with my refusals? 'I don't think . . . ' I began.

Jay cut across me. 'We'll do whatever is necessary to make it a success, Barry. None of this need be real, need it? Stars date each other all the time to make a story for their publicists.'

Hungerford nodded and smiled at his star pupil. 'Exactly: no real pain involved for any of the parties, just good photo opportunities. I'll talk to Marcus's people about it.'

This was getting out of hand. I stood up. 'No.'

'No what?' asked Hungerford, his smile dimming.

'I will not use my relationship with Marcus to launch our band. You'll have to find some other way.'

'Sit down, Angel. We'll talk about this later,' hissed Jay. 'Don't worry, Barry: Angel's impulsive. Take no notice.'

Hungerford gave me a quizzical look. My fingers were shaking where I rested them on the tabletop. 'Let's leave that aside for now. Return to it after we've laid down the track in the studio.' He moved on to less inflammatory matters, touching on the next few months, how we would work on the first album, write or sample new material. Matt tugged at my shirt to get me to sit. He put his arm around me and gave me a quick squeeze.

'I won't let them do that to you,' he promised. 'Remember, Marcus would have to agree too and that is no more likely than he'd agree to go on stage naked. Let him put these guys off. You don't have to take the flak for it.'

I nodded. Of course Matt was right: Marcus wouldn't compromise his art for a story. Dislike him as I did, even I knew he had more integrity than that.

At the end of the meeting, Ali opened the champagne and called in a waiting photographer. Hungerford made sure I stood in the middle as we toasted our agreement. Jay was the one who shook hands with him over the pages of the unsigned document; Hungerford insisted on kissing my wrist, laughing at his courtly gesture but clearly enjoying himself rather too much.

Jay sidled up to me. 'Angel, I just want to say that I think it's great—the name change, the contract, everything.'

What was his agenda here? Ever ready to be suspicious of him, I waited for him to explain. 'Really?'

'No really, I do. I realize I've been a bit unfair to you in the past.'

'A bit?'

He ruffled his quiff, apology-mode not a natural one to him. 'A lot then. And I'm sorry. I guess I was jealous.'

Now that seemed like the first honest thing he'd ever said to me. 'Of what?'

'You—I knew you had the potential to outshine the rest of us and that scared me.'

I didn't trust this laying-his-soul-bare Jay, but at least I had an answer to that concern. 'But Jay, I've always liked being in a band because, well, because we're a band. It's the sound we make together that's the thing I like—up front or backing, that's not important.'

He looked sceptical.

'It's true. Whatever we're called, we make our own music together, and that's what's going to make us succeed. And I really believe we can. At Rockport, we started to go places.' I refused to give in to the niggling doubt that my performance had only excelled because it had been Marcus-enhanced.

Jay patted my arm awkwardly, respecting my personal space. 'So new start then, Angel? For us I mean? We work as a team? No one gets left behind?'

'Sure, Jay.'

As we filed out, I tucked the contract deep in my bag.

'I'm getting this looked at,' I whispered to Matt, 'separately from Jay. I appreciate he's trying to make this work, but I wouldn't put it past him to sell his mother out to get a break, let alone us.'

Matt gave me a peck on the cheek. 'Good thinking. Cover our backs for us, Angel?'

I gave a firm nod. 'You bet.'

We parted by the railings around the centre of the square, Matt heading for Piccadilly as I cut through the garden towards Oxford Circus. I hadn't got very far when I heard someone running up behind me. Thinking it was Matt who had forgotten to tell me something, I turned.

It was Marcus. He was looking amazing in his grey jeans and white shirt over dark blue T-shirt. Why did he have to be so gorgeous? It undermined my common sense every time.

'Angel!' He stopped short of me, hesitant as to whether I'd welcome him to come closer.

'Oh, hi. What are you doing here?' My eyes flicked up to Hungerford's office. Of course. 'You were up there?'

He dug his hands in his pockets. 'Yeah. In Barry's office.'

'Did you set that up for us—ask for the meeting as a favour?'

'No. Barry told me after he'd spoken to Jay.' He rubbed the back of his neck. 'You happy with the deal?'

'Ecstatic,' I said flatly, folding my arms.

'The name change and everything?'

'That part was very embarrassing. My band mates are going to hate me.'

'No they won't—not when you take them to the top.'

My brain was doing a fast catch up. Marcus knew about the details of our deal—had known before I did. 'You complete arse!' I swivelled on my heel and stomped off.

'What?' I'd caught Marcus by surprise. He hurried to catch up with me. 'What did I do?'

'"*Oh Angel, I don't suppose you can engineer a little falling out with Marcus on single release day?*" Was that your idea too? You'd use our . . . our relationship so casually to sell records? I thought you had more integrity than that.'

He caught me at the gate and pulled me off the path onto

the grass so I had to face him. 'No, Angel: it was nothing like that at all. You have to believe me.' He brushed his fingers down my cheek. 'Barry suggested it and I told him to see what you said to the offer. I'm proud of you for refusing.'

He had been listening in.

'You were testing me?'

Marcus shrugged. 'I guess it might seem like that—but I had to know.'

'Know what?'

'If this was real.' He gestured between us.

Had I not done enough to prove that to him without jumping through yet more hoops he cared to put in my way? I pulled his fingers off my arm where they anchored me. 'What's real is me walking out on you, Marcus. Shame there are no cameras to capture the moment, hey? Barry coulda got his story today and done a quick release of the single. By the time "Star-Crossed" comes out, we'll be history.' I started walking away.

'Angel!'

I whirled round. 'No! Don't you Angel me, Marcus Cohen! You've treated me like dirt—suspicious ever since we met. Testing me is the final straw. You've never thought about how your behaviour affects me—not once. You never understood that all I wanted was to be allowed to love you.' You are not going to cry; you are not going to cry, I chanted inside. 'Just leave me alone from now on, OK?'

I can't.

Using telepathy was a low blow after all the times he had refused. 'I think you'll find you can.' I set my shoulders and walked away.

229

Chapter 19

It felt like entering a dream world to go back to school on Tuesday after the life-changing events of the last few days. The summer term in the lower sixth is an odd time at best: we were relaxing after AS exams, some drifting off on work experience, teachers starting the A-level syllabus and trying to convince us to concentrate even though the sun was shining. Add on to that the fact that I felt I no longer belonged there. I moved slowly about between class and sixth-form block as if nothing was quite real to me, like the diver I'd seen swimming in an aquarium behind plate glass, separate from the visitors watching her feed the fish. The common room realized something was going on too. They treated me like their own little celebrity, enjoying the reflected glory of my brief brush with the stars. One showed me Fresh's much retweeted tweet that had claimed I was going to play for Gifted. I laughed it off with a joke but it hurt to do so. I kept quiet about my offer of a record deal, having passed the papers to Mum to get checked out with a savant lawyer friend of hers. I was not going to blurt it out and then have an embarrassing climb down if it fell through.

So I was sitting in the music block staring out of the window in composition class, dreaming of the future, when the head teacher appeared at the door. I hadn't wanted to put on the school headphones—not after my experience in the boot of Davis' car—so had been delaying starting work on my piece; that made me the first to hear his knock. An extremely short man, Mr Herriot had to go up on tiptoe to look in the glass panel just as I did, his spectacles flashing in and out of view like a lantern buoy bobbing on the waves. This shared humiliation was one of the reasons I was fond of him.

'Mr Garfield, apologies for interrupting your class,' the head said, opening the door and tapping the teacher on the shoulder.

The music teacher took off his headphones: he'd been working on the keyboard and hadn't noticed the new arrival until Mr Herriot touched him. 'Sorry, Mr Herriot, can I help you?'

There were six others in the class and, naturally, they all took off headphones to eavesdrop. Mr Herriot appeared extraordinarily agitated, flyaway red hair looking like he had just been standing in the backdraft of a jet engine.

'Yes—I mean, no, Mr Garfield. I have a very special visitor who would like to talk to Angel. Ah, there you are, Angel. Would you mind stepping out of the class for a moment?'

My first thought was that Marcus had come to find me—but no, Mr Herriot wouldn't even know who he was and certainly wouldn't walk him around the school like he was royalty. Still wondering, I stood up. Before I could come out from behind my desk, Kurt walked into the room. The gasp from my classmates was audible. Shocked, I leant my hands on the keyboard, producing an ugly chord.

Kurt grinned. 'Ow, Angel, I thought you were musical?'

I couldn't think of a single thing to say. Fortunately, the head teacher stepped in.

'Class, as I'm sure you will have noticed, our special visitor is Kurt Voss. And yes, it really is him.' Mr Herriot rubbed his hands together, no doubt checking his memory banks for 'suitable words to say to gob-smacked sixth formers when rock god comes to school'.

'Hi, guys,' Kurt gave them a relaxed wave.

What are you doing here? I asked him, using telepathy so as to keep this private.

Impressing the hell out of your classmates it would seem. He winked at me. So he had come to terms with the fact that he was telepathic, had he? Kurt turned to my music teacher. 'So you're Angel's teacher? Mr Garfield, like that fat ginger cat?' Only Kurt would be so brazen. Of course Mr Garfield's nickname was Fat Cat; he was a portly man so was crying out to be so christened by generations of pupils. I hope Kurt hadn't picked that out of my head.

'Er . . . Kurt . . . Mr Voss . . . it's an honour.' I'd never seen Mr Garfield so star struck as he shook hands. '*Jagged* is my favourite concept album ever.'

'Thanks, man. Call me Kurt, please.'

Mr Herriot was beckoning me to find my feet again. 'Hurry up, Angel. I'm sure Mr Voss—Kurt—is a busy man.'

Kurt shrugged. 'It's fine, Nick.' Nick? The head teacher was called Nick? I'd always thought his colleagues knew him as Nicholas. 'I've a few minutes. I was planning on spiriting Angel away for the afternoon if that's OK with you? I've got her parents' permission.'

'Yes, yes, they rang me. Well then, er, Kurt, perhaps the students have some questions for you about the music business?'

That's right, Mr Herriot: turn this excruciating moment into an educational opportunity, why don't you?

'Sure. Fire away, guys.' Kurt perched on the corner of Mr Garfield's desk as I quietly packed my school bag. My friends lost their shock-and-awe expressions and dug up some decent questions about how Kurt became the mega-success he is.

None of them succumbed to the temptation to squeal 'We love you!' and 'Can I have your babies?' though I thought Mr Garfield looked quite close to it.

The bell rang for the end of lesson. The school erupted into movement as a thousand of us began to shift rooms. Mr Herriot said some appropriate words—don't ask me what— then dismissed the rest of the class.

'You coming, Angel?' asked Kurt.

'Where?' I asked. I pulled what I intended to be an earnest face. 'I mean, I have biology next.'

Mr Garfield and the head teacher looked shocked at my hesitation but Kurt must have guessed I was only joking because he smiled. 'I thought I'd take you to lunch—in Paris.'

'Seriously?' My voice squeaked. Though I was still cross with him for expecting me to play after my ordeal, I couldn't help but be impressed.

'There she is—the old Angel.' Kurt appeared relieved to have surprised me. 'Dead serious. Margot's just picking up your passport from home. We're flying over to a favourite restaurant of mine.'

'This is so cool!' I regretted my classmates had already left to spread the word of my treat.

'I take that as a yes. Thanks, Nick—Mr Garfield. Let's go.'

Mr Herriot escorted us off the school grounds to where Kurt's car was waiting. We had to pass through the crowds of students on lesson change-over and I could hear the gossip doing the rounds. Kids came running from all directions just to get a glimpse of Kurt. I was both thrilled and embarrassed to be running the gauntlet like this. The embarrassment racked up a notch or two above thrilled when I heard Mr Herriot mentioning the fundraiser for the new school auditorium. He had to do that to me, didn't he?

'Well, if you are producing talent like Angel here, you're

gonna need a decent performance space, Nick,' Kurt agreed. 'Contact my people about it, OK?'

We got in the car and I bent my head to my knees and groaned. 'Tell me he did not do that. My head teacher did not just beg money from you?'

Kurt laughed. 'Of course he did. It's his job, darlin'. I'll have him calling it the Kurt Voss hall before I'm finished. John, take us to the airport please.' The car pulled away. Through the blacked-out windows I could see the stunned school population watching us leave. The leather of the seat squeaked as Kurt turned to rest a warm hand on my hair. 'Forget about it, Angel. Tell me how you've been after that psycho took you prisoner?'

I sat up and brushed my hair off my face. 'I'm OK, I think.'

Kurt nodded grimly, studying my expression. 'You're not totally OK but you'll get there. I'm sorry I didn't get how bad it was for you. Victor only told me the full story after you left. Must have been terrifying.'

'It was—but no permanent damage done. I didn't have to do anything to reveal my gift to anyone.' I felt a little less angry now I realized he hadn't grasped the severity of what had happened when he had appeared in Marcus' trailer.

He sucked on his lower lip and looked away.

'I'm sorry you found out about us that way. It's not always like this, Kurt. Savant skills are usually just nice gifts to have. People don't normally hunt us down like rats just because we can do a few little extra things.'

He turned back to me and gave me a superstar grin. 'I know, darlin'. I was worrying about you. I know that cold dude Victor has a plan to get Davis off the streets but I won't feel happy for me and mine until I know he's neutralized.'

Me and mine. It was heartwarming to hear that Kurt counted me in that group. 'Have you worked out what your gift is yet?'

He gave a gruff laugh. 'It seems you called it right. Will thinks I have an instinct for people's motives, like a tracker dog sniffing out drugs. I can live with that—I always have.'

'So how did you not guess about Jennifer?'

He grimaced. 'I knew about her being untrustworthy but not why. I told Brian she was using him but he liked the ... well, being her guy.' He shook his head. 'We've all had our fair share of girlfriends who have complicated reasons for being with us—most are attracted by the fame. I put her in that group and kept away from her as much as possible. Margot did the same. She said they had a professional working relationship rather than a friendship.'

That was true. I'd not seen Kurt or Margot hanging out with Jennifer at any stage. She'd been Brian's girl, not one of the band's inner circle.

'What have you told Brian?'

'That Jennifer had been working for a journalist. That's the truth, isn't it?'

'Yes. Oh, poor Brian.'

'He's philosophical about it. Many more fish in the sea.'

'Yeah, and hopefully the next one won't be a two-faced savant-hating bitch.'

Kurt bumped knuckles with me in agreement.

The car turned into RAF Northolt in west London, an airstrip occasionally used by private jets that wanted to avoid queues at Heathrow. A white plane with the Gifted logo stood waiting on the tarmac. Inside I was dead impressed but I couldn't let Kurt get away with such flaunting of his wealth.

'Own jet, Kurt? My, aren't we getting big for our boots?' I teased.

'Hired—for the tour, darlin'.' Kurt tweaked my nose. 'Marketing idea for the name to be painted on it.'

'Can't hear you screaming your protests.' I grinned.

'Course not. Boyhood dream come true.' He got out and guided me across to the steps up.

I looked about me. 'What, no border controls?'

'Margot's sorted that out for us.'

Entering the cabin I found Margot and Will waiting for us, both looking very happy to be there. Clearly this was something of a treat for them too. 'Hi, guys, how are you?'

Will got up and hugged me. 'We should be asking you that. Ready for a trip to Paris?'

'Beats dissecting lamb hearts in the biology lab any day.'

Will smiled. 'Yeah, I can see how it wouldn't be hard to give that a miss.'

Kurt came up behind me and slapped me on the back. 'What's that? You want me to order lamb hearts for you at the restaurant to catch up?'

'Don't you dare!' I took my seat and buckled up.

The restaurant proved to be at the top of the Eiffel Tower—trust Kurt to go for something so sensational. I had no idea why I was there during the middle of an ordinary school day. I was completely inappropriately dressed for the upmarket dining room with sweeping views across the city, wearing my usual school casual of jeans and shirt. Kurt wasn't much better but he was a rock star so could get away with the scruffy T-shirt and leather jacket. Margot and Will had both spiffed up for the occasion, having had more warning. As it didn't seem to bother any of them or the waiters, I decided to ignore it. The only sneaky regret was that Marcus wasn't there. It would have made for one very romantic rendezvous.

Stop it. That relationship is history. Don't pine after him, you spineless girl, scolded Sensible Angel.

The waiter put my crème brûlée in front of me. To think normally I'd be eating crisps and an apple in the common room right now.

'So, Angel, as you might guess from all this, I've an offer for you.' Kurt sipped his espresso.

I tore my eyes away from the seagulls crisscrossing our window. 'An offer? You know about the record deal with Mr Hungerford, right?'

'Yeah, I told Barry he needed to snap you up before others got after you. Was the offer fair?'

I thought through the pages of legalese that my mother's friend was checking. 'Not sure yet. He seems to want to shove me up front, which isn't going down so well with our old lead singer.'

'Yeah, I guess not but Jay strikes me as the kinda guy who'd adapt when he sees what he stands to gain.'

I nodded and broke the sugar glaze on top of my dessert with my spoon.

Margot leaned forward. 'What we have in mind won't cut across that deal, Angel. It's about Saturday.'

'We want you to play like you should have done at Rockport,' said Kurt, 'if that head case hadn't half drowned you.'

My spoon stopped halfway to my mouth.

'They want you to play at the O2,' said Will, realizing I needed it spelling out before I would completely grasp what was going on.

'Really?' I asked.

'Yep. How does that sound?'

I closed my eyes briefly, remembering that Marcus would be there. I wasn't ready to see him yet, the wounds too raw. But I could avoid him, couldn't I? The arrangement was to play with Gifted, not Black Belt.

'OK, yes.'

Kurt's smile went crafty. 'Just "yes"—not YES PLEASE, YOU SERIOUSLY WONDERFUL ROCK GOD!!!'

He was listening into my head. 'Cut out the telepathic snooping. Just because you've learned how to do it, doesn't mean you should.'

He grinned.

'Jeez, we need to send you to savant school.' I waved my spoon at him, sending my crème brûlée slithering to the tablecloth. Oops. I scooped it up before a waiter spotted it. 'If you eavesdrop on me, I'll get Summer to do the same to you.'

At least that got him worried. 'OK. Won't do so again, promise.' But it was hard to believe him when his eyes were glinting with mischief. Like Marcus, he appeared to have much stronger telepathic powers than me, which came with the ability to snoop into other people's thoughts if you didn't watch what you were doing. 'So you'll play?'

'I'll play.' I nudged him with my elbow. 'You know, Kurt, I'd've said yes even if you just took me to MacDonald's, you know? This is a bit over-kill.' I gestured to the incredible view, amazing food and hovering waiters.

He chuckled. 'That might be what you think you're worth, but I thought you deserved this.'

On the flight back I had time to catch up with Will. Uriel had good news: Tarryn had secured the job in Colorado so there was another savant couple that had managed to mesh their life plans. There was talk of a wedding later in the year.

'And what about you and Margot?' I probed.

Will reclined his seat and pretended to sleep.

'William Benedict, you *will* satisfy my insatiable curiosity.'

He opened one eye. 'Why? You are so easy to tease.' He folded his hands on his chest. 'It's early days yet, Angel. We've only known each other for a week.'

'But I bet it feels much longer.'

He raised a brow.

'I mean that in the totally positive sense that you are so prepared for each other it just feels like she's always been there.'

He sat his chair back to the upright position. 'Yes, you're right. I've hit the jackpot with her, haven't I?' His gaze sought her out. She was sitting with Kurt going through some business papers. 'Her gift is fascinating. She just listens to how someone sounds to her and she can tell so much about them, like how good a person is.'

I giggled as a funny idea struck me. 'Like those squirrels.'

'What squirrels?' Will looked puzzled.

'In *Charlie and the Chocolate Factory*—they tapped on the hazelnuts to tell if they were rotten. Violet Beauregarde wanted one as a pet but got chucked away as a bad nut instead.'

Will chuckled. 'You do have the oddest brain, Angel. Yeah, a little like that, though she's also learned to pick up signs for musical talent as well as character—incredibly helpful in her business. She says it's the sound equivalent of Sky seeing colour auras around people telling her what they are feeling.'

'So how are you going to work out where you live?'

'She says she can move from Amsterdam if we need. My business is only just getting on its feet but the personal protection game moves with the client so I'm not tied to one place either.'

'Looks to me as though there's a new savant who's in need of a special kind of protection so he doesn't blow the whole shebang in front of the world's media.'

Will rubbed his chin. 'That thought had kinda crossed my mind, but baby steps, remember?'

I sighed. 'I wish I had remembered.'

'You really messed up with Marcus? No getting back on track?'

I slapped his stomach. 'Excuse me: Marcus messed up with me! He set me a test of loyalty, can you believe it?' I told him all about the events in Barry Hungerford's office.

Will didn't look as annoyed for me as I expected. 'Poor guy. He's really not got your measure yet, has he?'

'What about poor Angel? I don't want to see Marcus ever again.' Liar.

'Don't blame you. But when you do—'

I opened my mouth to protest.

'You will, Angel. You know you will. It's inevitable: he's your soulfinder. *When* you do, make him beg your forgiveness. It will do him good to feel the petitioner, not the one granting the favour.'

'What do you mean?'

Will gestured to the quiet cabin of the private jet. 'All this stuff—celebrity trappings—does a guy's head in. Marcus has got so used to it that he now suspects everyone who makes friends with him of wanting a slice of the pie. He has forgotten how to use his instincts about people. Margot and Kurt have been saved from that by their gifts. I guess that's why Kurt's not got too puffed up over the last decade since he made the big time.'

'And what does the Savant Net think about having a new savant on the books who is a headline every time he sneezes?'

Will shrugged. 'Too late to turn back the clock. As long as he isn't famous for being a savant then I guess we can live with it.'

'And Marcus—his gift is on show.'

'Nobody puts it down to a special power so that has to pass too. We'll talk to him about control when he's ready.'

I rattled the ice in the bottom of my glass. 'Have you tried yet?'

'Angel, ever since you took off on Saturday, Marcus has

been locked in his hotel room writing, only emerging to growl at everyone and perform the last tour dates.'

I could just imagine the kind of lyrics he was writing. Ouch. 'I think I'm bad for him.'

Will laughed. 'No way, Angel: you are the best thing that will ever happen to him. He's a nice guy but he takes himself way too seriously. With you to even up that side of his character, you'll both do fine: you're the fuel in the relationship's engine, he can be the ballast.'

I tried to imagine our ship one day chugging away across the seas ahead but it seemed impossible. 'But neither of us are at the wheel at the moment—that boat's still in dry dock.'

'No: you've set sail, both of you, you just haven't quite got to grips with the fact.'

I hit him again for good measure. Smug I've-found-my-soulfinder-and-everything-is-going-well savants need taking down a peg or two.

He rubbed his stomach, pulling a ridiculous face. 'You are an evil girl. I've eaten too much to be beaten up by an annoying pixie.'

'And you are an attention-seeking fibber: I didn't hit you that hard.' I leaned closer. 'Anyway, William, I thought you bodyguard types had six packs of iron muscles.'

'Not just after lunch.' He ruffled my hair. 'Pest.'

Chapter 20

Standing in front of the dressing-room mirror, I checked my concert outfit for the twentieth time. Jennifer had wanted me to wear black at Rockport so naturally that was the last colour I was going to pick for my big night at the O2. I'd chosen a short white halter-neck dress, high heels, and silver belt. My hair was newly trimmed, touching my shoulders but swept up at the sides and fastened with diamante clasps in the shape of wings. I'd got make-up tips off a local beautician so my eyes were huge behind the silver and blue shadow she had sold me. Tiny crystals outlined the lids. I looked otherworldly. Only the battered shape of Freddie brought me back down to earth but I wasn't going to change him—he was as much a star of this piece as me, providing the voice to the breath I played into him with the bow.

I went through the steps of my pre-show ritual. I had deliberately asked to arrive late to the performance so I did not have to rub shoulders with the other members of Gifted and Black Belt. Marcus and his guys had already been onstage as my car dropped me at the performers' entrance. I had heard the familiar strains of their songs even from outside the huge white circus tent dome on the banks of the Thames. The sell-out crowd had been lapping it up. Marcus had evidently emerged from his cave and ceased growling in time for this big show.

Stop thinking about him. This is your night—your chance, Angry Angel had bellowed, kicking Lovelorn Angel out of her wallowing spot.

So now I was in front of my mirror alone in my dressing room, aware that all my family and friends were in the audience rooting for me. I was not going to think about my poxy soulfinder; I wasn't even going to think about how I was not going to think about him, OK?

Dang it all: I was rubbish at this not thinking malarkey.

Concentrate on your preparations. Great: Calm and Sensible Angel had made an appearance in my head after a long absence. I poured water into a beer glass and began the swirl and fountain mental exercises that focused my brain. I had just reached the high point—water roping around the glass like an eel—when there came a knock on the door.

'Blast!' Losing my grip, the water splashed over the dressing table, soaking the programme Margot had given me. 'Come in!'

Hoping against hope it was Marcus—you are not thinking about him, Angel!—I was briefly disappointed to find his band mates, Michael and Pete, in the doorway.

'Hey, how's our favourite violinist?' Michael asked.

'All right, Angel?' added Pete gruffly.

I wadded some tissues to soak up the worst of the water. 'Hi, guys. How did it go?'

Pete grinned. 'We were smokin' hot.'

I laughed. 'Good.'

Michael joined me in clearing up with a towel grabbed from the sink. 'You didn't listen?'

I looked away, not wanting to admit I had purposely avoided the chance to hear the first half of the concert. 'I couldn't sit still—too nervous.'

Michael threw the damp towel in the basin and gave me

a one-armed hug, careful not to rumple my costume. 'I can imagine. I threw up before our first time performing here.'

Pete winked at me. 'And today is our first time at the O2.'

I felt bad: I'd forgotten they were relative newbies too. 'Oh, Michael, you poor love. Do you want a mint?'

Michael shook his head. 'I'm fine now. But if you are feeling sorry for me, how about a kiss better?' He grinned and pointed to his lips.

I kissed his cheek and patted his shoulder. 'There—all better now.'

Pete slapped him around the head.

Michael gave a put-upon sigh. 'It was worth a try. Marcus hasn't put up any "No trespassing" signs yet.'

'Let's leave her to finish getting ready,' said Pete, tugging the back of Michael's T-shirt. 'We'll be watching. Hope it goes really well.'

'Thanks, Pete.'

Having shoved his friend out into the corridor, Pete hovered by the door.

'What is it?' I asked, catching sight of him in the mirror as I touched up my lip gloss.

'Don't I get one of those too?' He pointed to his cheek with a twinkle in his eye.

I went up on tiptoe and kissed him.

'Take no notice of Michael,' Pete whispered. 'Marcus has planted the signs but he just hasn't owned up to it yet.'

'Thanks, big guy.'

The two Black Belt band members headed off down the corridor to their dressing room. I told myself to be pleased that Marcus hadn't come. That would just have messed with my head, wouldn't it, and I needed to be clear thinking for this.

I glanced at the clock. Almost time. My song was to come near the end of the Gifted set at ten to ten if the concert was running to plan. I scrolled through my texts. Misty and Summer had both sent me good luck messages, as had every Benedict brother and their soulfinders except for Victor. He didn't do that kind of thing. School friends had also texted—as had my parents. Eek—so many people I could let down. My fingers suddenly felt like sausages, too clumsy to find the strings.

Why wasn't someone here to stop me getting all Angelish before I went on?

Angel: you'll be fine. Summer's message reached me loud and clear. She was with Misty and Alex out front.

I'm panicking here.

Of course you are. I'd be worried if you weren't.

How does that work?

Because—that was Misty joining in—*you'd not be your normal self. And it is your normal self that panics then plays so well. Alex, tell her.*

You'll be amazing. Alex was using a little touch of his persuasive gift to convince me. *You know what you're doing and that's all that is expected of you.*

I could feel myself purring under his touch like a cat being stroked. He is such a cool guy.

Thanks, everyone.

And even if you do mess up, added Misty briskly, *you'll do it in such a loveable way that no one will mind.*

But I don't want to mess up!

Then you won't, said Alex. I could sense he had just elbowed Misty to stop giving me so much truth.

Just do your best, Angel, said Summer.

I'll try. That was a promise I could make.

The stage manager tapped on the door.

'Miss Campbell, are you ready?'

I gave her a sassy grin. 'Ready as I'll ever be.'

'I like your shoes,' she said as she walked me to the wings. 'Where did you get them?'

I knew she was distracting me from my nerves but it worked. We chatted about the shoe stall in Camden Market for a bit then we were there. The noise as we went through the last door was incredible: Gifted were playing one of their most famous anthems, producing a tidal wave of sound that swept into the gut and took you bodily along with it.

'Wow!' I whispered but no one could hear me as the sound was deafening. The nice stage manager gave me a thumbs up. I returned the gesture.

'Ready on my mark,' she said, holding her earpiece to her right ear.

Kurt was now talking into the mic, saying something about a special treat for fans, a rising star going to be playing with them for the first time, so give it up, London, for Angel.

'Go!'

The shove in my shoulder blades got me walking. Do not trip up. Do not do a Jennifer Lawrence at the Oscars, I told myself. I came on stage into a wash of warm applause. That was OK. I could do this. I smiled and waved, heading over to my spot at Kurt's left hand. The performing area was huge: it felt a very long walk. Banks of lights blazed down on us, preventing me from seeing anything in the crowd apart from the raised phones with their lit screens filming the moment, a thousand fallen stars. Kurt gave me a kiss as I passed.

'Brace yourself,' he said in my ear.

Puzzled, I took up my stance, waiting for the introduction to the new song he had rehearsed. But he was leaving that script behind.

'As you guys know, I have collaborated with various songwriters, but none have come anywhere as close to understanding me as my most recent partner. The new song we're going to play was written with him and I've asked him to return to the stage to sing with us. Please, give a big London welcome to Marcus Cohen!' Sweeping his hand to the opposite side I had come from, Kurt gave me a wicked smile. Behind me, Marcus stepped out into the lights. The applause went up a few notches. I turned slowly.

Do not embarrass yourselves, I told all my inner Angels: the Lovelorn, the Angry, the Calm and Professional, the Impulsive. Especially the Impulsive.

Marcus was carrying his guitar. He was wearing the same clothes he had worn on the beach: faded jeans and same blue T-shirt under an open shirt. Was this a signal to me? A reminder of when things had been on track?

He crossed to me and brushed my arm. Bending to my ear, he said. 'I would have worn the tutu but Kurt said you'd never forgive me.'

So he remembered his vow: that he'd wear one if Kurt ever spoke to him telepathically?

I cleared my throat. 'Good call.'

Passing in front of Kurt with a grin, Marcus took up position at the central mic. 'The new song you're going to hear is called "Stay Away, Come Closer", and it's dedicated to a very special girl.' He turned to me. 'She's standing right there.'

The crowd whistled and stamped. I could feel tears pricking my eyes but told them to go away until I could howl in private.

Brian took up the intro and then the music wove its spell. I didn't have to shout at my conflicted inner selves; the melody made me enter a space where I was whole. It was the place Marcus took me to with his power, where I could be more of a musician than I ever could on my own. Three verses passed and it was time for my solo. I lifted Freddie to my chin and relaxed. I forgot I was on stage, that I had an audience of thousands, even that I was in the O2; all there was for me was

Marcus's steady blue gaze holding me with him in the web of notes. I put into my part all the regret for my hastiness, my sadness that we'd hurt each other, the distance between us that I'd been unable to bridge. The violin said it all far better than I could and I knew that Marcus understood from the tiny smile he gave me at the end.

He returned to the mic for the final verse, but the words had changed from when I first heard it.

Don't stay away, 'cos I'm closing in.
Just can't fight you.

He turned to face me. My head was spinning: this was his declaration, his apology! And my reticent Marcus had chosen to do it in front of thousands.

You know it's said that fools rush in
Where angels fear to tread.
Then I'm a fool;
Angel, I'm your fool.

Blue eyes locked with mine, filled with hope and fear— hope that I'd forgive him, fear that I'd give him the biggest, most public rejection of his life. Freddie dangled at my side in nerveless fingers as the song ended, the words rolling through me. Kurt plucked my poor violin from my grip as Marcus took off his guitar. He leant to the mic.

'Excuse me guys: there's something I've got to do.' Not waiting for a sign from me, Marcus closed the gap between us and gathered me up in his arms for a kiss. Bending me back over his arm, the kiss went on and on, encouraged by the cheers and whistles of the crowd. Of course, I'd forgive him. I'd choose hope over hostility any day. Then the chant 'encore,

encore!' struck up in the huge inverted bowl of an arena. It was Kurt who answered the cry.

'Sorry, guys, but Marcus will be otherwise occupied. You'll have to put up with us playing our final number.'

Taking that as permission, Marcus swept me up into his arms and strode offstage with me. This produced the biggest cheer yet.

I pressed my ear to his chest, listening out for his heartbeat.

'Do you want me to put you down?'

'Never.'

'An attractive if somewhat impractical plan.' He kicked open a fire door and strode out onto a balcony overlooking the Thames. He set me down on the plinth but didn't remove his arms. We just stood together watching the dark waters unroll beneath us for a few magical moments.

'I can't believe you just did that,' I admitted.

He gave a self-mocking laugh. 'Neither can I. Did you like it?'

'I loved it.'

'And have you decided to forgive me for being an idiot?'

'I don't bear grudges—it's just not something I'm good at.'

'That's a relief.' He kissed the tip of my ear. 'I didn't get a chance to explain. I didn't ask Barry to test you. I told him he was wasting his time, but I handled that all wrong. I should've stopped him before he opened his mouth but I couldn't interrupt the meeting in case you thought I was behind your success—asking him to see you as a favour.'

'Oh.' I'd accused him of not trusting me when in fact I had been the one rushing to judge him. Didn't that make me feel about a centimetre tall? 'Then I guess I owe you an apology.'

He had worked his way down to my neck. 'I can think of all sorts of ways you can show me how sorry you are, starting with this.' He put his lips to mine, waiting for me to initiate a kiss. I did so.

'I'm sorry.' I kissed him again—and again. 'Just piling up some useful forgiveness tokens as I'm going to need them.' I turned to lay my head against his chest again. 'I'm sorry I'm impossible to live with.'

He smoothed my hair away from my cheek. 'That makes two of us. I get all moody when I'm writing.'

'So I suppose we're doing the world a favour taking two such difficult people out of the dating pool?'

'I'd say so. And Angel, I have every confidence you'll learn how to handle me—and me you.'

'You do?'

'Yes, because I've finally figured it out. We've got something major in our favour. Not the soulfinder thing—though that's a bonus—but the fact that I've fallen in love with you.'

I frowned. I couldn't believe anyone would—not a boyfriend. I was too much for most people to handle. 'You sure?'

His shoulders shook as he laughed. 'You're not supposed to say that. Yes, I love you. I think I did the moment I saw you dancing on the table making everyone have a good time. The colours are brighter when you're by my side, the laughter more infectious, the fleeting moments of perfection more poignant. Life is just *more*.'

I sighed. 'What wonderful words. They could be a song.'

'Maybe they will be.' He waited, stroking my arm. I knew what he wanted but I was trying not to give in to my tendency to rush things, savouring his words. 'Angel?'

I wouldn't make him wait too long. 'Marcus Cohen, you are gorgeous—both on the inside and out—but as a wise man once tried to tell me, it really is the inner kind that matters. You are thoughtful and generous, caring of others, and incredibly talented. When you sing I feel you've climbed inside my heart and found all the keys to my soul, opening every corner, every pathway. And I love you, too.' He went still, chin pressed tenderly to the top of my head. 'I'm sorry I rushed you into this far too quickly at Rockport. I'm an idiot as I caused us both hurt, but I'm not sorry—not for a millisecond—that you're my soulfinder. In fact, I'm very, very . . . ' I grinned up at him then turned back to the river. *Jump*, I commanded it. A ribbon of water coiled and span into a circle, sparkling with white lights. Another smaller ball briefly taking the shape of a cow flew over it, landing with a splash that sounded just a little like a moo. 'Over the moon.'

Then Marcus roared with laughter. Holding me to him, he shook with it, interspersing fits with kisses and hugs. I'd never seen him give way to his sense of humour before as he'd always held something back. He had tears running down his face by the time he had caught his breath.

'You are one in a million, Angel. No, I'm wrong: one in seven billion and I'm the luckiest guy alive as I get to keep you.' He kissed my fingers. 'First thing into the fire when I get home tonight: the words to "Demon Angel". I couldn't have been more wrong.'

I jumped down from the wall. 'No way: that's a good song! *Sent to torment me*,' I sang. '*Fly back where you belong.*'

He groaned. 'You really did hear it all then? I was hoping you'd forgotten.'

'Hardly, the words are graven on my heart, Marcus "OMG" Cohen.' I pulled him towards the stage door, aware there would be people waiting for us inside. 'You'll need them when I annoy you, which I've no doubt I will. Besides, good music is good music.'

His hand slid from my waist to my hip. 'I'll just have to write another song then—the one where the guy wakes up and realizes he's the shallow fool for getting her all wrong.'

'Or you could write me a song where I get to answer back.' I pushed open the fire doors that hadn't closed properly behind us. The warmth of the stage and the buzz of people reached out to wrap around us.

He patted my hip in approval. 'Great idea. I'll write you one then our bands can duel for that top spot. Him and her.'

'Black Belt versus Angel Dares? That's one story I don't mind being part of.' I headed for the green room.

'Sorry, but you don't stand a chance against us highly trained guys.' In the corridor just outside the lounge, Marcus feigned a judo move to throw me, giving me plenty of time to skip out of the way.

Backing into the room laughing, I shook my finger at him. 'Uh-huh, we'll just dance out of your reach.'

Cameras flashed—and yes, that was the second picture that made it into the press the next morning along with the onstage kiss: Marcus and I fooling about in the doorway to the green room, both laughing, me holding him off, him with his hands outstretched to grab me.

'Oops.' I blushed and quickly checked my dress was straight after our tussle.

'Yeah, the backstage press conference.' Marcus cleared his throat, looking more amused than embarrassed. 'I forgot about that.'

I turned to take in the avid looks of what appeared to be at least fifty journalists. Marcus closed the gap between us and slung an arm around my shoulders. 'I think they'll want us down the front with the others.'

Kurt, his band mates, and Pete and Michael were all smiling at us.

'You did say "send in the clowns—there oughta be clowns"?' I said brightly.

'Don't worry: we're here,' finished Marcus. I just knew that before me he would never have made a joke like that at his own expense.

'Thanks for the floor show, guys,' said Kurt. 'Come closer.' He patted the sofa beside him where they had left room for two.

'Not stay away?' grinned Marcus, pulling me down onto this lap.

'Definitely not stay away. Right, Margot, over to you to pick the questions.'

As Margot took the floor to control the interview, I relaxed back against Marcus. Kurt refused anyone who asked about Marcus and me, making clear this was about music, not about our private lives. That was sweet of him but I guess Marcus had kinda blown the private part when he did his apology in front of thousands. From my perch I was able to take in some of the details that had escaped me before. Will, Uriel, and Victor were in the room, standing at the edges, eyes on the journalists rather than us. I could see Alex also, standing next to Uriel, Misty just behind him, visible only because I could see her hand wrapped in his. That left Summer. I spotted her sitting on a chair behind Victor, eyes closed as she concentrated. What was she doing? When I'd seen that expression on her face before, she'd been using her gift. She can get into just about any head unless they have formidable shields. As I watched, she got up and whispered something to Victor. His eyes focused on a man in the middle of the crowd, face hidden behind a large camera that he didn't lower.

I sat up, not believing the man's gall. Eli Davis had dared to come to our press conference! Was he that stupid to think we'd let him walk in and out with impunity? I sagged a little. Of course, we had nothing to charge him with. We couldn't stop him as I'd been unable to prove he'd been behind my abduction.

Marcus noticed my reaction. 'What's wrong?'

Eli Davis—the guy with the black Gifted baseball cap and checked shirt.

Marcus stiffened and started to shift me off his lap. I'm not sure what he was planning to do but tearing the guy limb from limb appeared to feature heavily in his thoughts.

No, not here, I begged. *Let's not give him the story he wants.*

Kurt stood up and signalled that the question and answer session was over. 'Thanks for coming, everyone. There are drinks and stuff in the waterfront bar. We'll be over for the party when we've had a chance to wind down, OK?' Gifted were famous—and well liked—for their hospitality to the music press. These parties were a regular event at the end of a tour.

As the press filed out, Victor and Will moved in on Eli Davis. Victor relieved him of his camera as Will took a firm grip on his arm.

'Mr Davis, I believe we need to have a word in private,' said Victor coolly.

Davis' eyes flicked to his colleagues heading for the free drinks. 'You can't do anything, Benedict. People know I'm here.'

'I believe Mr Voss would like a word too.' Victor marched Davis up to where Kurt, Marcus, and I were still sitting. Margot moved to Will's side; Alex, Misty, and Summer stayed in the room but kept back. None of them looked surprised at this confrontation.

Did you know about this? I asked Marcus.

No—but I think I like what I'm seeing. He settled me protectively against him. *Just sit back and enjoy the show.*

Kurt glanced down at us to check we were OK then turned to face Davis.

'Davis, I have some bad news for you,' he said.

'What? That you're one of them?' Davis spat at Victor's feet. Victor raised a brow but said nothing.

'One of what?' asked Kurt blandly. 'I've no idea what

you're talking about. No, what I mean is that my lawyers are delivering an injunction against you and your newspaper.'

Davis' eyes darted to me, then to the door. 'Nothing can be proved.'

'Sadly, we are aware that we can't pin attempted murder on you, you scum, but that is not the charge I am bringing against you. I have presented evidence of phone hacking to the police here and in the US. So desperate to get celebrity gossip, you stole a phone off a new associate of mine and dug through her contacts for our numbers. One of those stolen was mine and I know you attempted to break into my voicemail—I had my security team watching for it.' He gestured to Will. 'And Mr Benedict here also has something to add.'

Will passed Davis an envelope. 'You also hacked into my account and picked up a message left for me by my brother four days ago. Taking his number, you attempted to do the same to his voicemail. Unfortunately for you, his phone is FBI-issued, which bumps up the charges to attempted espionage on a government official. Homeland Security has got very interested in you. When you've got through the court case here, I imagine the US authorities will be asking for you to be extradited to face further charges at home.'

Davis went white. I had no sympathy—not a scrap. He had brought the whole stinking bucket of gunk down on his own head by forgetting to behave like a journalist with any morals and almost killed me in the process. Margot spoke into her walkie-talkie and two uniformed police officers entered the room.

'You can't do this,' spluttered Davis. 'I've got rights!'

'Excuse me, sir, I was just about to read you those now,' said the senior officer as she approached. Victor gave her a nod and stepped back. Davis had forgotten in his mad dash to expose us that Victor had friends in most major police forces in friendly countries. He was now about to find out just how unpopular the charge of celebrity phone hacking was going to make him.

He was led away, shouting out about savants and plots. Kurt stood between Will and Victor, savouring the moment.

'Ah, that felt good.' He turned to me. 'You OK seeing him again? We thought you'd like to be here when he was brought down.'

I bounced off Marcus's knee and did a little happy dance. 'Yay, score for the good guys!'

Marcus got up and spun me once. 'And it was all thanks to you.'

'Me?' I squeaked. 'No, it was these wonderful people.' I gestured to my friends.

Victor gave me a wry smile. 'No, Marcus is right. It was your phone that did it.'

Misty approached hand in hand with Alex. 'None of us planned it that way but he had stolen it off you already so Alex here had the totally brilliant idea of using it as bait.'

Alex cleared his throat. 'I might've made a call to your old number suggesting persuasively that whoever was listening go through your contacts and focus on Will and Kurt.'

'And Summer tracked him for us tonight so we knew he would be here,' beamed Misty.

'And believe me: you owe me for that. His is one horrible little mind to shadow,' said Summer. 'I've had to live in his head since he walked through the doors.'

I hugged Marcus tight as I looked round at them all. 'So what you're saying is I was totally amazingly cunning to get him to steal my phone—and even cleverer not to passcode it?'

'Just this once,' said Victor, 'but yes.'

Marcus laughed into the crook where my neck meets my shoulder, sharing my happiness. 'You genius, Angel.'

'Your genius,' I corrected. Holding out my hand to my friends, I smiled at them all. 'And do you know something? I think we deserve a party to celebrate our combined brilliance.'

Kurt came up to us and hugged both Marcus and me to him. 'So it's just as well I've got one already laid on out front. Let's go, people.'

Joss Stirling lives in Oxford and is the author of the bestselling **Finding Sky** trilogy. She was awarded the Romantic Novelist's Association's Romantic Novel of the Year 2015 for **Struck**.

You can visit her website at **www.jossstirling.com**.

Want to know how Angel's friend, Misty, got together with her soulfinder, Alex? Discover all in Misty Falls.

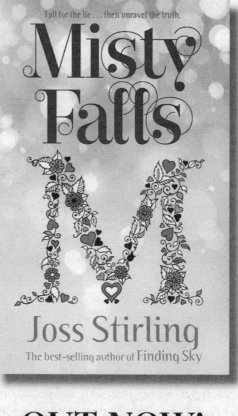

OUT NOW!

Heard the buzz about Struck, winner of the 2015 Romantic Novel of the Year Award? Read on for a taste!

A black eye. Great.

Raven Stone studied it in the mirror, lightly probing the developing bruise. Ouch. The strip light flickered over the wash basin, making her reflection blink like the end of an old newsreel. The tap squeaked a protest as she dampened a cold compress.

'You look about seven years old,' she told her mirror-double.

Ten years on from the schoolyard of scraped knees and minor bumps, Raven considered the injury more a humiliation than a pain. She tugged a curl of her spiralling black hair over her face but it sprang back, refusing to hide the cloud gathering around her left eye. She wondered whether she could hide in her room until it faded . . . ?

Not possible. All the students were expected to attend the welcome-back supper and her absence would be noticed. Anyway—she threw the flannel in the sink—why give her enemies the satisfaction of knowing they had driven her out so easily? Cowardice was not part of her character résumé. She had far too much pride to allow it.

Raven stripped off her tennis kit and pulled on a towelling robe. She tossed the dirty clothes in the laundry basket by the door with a snap of the lid. It was tough keeping her promise to herself that she would be strong; easier when she had someone at her back. But the second bed in the room was empty—no heap of untidy belongings or suitcase as she had expected. What was keeping Gina? She was the only one Raven wanted to talk to about what had just happened. Raven flopped on her bed. How had it come to this in a few hours? Until the black eye, life had been skating along fine, a smooth place after years of rough. Westron, as run by the head teacher, Mrs Bain, had been weird sometimes, putting too much emphasis on wealth and parents, celebrity pupils and privacy, but teaming up with Gina, Raven had been able to laugh off most of those absurdities. She would have said no one in the school wished her ill. In spite of owing her place to her grandfather's presence on the staff, the other students had not appeared to mind her numbering among their privileged ranks. Now she knew better.

The realization had come out of nowhere, like the tornado spiralling Dorothy's house off to Oz. When Raven opened the door to the changing rooms, everything went skipping down the yellow brick road to Bizarre City.

Hedda's question had seemed so, well, *normal*. 'Hey, where's my Chloé tote?'
The other girls in the locker room getting ready for the tennis competition had made a brief search among their belongings. Raven had not even bothered: her little sports bag, a much mocked airline freebie, was too small to hide the bulky taupe leather shoulder bag. Hedda had been flaunting it all morning like a fisherman displaying a prize catch. The flexing, polished surface had gleamed like a sea trout in her manicured fingers: *so many pockets and you won't believe how much it cost!* Hedda had thought it a bargain but it had come with a price tag more than Raven's grandfather earned in a month as the school's caretaker. Something so pointlessly expensive had to be a rip-off.

'Hey, I'm talking to you, Stone.'

Raven felt a sharp tug on her elbow. Standing on one foot to lace her tennis shoe, she toppled to one side. Why had Hedda suddenly taken to using her surname?

'Whoa, Hedda, careful!' Raven balanced herself against the wire mesh dividing the changing areas and tied off the bow. 'You almost knocked me over.'

Stick thin and with an abundance of wine-red hair, Hedda reminded Raven of a red setter, sharp nose pointing to the next shopping bargain, a determined little notch in her chin that gave her face character. Hedda put her hands on her hips. 'Where have you hidden it?'

'What?' Raven was too surprised to realize what it was that Hedda was accusing her of doing. 'Me?'

'Yes, you. I'm not stupid. I saw you looking at it. It had my phone—my make-up—my money—everything is in that bag.'

Raven tried to keep a hold on her temper and ignore the hurt of being accused with no proof. She had had enough of that in the last school she had attended before coming to the UK. She tried for reasonable. 'I haven't done anything with it. Where did you last see it?'

'At the lunch table—don't pretend you don't know.'

The changing room fell silent as the other girls listened in on the exchange. A flush of shame crept over Raven's cheeks even though she knew she was innocent. Memories of standing before the principal in her old school rushed back. She felt queasy with the sense of déjà vu.

'I'm sorry: are you saying I stole it?'

Hedda tipped her head back and looked down her long nose at Raven. 'I'm not saying—I know you took it.'

Raven dragged her thoughts away from her past and focused on the accuser. What on earth had happened to Hedda? She had missed most of last term and had come back with what seemed like a personality transplant—from clingy, whingeing minor irritant to strident, major-league bitch.

Raven told herself not to back down; she'd faced false accusations before and this time she wasn't a traumatized little girl. What was the worst Hedda could do? Wave a mascara wand at her?

'So you think I took it? Based on what? On that fact that I just *looked* at it? Looking doesn't mean stealing.' Raven appealed to the other girls, hoping to find someone who would join her in shrugging off the accusation as absurd, but their expressions were watchful or carefully neutral. *Gee, thanks, guys.*

Then Hedda's friend, Toni, joined in the finger pointing. 'There's no point claiming you're innocent. Things were going missing all last term.'

'I had nothing to do with that. Some of my stuff was stolen too.'

Toni ignored her. 'We all noticed small things disappearing but didn't like to . . . I mean we *guessed* it was you but we felt sorry for you, so . . . ' Toni waved her hand as if to say *that was last term, this is now.*

'Sorry for me?' Raven gave a choked laugh. One thing she never wanted was anyone's pity. Even at her lowest moment after losing her parents, she hadn't asked for that.

Hedda got right up in her face. 'But taking my brand new Chloé? Now you've gone way too far. Give it back, Stone.'

Ridiculous. Raven turned her back on Hedda. 'And what am I supposed to be doing with these things I'm stealing?'

'Your grandfather has a new car—if you can call a Skoda a car.'

Toni snorted. Raven felt a surge of anger: taking a crack at her was one thing but Hedda had better keep her granddad out of it or there really would be trouble!

'So I, what? Steal from the rich to give to the poor? Now why didn't I think of that?' Raven's irony was lost on the literal-minded Hedda.

'Stop denying it. I want my bag and I want it now.'

Hoping that if she ignored the infantile rant Hedda would back down, Raven shook her head and dipped her fingers inside her jeans pocket for a band to tie up her hair.

'Don't you ignore me!' With a grunt of fury, Hedda shoved Raven hard into the mesh, right onto a peg that caught the corner of her eye. Even though the hook was padded by clothes, Raven saw stars. Clapping a hand to her face, she swung round, temper threatening to gallop away riderless.

'Look, Hedda, I don't have your stupid tote!' She gathered herself in the defensive stance she had been taught. Raven had to be careful, knowing she could do a lot of harm with the self-defence training her father had insisted she take. It had come in useful for fending off the predators who roamed the corridors in her American public school, but she guessed it would be frowned on at refined Westron and would earn her a reputation as a thug.

'Yes. You. Do!' Hedda shoved Raven in the chest with each word so her back collided with the mesh. Someone giggled nervously while two students hurried out to fetch the PE teacher.

That was outside of enough. It was time Hedda learnt there was one girl in the school she couldn't bully.

'I've had enough of your idiotic—' (push) '—accusations!' Raven thrust Hedda back a second time, measuring out exactly the same force as Hedda had used on her.

Then Hedda went for a handful of hair. Big mistake.

BOOKS BY
Joss Stirling